AMBITIONS

This paperback edition published in 2025 by Tweedlecoate.
tweedlecoate.co.uk

Cover Design by The Tweedle

Printed and bound by CPI Group (UK) Ltd, Croydon, CR0 4YY

ISBN 978-1068644566

AMBITIONS

Val Owen

Tweedlecoate

With thanks to the members of the Copper Writers group for their help during the gestation of this novel. Thanks also to my husband Tony for putting up with the whole business.

"Ambition should be made of sterner stuff"

Julius Caesar
William Shakespeare

"They have to be made to pay the price."

All the old men were leaning forward and looking intently at Flint.

"We have waited a long time to find someone with the skill and knowledge to carry out the task. Now you are the one. You must make it your ambition."

Part One

Chapter 1

That night Flint lay in bed listening to the distant roar of the waves and pondered.

What is ambition? Where does it come from? Is it something built into a person's character or is it something instilled by background?

Flint heard his mother washing the pots and pans outside the open door. She would have said her ambition was to have a house with running water. His father would have said they were surrounded by water. They had a well in the village. That was enough.

Where would Flint find his ambition? Perhaps he would have said it was something that was being instilled and encouraged by his community.

At university Flint knew the professors were pleased with him, his enthusiasm to learn, his keenness to gather and understand all the information and now, his interest in this deadly infection. Yes, this outbreak of cholera was unusual. The virulence of the disease was exceptional. No one had experience of an infection that killed everyone who contracted it. There was also the speed. The victims were dead within a few hours.

Anxious to probe for every last scrap of knowledge, Flint asked, "Most of the deaths were children or adults who had been in poor health at the charity home. Would people in good health, on a good diet have died?"

"There was a young woman who had just arrived from England. She was amongst the dead. I presume she was in good health but her resistance to tropical diseases and the bacteria we have in our environment would have been less." The professor allowed his thoughts to run on. "Someone from England, in fact any northern European, would probably be more susceptible."

Flint's thoughts were racing ahead, but his practice of constraining the outward signs of his feelings had prepared him for moments like this. He ran his fingers down the side of his textbook on environmental microbiology. "Next term we have to complete our individual research projects. If the department is going to study this outbreak, try to sort out what made the disease so bad, could I be involved in that study? I would like my research project to make a real contribution to public health."

Flint knew he was impressing the professor.

"The projects have not been assigned yet, but I will see what can be done. In the meantime samples have been frozen and will be available for study at some time in the future."

As it was, no work was done to elucidate the cause of the outbreak, the deaths. Although Flint did not get his wish to study this bacterium, he did make sure that he knew where the frozen samples were stored and how they were labelled to identify which test-tubes contained the samples likely to have the most dangerous bacteria.

Flint felt confident that he had found a building block to start constructing his ultimate plan.

As a young boy Flint always wanted to see what his father was doing.

"Why is he constantly asking questions?" his mother had asked.

"Because he is curious about everything. He wants to know how everything works. That's why I let him help me with the repair work on the boat engine," replied his father.

"And he got covered with oil!" was his mother's retort.

Flint had travelled between the islands with his father. He loved the ferries which would be crowded with people carrying local produce. There would be sacks of sweet potatoes or breadfruit and crates of chickens, even freshly caught fish. Flint's father would greet friends from the various islands and Flint listened to the conversations about matters of importance to these people.

Occasionally they went to the main island, a place of crowded streets, traffic and noise. Flint had seen large buildings, constructed of concrete. His father had pointed out the university and told him that one day he would study there. He would leave his home island and live in this place of people and turmoil.

They would stay overnight with friends during the visit. Flint remembered the morning when he awoke to find a huge new building had suddenly appeared overnight. It was much bigger, much taller than anything he had seen before. Flint thought it was a miracle but his father explained it was a cruise ship full of foreign visitors who would come and spend money. Flint begged his father to take him to see the ship. His father explained that they would not be allowed to go on board but they could walk down to the dock to get a better view of everything.

Flint marvelled at the size. He could see people walking about on the top deck and they looked so small. There were people all over the ship, so many people. Then Flint saw that part of the side of the ship had opened up and there was a stream of passengers coming ashore.

"Where have these people come from?" Flint asked.

"It is an American cruise line so probably they are mainly Americans but could be from anywhere over the world," his father explained.

'Anywhere over the world,' Flint thought about that. Could he perhaps go 'anywhere over the world' when he was a bit older; when he was grown up? His father assured him that he was clever enough.

The knowledge that he was clever and would be able to travel stayed with Flint.

On one visit to the main island Flint and his father arrived to find a cruise ship already in the harbour. Immediately Flint asked if they could have a closer look but this time his father had said no. The ship had come from England and many of the passengers would be English.

Flint understood why his father had such a hatred of the English but he did not think it would do any harm just to have a look at them, just to see what they looked like. He said he would walk up to the university buildings while his father was busy. As soon as he was out of his father's sight he ran to the dock area. There was the beautiful ship towering over the buildings of the town. The passengers had already started to come out of the hole in the side of the ship. Many of them were getting on to buses or small boats to tour the island but some were walking out of the dock area. Flint crept closer. The visitors looked much the same as those who had arrived on the American ship although many of them were old and pale. Flint did not think they looked terrible but he was too afraid to get close. After a few minutes he ran away up to the university buildings so he would have something to tell his father.

Flint marvelled at the number of buildings. There were students everywhere, how wonderful, how exciting. One day he would be one of those students.

He ran back to tell his father about the university and the students.

"Yes, you will be there after you have finished at school," smiled his father.

Flint did not say anything about the ship and the English.

CHAPTER 2

During his young life one of Flint's greatest pleasures was to go fishing with his father and the other men from the community. Flint loved the feeling as the wind caught the sail and the boat skimmed across the waves. Then there was the sense of achievement as the fish they had caught were taken ashore and given to his mother to cook for that evening's meal. Flint felt like one of the men, he was doing a man's work.

Then came the day when Flint's father went out alone. Flint was at school and most of the other men had gone to the main island. Flint's mother had assumed he had gone fishing in the lagoon; however by evening there was no sign of him. Sunset and darkness came very quickly so there could be no thorough search until the next morning. Flint told himself that the next day he would see his father sailing home but it did not happen. Nor did it happen on the subsequent days. Although there was a thorough search nothing was found. Eventually there was the acceptance that he would not be coming back; he had been lost at sea, taken by the waves.

Flint walked down to the beach, to the water's edge. He felt the waves run over his feet and legs. He felt the swell dragging him into the sea. Should he allow himself to be pulled out there to join his father? Then he heard his sister's voice calling him. He turned and looked at her. Although she was only four years older than Flint her quiet confidence meant she was mature for her age. She was a younger version of their mother. She was the one who was supporting the family through their grief at the loss of their husband and father.

"Our mother needs you at home," she said.

Flint turned and walked away from the water's edge. He still had a life with his family and with the community. They needed him. He would continue along the path which his father had wished for him. He would do well at school and he would go to university. Then perhaps he would go across the sea to anywhere in the world.

The ideas of university and then travel drove Flint at school. He found if he concentrated during lessons he could do well, he could do very well, he could come top of the class.

The elders in the community encouraged him in all his activities. Flint was not sure whether they took such an interest in him because he was fatherless and needed male support or because he was the cleverest and most talented at school.

Flint was indoctrinated with the history of how their island, their homeland, had been taken by the English soldiers. How they had been told that everyone would have to move to another island, to a strange place.

The military came and forced everyone onto ships. Those who resisted were shot and their bodies dumped into the sea.

Flint was told how families went to the graveyards on the island and dug up the bones of their ancestors so they would not be left abandoned to the coming contamination which would be visited upon the whole island.

The population was taken to a new, uninhabited island. They were left there to manage as best they could. It was a time of great hardship. The elderly died, the children went without education. It was only the resilience of the people which meant that enough survived to built a new community.

The bones of the ancestors were buried in a communal grave on the new island and Flint remembered his grandmother squatting by the grave, her hands over her face. She would rock back and forth issuing a long low moan. Flint's mother told him she was calling back to the old island, calling back to their home.

During his last year at school Flint's marks were excellent and he was invited to visit the university to talk to tutors in the various departments and to visit the hall where the first year students lived.

"So Flint?" his mother enquired when he returned home after the visit.

"There's so much," enthused Flint, "I saw the labs and there is so much stuff, so much equipment. There're so many places for sport and a gym. Everyone was friendly and helpful; they even talked about the jobs we might get after we get our degrees and the pay we might get."

His mother smiled, "So you are going and you know what you want to do?"

"Yeah," summed up Flint's decision.

He had chosen to do courses which included biochemistry, genetics and marine biology. He wanted to know more about the coral reef at home, all the animals that lived there and how they interacted. He began to realize that the studies and experiments in biochemistry gave him a fuller understanding about how life worked. He especially enjoyed the laboratory work.

Genetics, he felt, gave the key to everything. The genes, the DNA contained the information which allowed all life on earth to function. He wanted to know more.

Flint found he was not prepared for the reality of university, the number of people and the confusion of buildings. Life was a whirl but he was desperate to succeed. He had to be able to manage all the different subjects. He needed to reach the required standard.

It was not until after the first set of university exams that he was confident that he was reaching the necessary level. Growing confidence allowed him to talk to the professors about the details of the courses and, perhaps more significantly for Flint, he relaxed into the sporting and social life.

Flint enjoyed the full happy life, a life much more exciting than the one he had on his home island. The only thing he missed was the comfort and familiarity of his home. His student room was stark and the food was boring, tasteless compared to his mother's cooking.

Gradually Flint formed a circle of friends and the closest of these were Howy and Tep. Howy came from a small island and his experience was similar to that of Flint.

"All the noise. It goes on the whole time. Don't people ever sleep in this place? Then there's the smell, the cars and things stink," was Howy's complaint every evening.

"You have to put up with all that if you want to be at university," rationalised Flint.

Tep had talents in different directions. He was from the main island and he lived at home with his parents and three sisters. Flint became a frequent visitor enjoying the home atmosphere. Then there was the fact that Tep knew the island. He knew the best places to swim and where to find tasty cheap food. Tep also knew how to make money.

"The visitors who come on the cruise ships are walking gold," he told Flint. He explained about working on the boats which took the tourists out to different beaches to swim, fish or just lie in the sun.

"But I'm not old enough to do that sort of work," complained Flint.

"Most of the captains on the boats don't ask about age," assured Tep. "They just want someone who'll turn up and be nice to the visitors. You can always lie about your age."

"I heard the pay was not that good."

"Don't just look at the pay. It's the tips that make the money good. You just have to be nice and helpful to some American woman and you get a good tip. The British are not much use."

"But how do I get that sort of job?" asked Flint.

Tep smiled, "I'll get you something."

A few days later Flint was introduced to the captain of a catamaran which ran trips for the tourists. Initially the captain looked Flint up and down as if assessing him as a piece of meat.

"He's a very strong swimmer and knows a lot about the wildlife on the coral reefs," Tep tried to convince the captain.

The captain turned to Flint, "You done any sailing?"

"Yes, used to go out with the men on my island. Not on a thing like that," Flint said as he looked at the gleaming catamaran, "but I know the feel of the wind in the sails and how to steer a good course."

"You'll have to deal with a lot of tourists. Some say they can swim but they have never been in the sea, just swimming pools. They don't know about waves and currents. They don't know they must not touch the coral because they can get scratches and infected," explained the captain.

By now Flint was beginning to think he was ill equipped for work with visitors to the island. All the people he had known in his life had grown up next to the sea and knew all its moods and dangers.

"Okay, you can come along and I'll see if you are any use," grunted the captain.

"You'll be just great," Tep stated as they walked away from the catamaran.

Two days later Flint was helping tourists onto the boat.

For Flint the experience of sailing on the catamaran was wonderful. It seemed to skim across the sea, high above the waves.

Some of the tourists were very knowledgeable about life on the coral reef and Flint was able to discuss some details. However, most of his time was spent watching everyone. The captain had said that they were taking thirty two passengers out and they needed to return thirty two passengers back to the ship, all uninjured.

This task was accomplished.

"Yes, you'll do," said the captain as he paid Flint and made sure he was given his share of the tips.

Flint was tired, happy and wealthy. He had a job, all thanks to Tep.

On Flint's next visit home he told his mother all about the job. "The catamaran is great; beautiful to handle and fast when we get it out in the breeze. Most of the tourists are very friendly and want to know about the islands and the coral. Some of them live a long way from the sea and the cruise is their first experience of an ocean. One even asked why the water in the ocean was salty as he lived by a great lake, a huge lake with ships on it, but the water was not salty. He said you could drink the water from his lake if you got away from city pollution." Flint's mother listened with interest and nodded while her son explained.

"But did you find out about the water?" his mother smiled knowing that her son would find the question interesting.

"Yes, I looked it up that evening and found a paper about it. It's because salts from the rocks, on land, are washed into the sea and they dissolve there. The rivers and lakes get their water from rain mainly, so no salts," Flint explained in detail.

"But I hope all this is not interfering with your university work," she commented.

"No, not at all. I'm keeping up with everything plus the money works out to be good."

"Don't forget when you finish university you will need to do a proper job."

"I know, but Tep's talking about getting his own boat and doing trips for the people who are really interested in marine biology. He said I could work with him. We could work together to build up a business."

His mother frowned, "I'm not sure."

A few days later one of the elders of the community came to see Flint. "I have heard that you are doing some work with the tourists. I'm sure it is nice while you are a student, earning some money, but don't forget that the people of this island need you to do a job, a real job." The old man looked hard at Flint, a look that seemed to go through Flint's eyes and into his brain. Flint's mind was filled with the memory of his grandmother's grief.

"No, I have not forgotten and I'm trying to find an idea that will do what you want but, in the meantime," Flint's voice trailed off. He knew he was the chosen one and he knew what was expected of him, his mission.

Chapter 3

"So have you thought about helping me with getting the boat, building a business?" was Tep's first question to Flint after the holidays.

"I think it's a great idea but I really want to concentrate on the university work," replied Flint. "I would like to do some work with the tourists. Make some money, could help you. But trying to set up in business, no, I don't think so, not at this time."

Tep was right when he said the Americans were generous with their tips so most of the money Flint received was in American dollars but one day he was given a note which felt different. It was crisp and clean, and said Bank of England £5. Flint looked at the picture of a bad tempered man on the note. These were the people he must expect when he got to England. He decided not to change the note but to keep it until he went there. He wondered how long that would be.

Flint's ability to make money as a tourist guide gave him some financial freedom to enjoy the social life, at university, which was wonderful. Something he could not have imagined when he was at home. His height and athletic ability meant he was selected for sporting teams. His good looks also gave him an advantage with the girls. There were so many pretty girls and the parties on the beaches offered him plenty of chances to meet them. There were barbecues and music, and the students would dance down to the water's edge.

Tep was disappointed by the decision but assumed that Flint needed to concentrate most of his efforts on his studies; perhaps his plans were similar to those of Howy. Howy had a girlfriend back at home, on another island, and he wanted to marry as soon as he had finished his degree. Howy was hoping to get a job with a company which exported fruit from the islands or with the main medical laboratory which served the population. These both offered good opportunities for people who had university qualifications. They were secure jobs with chances for promotion. Howy wanted marriage, a family and security.

Flint knew he had to spend more time trying to find a means of accomplishing his mission. He could not afford to get sidetracked into other options. He admired Howy's single-minded approach and, also, it did cross his mind that Howy might come across some dangerous bacteria in his studies, something that might eventually be useful in his mission.

"The course you said you would be doing, bacteriology. Would be interesting if you found something that caused serious disease in humans, something that seemed to be new," Flint joked with Howy.

"Yes, but I don't expect that will happen. It's mostly a matter of identifying the usual bugs quickly and accurately so it is possible to treat the patient before it becomes a serious disease and spreads through the population," smiled Howy. He always had clear steady ideas. He was the opposite end of the drama spectrum when compared to Tep's impulsive temperament.

Flint and Howy discussed the importance of studying the bacteria which could infect humans. Howy recommended the most appropriate course at university and Flint signed up for it. At the same time Flint was finding genetic engineering interesting and made sure he was enrolled for the course which dealt with the use of genetic engineering in modifying crops to resist pests and to increase the amount of food produced. He became fascinated by the ability to move genes, DNA, from one organism to another. Was it a way of speeding up normal plant selection and breeding, the process that people had used for thousands of years, or was it playing God? Flint decided on the former.

He had always been intrigued by the life in the sea, the fish and the whole variety of organisms which live in the coral reef but now he had been taught about plankton, the tiny creatures which float in the ocean and were only visible using a microscope.

Education was opening up so many doors in Flint's mind, so many ideas, so much new research. One evening he lay in bed thinking how wonderful that something so small as the plankton cell could exist. How amazing that they could grow and reproduce. There were single-celled organisms which could use sunlight to make their own food, to photosynthesise. Flint considered all the information which must be packed into each tiny cell to instruct it to do everything that was necessary for life. It seemed to him that every living cell had a computer which ran all the operations of the organism, how wonderful! He looked at his laptop and thought how little information was contained in that compared to these tiny organisms. Could humans ever construct something which was so compact and clever? What a wonderful project to work on, to do research into, he thought. Perhaps one day, after he had completed his mission, he could find somewhere that was looking into that. He fell asleep asking himself if anywhere existed that was trying to use biology as a model for a new generation of computers.

A few weeks later the students in the bacteriology course were all discussing the latest news.

"I don't understand why it was not sorted out quickly when they first started to get ill," said Howy.

"But it happened very quickly. Perhaps there wasn't time and they did not realise how serious it was going to be," suggested Flint.

"We've got very good health services at home," defended Howy. "They could have got a doctor or someone from the hospital."

Howy and Flint agreed that they did not know exactly what had happened or how long the delay had been in getting help when the outbreak of cholera started on Howy's home island.

"It was just in that one place that had its own well. Wasn't it?" asked Flint.

"Yer, a bit isolated, a sort of charity home," explained Howy.

Several people had died very suddenly and it was established that the disease had come from the water in the local well. Samples of water from several wells had been brought across to the university for investigation. Flint agreed with Howy that this was going to be a very interesting, significant study. What had caused this deadly disease to act so fast?

"Could it not have been prevented in the first place?" Flint asked.

"Oh, yes, if they had observed better precautions with the water from the well but they don't seem to have taken any steps to check the water or sterilise it. Any proper water purification process would have prevented this outbreak."

"Strange that something like that should suddenly appear," mused Flint. "Was it brought in from somewhere else or could it have just been a mutation?" He did not say anything to Howy but he did wonder if the mutation could have allowed the bacteria to pass through a water purification system and still infect people, or was that just his wishful thinking.

"It would be good to see what the people in the department thought happened," suggested Howy.

"The prof. will have some views and ideas I am sure. Would be good to have a session with him," was Flint's comment.

Flint and Howy sat late into the evening discussing this sudden outbreak of such a lethal disease. Flint wanted to understand how better water purification would have prevented the outbreak.

By the end of the evening they had both decided that they would like to have a seminar on the subject and they would tell their professor about their interest in the subject.

The professor explained that the World Health Organisation had been contacted and they had no records of similar outbreaks anywhere else in the world. In that case Flint wanted to know why and how it had happened.

"It was probably a mutation in the usual organism which means that a dose of a few bacteria can cause a very toxic effect. The body does not have time to develop and turn on its defences."

"But could the patients not have been treated?"

"Everything happened so quickly. They were dead within a few hours of the first symptoms. In a country with excellent local healthcare services it would be difficult, almost impossible to deal with this in time. Even a country like Denmark probably could not respond adequately, in time."

Flint noticed how the professor always held up the example of Denmark as having a highly developed healthcare service. The professor had spent a year studying and working there and had formed the opinion that all countries should strive to obtain the high levels which had been achieved in Denmark.

"So this could this happen in Denmark?"

"No, no, their water processing is much too good. However, we have taken samples from the contaminated well and they are to be studied here and by colleagues in Denmark to try to find out more about this organism. It does seem to have been unusually virulent and was exceptionally fast acting. Very difficult to handle if it does enter the drinking water."

"If the organism evolved to withstand the chemicals added to water I suppose they could infect people via drinking water," mused Flint.

"I suppose it is theoretically possible," laughed the professor, "but the only things that withstand the sort of conditions used to keep water safe are probably the extremophiles which live in conditions of high temperature, extreme acidity or alkalinity, and high salt concentrations or in the presence of toxic substances. Organisms which cause disease don't live in those situations. Their genes, their biochemistry is quite different."

But their genes, their biochemistry could be modified thought Flint as he smiled and nodded in agreement with the professor's words.

Chapter 4

As it was no work was done to elucidate the underlying causes of the outbreak, the deaths. Although Flint did not get his wish to study this bacterium he did make sure that he knew where the frozen samples were stored and how they were labelled.

Flint spent his evenings wondering if something this deadly could be introduced into the water supply in England. Could something be done so it could pass through the purification system?

Although Flint was uncertain about the next steps of the technology he felt the quarry could provide the means to its own ultimate destruction. He would need to go to England to study, to find the route by which the blow could be delivered.

He used every source of information available. He accessed course details for English universities via the Internet. He looked up recent research papers to get a better feeling for what work was currently being undertaken. He sought the advice of members of the academic staff at his university. Everyone was impressed by the diligence of the young man and provided all the help they could. There were appropriate courses available at British universities and he should be suitably qualified to enter most of these, but it would all be very expensive.

All his research led him to one conclusion. There was one university which offered a course covering the subjects which would be useful to him. He would be able to get the technology and the ideas finalised.

Sillfield University was a centre for research into many aspects of the water industry. There was active collaborative research with a number of companies which supplied water across England, including London.

By the end of term, when Flint returned home, he had developed his ideas.

He had a meeting with some of the older members of the community.

As they sat round, in the cool of the evening, Flint described his plan. He reminded them of the devastating cholera outbreak on one of the neighbouring islands.

"But England has good healthcare, even the NHS could cope with water contamination," intervened one man who had lived in Birmingham for a time.

"No, I don't think so," Flint was respectful of the elders but had confidence in his facts. "You see the bacteria act so fast that there would not be time to get to the doctor or the hospital to receive treatment."

"But they have good public health provision and high standards of water purification."

"Yes, but every system has its failures and weak points."

Some of the old men nodded in agreement.

"They had several deaths from food poisoning in Scotland a few years ago. There was a particularly dangerous E. coli that was in some of the meat. Then there was an incident when too much of a chemical was put into the water supply somewhere in England. Although no one died directly, it may have affected people's health."

By now all the old men were leaning forward looking intently at Flint. Clearly he had studied his subject thoroughly.

It seemed everyone was beginning to understand the idea but some doubted the feasibility. They expressed their concerns.

"Well, this is my plan."

The group fell silent to listen to Flint.

"I know where the water samples from the well are stored. I could get to those. I have identified the course at Sillfield University where I can learn new techniques; find out about the water supply systems to London." Flint got up, crossed the room and collected a sheaf of brochures. Putting these down on the table in the middle of the group he selected a glossy booklet. "This is from Sillfield and," opening the booklet, "this is the course."

The booklet was passed round the group, each member studying the page with the course details, then flicking to the other pages, looking for details to question him further.

Flint gazed out through the open door of the house. He could see a pair of booby birds skimming the waves out to sea. Would they have similar birds in England? Yes, England was an island so they would have something similar, he thought.

"Where in England is it?"

"Just north of London."

"Where will you live?"

"There is a student residence or they help you find a flat."

"Will all the other students be English?"

"No, they say about a third of the students are from other countries."

One of the elders turned to a page showing a group of young people sitting on the side of a swimming pool, "I am not sure," he began to express doubts, but before he could continue he was interrupted.

"What will it cost?"

"I have worked out the cost in pounds and our currency. Everything, fees, travel, accommodation, everything! It is very expensive for a student from outside England." Flint passed round a paper showing details of all the costs.

A black feathered cockerel strutted past the open door but it was ignored by some nearby hens which were scratching in the dust.

There were furrowed brows and gasps of “So much”.

“Have you got your passport yet?” asked one of the elders.

“Passport, oh no,” confessed Flint.

“Well you better get that organized and do you know if you need any special visas?”

For a moment Flint looked blank. He had been so busy finding out about courses in England that he had forgotten about travel documents he admitted to himself. Now he wondered if there were other necessary things he had forgotten.

The discussion lasted late into the night. The enterprise was very expensive and there was no guarantee of success, but if they did not follow this path would they ever achieve the goal set by the community. It was obvious that no decision would or could be reached that evening.

Over the next few days individual members discussed their concerns or voiced their support to Flint. He was also aware that small groups within the community were forming and reforming to explore their attitudes.

Flint knew they had the financial resources to support his project but he began to feel they lacked the will to back his plan.

There were no words to express Flint’s disappointment at the lack of decision. He felt betrayed by the community, all the work, all the research, all the planning, for what? There was a group of old men who did not have the courage of his convictions.

The days dragged as he awaited their decision. All the energy and enthusiasm which had driven his last three years as a student were draining away. He felt he could not sit around at home waiting for a lot of old men to make up their minds. Had they forgotten what happened? How their island, their homeland had been taken by the English soldiers. How they had been told that everyone would have to move to another island, to a strange place. How those who resisted were shot and their bodies dumped into the sea.

Flint had learnt that the past must not be forgotten, not forgiven.

Why did the elders procrastinate when he had devised a plan to use deadly cholera bacteria which could escape premature detection and would accomplish the desired end?

"You must be patient," was his mother's advice. "These men have waited so long; it is so important to them: they need to be certain in their own minds."

But patience is not a characteristic of the young and ambitious.

"But they chose me."

Part Two

Chapter 5

Yes, she remembered the day when she had been awarded a place at Sillfield University. Louise could not find words to describe her happiness. This was the news she had been awaiting but hardly daring to believe that it could happen. This was the next step along the path to her ambition, the realisation that she could, she would decide her own future and work towards it. Where had this ambition come from? There was nothing in her background which drove her. No one in her family had gone to university. The assumption had been that she would leave school and get whatever job she could. Of course she would marry, have children, but all this would happen in the tight knit community in which she had grown up.

Louise tried to decide what had made the difference. There was perhaps one single event that had changed things. It was over eight years ago when her friend Emma's mother had been taken ill and was going to spend some time in hospital. Life might have turned out very differently if Emma's mother had not needed an operation. Emma's father said he would not have time to look after his daughter so he would take up the offer from his sister to look after Emma. Emma had announced that she was not going to stay with an aunt she hardly knew, nearly two hundred miles away, unless her friend Louise could go with her. That is how Louise found herself in a car, with Emma, on the first day of their school holidays. They were heading down the motorway away from the village where both the girls had grown up.

Louise looked out of the car window at the seemingly endless miles of countryside. They did not pass through any towns or villages. There was nothing like the mining village which had always been Louise's home. Even when they turned off onto a country road the villages they passed through were different. Louise's village had rows of narrow red-brick terraced houses, but here there were individual cottages built of a warm coloured stone. Some even had thatched roofs.

"We'll soon be at Sally's place," said Emma's father as he drove his old, battered car into the small town. "I think this is their street."

It was not a street but a wide road with large houses on either side. Each house had a generous garden with mature trees. Expensive highly polished cars were parked in the drives outside the houses.

Louise began to feel a nervous excitement. Emma had said her aunt and uncle, Sally and Paul, were rich but the people who lived in these beautiful houses must be very rich.

The house confirmed Louise's view. The wide front door led into a light spacious hallway. There seemed to be a confusing array of rooms, all beautifully furnished with highly polished tables and cupboards. Everything was very neat and tidy. The kitchen was huge and contained an amazing range of appliances, but Louise was very relieved when the evening meal Sally cooked turned out to be beef burger and chips which they ate at the kitchen table.

"This house is fantastic. I cannot imagine having a house like this. I mean somewhere so posh and expensive," said Louise as she settled into her bed in the room she was to share with Emma.

"Sally and Paul have their own company. Don't know what they do but we'll see it tomorrow. Sally's got to go into work in the morning and we are going with her as Paul is away," explained Emma.

The drive to the office took only a few minutes the next morning. Louise and Emma were sorry it was such a short journey as they felt like princesses sitting in the shiny new car that Sally drove.

The office was in a glass and concrete building surrounded by smooth lawns and neat flower beds.

"Trudy, this is my niece Emma and her friend Louise. Could you show them around and explain what we try to do in this place? You said you did not have a meeting until eleven and by that time I should be free." Sally turned to the girls, "Trudy organises the conferences run by PSW, but she knows all about our other work so she can explain things to you and introduce you to some of the people in the office."

Trudy turned to Emma and Louise and, with a welcoming smile, said, "Yes, I would be delighted to show you round, but can you give me a moment while I send a quick email."

As Trudy tapped at her keyboard Louise looked round the office. It was a large square room with big windows on two sides. There were about eight desks in the office, each partly surrounded by screens. Five of the desks were occupied by people busy using their keyboards or talking on the telephone. Everyone looked very busy and there was a buzz of activity.

Louise's attention switched back to Trudy. She thought how neat and smart Trudy looked, more like something from a magazine or TV programme than from real life. Her glossy dark hair was pulled back into a short pony tail, her white blouse looked brand new, her make-up was light and expertly applied, not like some of the gaudy stuff worn by a lot of the young shop or office girls Louise saw at home. Trudy's only jewellery was some little earrings which perfectly set off her dainty face.

"There that's done. They should open that up first thing when they get to the office in Montreal," said Trudy as she stood up. "Now how much do you know about PSW, our history and our present work?" Neither girl replied. "Not much I suppose. Well, the company was set up about 10 years ago by Sally and Paul Walker because they realised that scientists, engineers and technicians, working in new high technology areas, had trouble if they wanted to set up a company and wanted to go into business. They were not always very good at explaining what they were doing. They did not always get their message across to other people. They had difficulty getting money for investment and did not understand how to handle the press and media to get the best image presented for their inventions and research."

Emma was already getting bored with the visit to the office. She did not care what scientists and people like that did.

Louise was curious about what went on here and why nearly half the desks were empty. Were so many people away ill? That was the explanation when there were empty chairs at school.

"The main activities are working with clients to prepare press releases, arrange conferences and other meetings, and help introduce our clients to investors and people who can help them with their business development," continued Trudy. "I do most of the conference organisation, booking places to have the meetings, arranging speakers, inviting people to attend, all that sort of thing. We are planning our first conference outside the UK, in Canada, in Montreal. It's proving quite a challenge to organize from a distance, but it's fun and I am looking forward to visiting Montreal."

Louise had never thought of work as fun or a challenge.

In the meantime Emma was trying to see an escape route from this office tour; perhaps she could say she needed to go to the toilet and could just stay there.

"Let me introduce you to Steve who is our expert in marketing. He helps our clients decide which market they should enter, the timing and will help them understand the barriers to market entry." Both girls knew what a market was but, somehow, this good looking young man with his white shirt and brightly coloured tie did not look like a market trader.

Steve sensed their confusion and explained that when a company was launching a new product it had to decide which country it should be sold in, should it be sold directly to the public or through an existing shop. Were there any regulations it had to comply with? There were a hundred and one decisions to be made before a new product could be sold, especially in the hi-tech area.

To Louise it was all new ideas and very interesting.

Meanwhile Emma's attention had been caught by a series of cartoons pinned to the partition next to Steve's desk. "What's that?" she asked.

"Oh, Jayne has done those as part of a marketing exercise for some new software. The software will help in the development of on-line shopping for people with disabilities which make it difficult for them to use existing systems."

Emma studied the cartoons and thought about the skill of the artist who showed so much with just a few pen strokes. She enjoyed art and design at school; it was the only subject she did enjoy. She then looked at another drawing pinned to the partition. This showed a strange spiral shape running into a dollar sign. "What's that?" she said.

"That one is for a new biotechnology company which is using genetic information to develop novel drugs," said Steve, then realising that both girls were out of their depth, "You know that scientists are working to find out all about the genetic information, the chromosomes, the genes we inherit from our parents. Then, using the results of this research, they can make better medicines to treat illnesses. This design shows a double spiral which represents the DNA, that's the stuff your genes are made of. Then this runs into a dollar sign so it suggests that money can be made using the DNA information."

Trudy sensed that the conversation was becoming much too technical and she wanted to make things more interesting for the teenagers. "Jayne does the design work. She works from home most of the time. She has a young family and working at home suits her well. Pity she won't be in today for you to meet her. She's a really nice person. Dr. Wild is in today perhaps you should meet him. He only comes in once or twice a week. Thanks Steve." Trudy shepherded the girls away from Steve as they muttered their thanks.

"Where are all the other people? Are they all away sick?" asked Louise as they walked between the empty desks.

"Oh no, they are working outside, visiting places, meeting clients. None of us spend much time tied to our desks," laughed Trudy.

Chapter 6

John Wild was an older man who was sitting at a desk in the corner of the office. Behind him was a bookcase filled with official looking books and files. As they approached John looked up from his book.

"John, this is Sally's niece Emma and her friend Louise. They are here on a visit today." Turning to the girls, Trudy explained, "John is a wonderful source of experience and knowledge for the office."

"A source of experience and knowledge, I don't know about that," laughed John. "Perhaps it's just a way of saying I have been round a long time. I don't work full-time for PSW, but I come in a few days a week to help write some of the more technical items for them and to do some market research. I have quite a good library of reference books and reports here which I can use." John waved his hand at the shelves around his desk. "There are a lot of government statistics which are useful. Also I have contacts across business and they come in handy. I ran my own business making sensors to go into planes and satellites, all exciting stuff, but we were bought out by a German company. They offered me a good job in the new organisation but it would not have been the same as running my own show, so now I act as a consultant to various companies. It keeps my hand in but also gives me freedom to select the work I prefer. I do not want to retire completely and I find this interesting."

Then he turned and looked at Emma and Louise more directly. "But tell me about yourselves. What interests you? What do you want to do in the future? What age are you?"

Neither girl wanted to respond to his questions.

"I have a granddaughter, about your age, she's fifteen. She is quite good at science at school but prefers languages. Says she wants to go into something in international business, wants to be able to use her work to travel. I tell her to get lots of good qualifications then the world's her oyster. So many opportunities for well qualified young people these days, an exciting time to be starting a career. So, what are your interests at school?"

Louise pondered what John had said. He looked quite old, as old as her grandfather. Her grandfather had given up work, something to do with a bad back, but there were comments around the family that the bad back was an excuse to get out of work. Her grandfather had always hated work. She wondered about this man who did not want to retire. All her experience was that most people disliked work or, at best, tolerated it. She had never heard anyone in her family say they enjoyed it and did not want to get out of it.

In the meantime Emma had decided it was her turn to hold the stage. "Art is my best subject at school. I want to be an artist, do drawings like the ones over there," she said waving her hand at the cartoons they had been looking at earlier.

Louise was surprised at this reply as Emma had never expressed any interest in a job as an artist. Emma's interests were shopping, certain television programmes and a boy in the year ahead of them at school.

"Commercial art and advertising, yes, a good area if you have the right talents. Of course you need to go to college to develop all the techniques and skills, that's if you have talent in that direction...good luck," observed John. "And what about you Louise? Where do your talents lie?"

Louise felt a sense of panic rising. She did not think she had any talents. She searched her mind for something sensible to say. "This office seems very interesting, perhaps I could work somewhere like this," she floundered.

Fortunately Sally reappeared at that moment. "My meeting finished early. Hope you have had a good look round and it has not been too boring." Sally thanked Trudy for showing the teenagers round.

"Your niece seems to be interested in commercial art. Perhaps we will see her work here at some time in the future," laughed John. "But I think Louise is still wondering about her path ahead," he said smiling at Louise.

As they got ready to leave the office Sally suggested lunch at a local pizza bar followed by a trip to a cinema. Both girls leapt at this chance.

Later, while Sally was finding a place to park the car, Louise turned to Emma, "You never said you wanted to do art when you left school."

"I had to say something. It was the first thing I thought of. I might try art. It would be great to see a drawing up on a poster, a big ad; but what about you?"

Again Louise was saved by the return of Sally and the business of selecting what topping to have on her pizza.

It was later when Louise returned to the question what about herself? She had never really considered the future, at least not beyond what clothes to wear tomorrow or what presents she might get for her next birthday. It had always been assumed that she would leave school as soon as possible and then she would get some sort of job. No one seemed to think that there was much choice in life. You had to take what was available. However, after the visit to PSW she was beginning to think that, perhaps, there could be a choice.

That evening, as she helped Sally clear the dinner table, Louise plucked up courage to try to find out more about what was needed to get a job in a place like PSW. Emma was already watching TV so Louise did not feel the risk of looking ridiculous in front of her friend.

"Well, we specialise in hi-tech areas so most of our people have degrees in a science subject and then, because we are helping clients with their public relations, they have qualifications or experience in some aspect of business such as marketing or advertising." Sensing that Louise was genuinely interested and not just trying to be polite to her hostess, Sally continued, "I did a degree in chemistry then research for three years and got a Ph.D. Ph.D. stands for Doctor of Philosophy. That's why people call me Doctor. It's different from being a medical doctor, although it does get confused and sometimes people expect me to treat their illnesses. I am a scientist not a medical doctor."

"I didn't know they were different."

"After university I worked for a chemical company, worked in a lab then became more interested in the business side of things. The how and why do people make certain business decisions. The chemical industry is a big industry. A few wrong decisions in a company and they can lose lots of money, lose lots of jobs."

Louise knew about job loss. The people in the village where she grew up understood job loss very clearly.

"I went back to university for a year to get an MBA, a Master of Business Administration degree. It was a lot of work for a year but opened up loads of new doors."

"Of course, most of the people in the company do not have as many qualifications as Paul and I, but they all have at least a first degree and keep up to date with all the technical and business developments. Trudy has a degree in history, but she has learnt the scientific terms. She is good at administration, very organised."

Louise had a very sketchy idea of what was needed to go to university and get a degree. Teachers at school had mentioned it but Louise had not thought all that stuff applied to her. None of her family had been to university. "Don't you have to be very good at school to go to university? Doesn't it cost lots of money?"

"Well, you need to work fairly hard and stick with it through GCSEs and A levels. Money, yes, that is becoming more of a problem, but there are grants, loans, holiday jobs. It's worth it in the long run. My family were not well off and I am the only one to have gone to university. It was difficult at times but it has been worth it. My career has been very interesting. I enjoy the work and we have been lucky, so we have a nice house and a good standard of living."

Louise and Emma enjoyed the rest of their stay with Sally and Paul. They were taken out every day and even spent a day in London visiting Madame Tussaud's. All the time, however, Louise thought about her conversation with Sally, she thought about PSW and about Trudy. It would be nice to look as smart as Trudy, to have an interesting job and a beautiful home. Perhaps, if she worked a bit harder at school, she could be like Trudy.

CHAPTER 7

After the visit to PSW the rest of the school holidays seemed long for Louise. For the first time in her life she looked forward to the beginning of term. Perhaps, just perhaps, if she worked harder she could do better at school. She discovered the nearest library. It took courage but she went in and looked at the shelves of books.

"You know that this is the reference section. You can't take these out but can read them in here," explained the librarian. His bright blue eyes seemed to dance as he spoke to her. She had thought that all librarians were old and dusty. "What section do you want? I can show you where it is."

"Things about going to university," Louise asked tentatively.

"We had quite a lot of prospectuses for different colleges and universities but you will find loads more on-line."

The next hour was spent pouring through glossy brochures and on-line sites filled with pictures of smiling happy students in gleaming laboratories, fabulous sports facilities, comfortable halls of residence and large lecture halls. It all looked wonderful, almost too good to be true. She looked at the array of courses offered at these wonderful places. The choice was overwhelming and confusing. She would need help understanding all that stuff, but she was not sure that university was the place she could get to.

She visited the library several times during the summer and started taking books out. Most were returned unread as they proved too difficult or boring after the first few pages, but some of the novels she found exciting. Once she had started reading them she could not put them down.

She found she preferred reading to watching television or hanging about in the local park with Emma.

When term started Louise was ready and prepared to test her abilities. She paid attention in lessons rather than gazing out of the window daydreaming. She did her homework and took a little extra time to make sure everything was done neatly and completely. She had never found school difficult but previously had been disinterested.

She found most subjects easy and her new sense of purpose made lessons more interesting. Soon her change of attitude was reflected in her marks and the perspective of the teachers. They took an interest in her work, were keen to discuss some of the finer points of her homework. By Christmas she had risen from somewhere close to the bottom of the class to something approaching the top group.

When the class was subdivided into study groups she found herself put together with the high fliers. She developed friendships with some of her brightest fellow pupils. She discussed the future with these new friends, Ann and Max. Ann had already decided she wanted to study medicine. Both her parents were doctors. Max was not so sure. One day it was law, the next it was journalism, and then again he wanted to run his own business, perhaps designing computer games. Louise mentioned a future in public relations. That seemed to impress everyone even if they were not sure what it was.

Her friendship with Emma was on the wane, their paths separating. Emma had become interested in a group of boys who were a few years older and had already left school. They liked to spend their time in the pubs. Emma discovered that a change of hairstyle and some makeup made her look old enough to join the drinkers. The last straw was when Emma confided in Louise that she thought she was pregnant. Louise insisted Emma should see a doctor and tell her parents.

"But me Dad will kill me and me Mum's illness will get worse if I tell them," complained Emma.

"They'll find out sooner or later, better tell them now."

The pregnancy was confirmed and a baby was born the following summer when Emma was just sixteen. Only half Emma's predictions came true. Her father did not kill her but her mother's condition worsened.

Louise held the baby and looked into its pretty little pink face, but then it started to cry. It cried most of the time so Emma got very little sleep and she was extremely tired. Louise watched her friend push the pram through the village and felt sad that Emma now seemed to have such a limited future, while she was beginning to plan her own exciting years ahead.

For Louise that summer was productive in a different way. She got a job during the holiday. It was not much, just working in a local shop. The pay was poor but to Louise it was a taste of financial independence. She had offered to give some of the money to her mother, but the offer was declined as it was decided that most of the money should be saved to help pay for her way through university. Suddenly Louise realised that her parents were suggesting that she could get that far.

At home there had always been the need for thrift and to have some emergency savings. Her parents had managed to buy their house, one in a terrace, and had never run up debts. They had encouraged Louise to follow a similar path.

Louise's parents were delighted and astonished by the change in their daughter. They had married in their thirties and it was five years before their only child appeared. Although they were devoted to their daughter, they had little idea about the needs of a child who had ambition and academic ability. No one in their families had gone to university. They were pleased by her blossoming but they did not wish it to change their own quiet routine lifestyle.

The school predicted good exam results so Louise needed to decide on subjects for A-level and what course at university. She found her academic aptitude stretched across a wide range of subjects, her abilities opened up the whole vista of possibilities but then she attended the lecture.

The lecture, by Professor Don Miller, was given a great build-up at school. It was made clear that the chance to be there would only be offered to those students who would gain the most by attending. It would be a wonderful opportunity for the chosen few to have this great privilege. Louise was amongst this select group.

Professor Miller, they were told, was a pioneering academic who was a leading figure in the development of biotechnology. He was presenting a limited number of lectures to groups of school children and would be explaining biotechnology, which was the use of biology in the service of mankind and its application to provide products and services to industry.

On the day of the lecture Louise joined the elite band on the bus taking them to the university some twenty miles away. The air of expectancy was growing by the mile. What secrets of science would this great man reveal?

On entering the lecture theatre Louise was surprised. She had expected an old fashioned environment with hard, dark, wooden benches, but, in fact, it had rows of comfortable padded blue seats. Between each seat, tucked away, was a writing surface. When this was pulled up it could be used as a little table to rest papers. At the front of the lecture theatre was a huge white board flanked on either side by large screens. In front of these was a raised platform with a lectern set to one side and on the other side a table and chairs.

Chapter 8

The lecture theatre was filling with groups of young people; the different school uniforms formed a mosaic across the rows of seats. Everyone's expectations were reflected in the buzz of conversation.

At the appointed time a side door opened and three men entered. The first was very smartly dressed in a dark suit. Was this the professor? The second man wore a crumpled corduroy jacket, rather baggy trousers and his shirt was open at the neck. Yes, this looked like an academic professor. Behind them there emerged a very elderly man walking slowly with the aid of a walking stick. What was 'Old Father Time' doing here? His dark suit hung on his withered frame. Louise could hardly see the face beneath the thick thatch of white hair. He shuffled slowly to the table and sat on one of the chairs.

"Oh shit, I hope that's not him," muttered Max, who was sitting next to Louise.

After a few moments deliberation the stage party of three crossed to the lectern. From where Louise sat it appeared that the man in the corduroy jacket was explaining the use of some controls and switches on the side of the lectern. The lights in the room were dimmed then returned to full illumination. The microphone seemed to be switched on and off. The white board and screens were illuminated momentarily by projectors at the back of the theatre.

The audience was getting restless.

"When are they going to get on with it?" was the stage whisper from Max.

At last the lectern operation instruction class came to an end and corduroy jacket and Old Father Time returned to their seats.

The smart suited man switched on the microphone and introduced himself as an official of the trade association which was sponsoring the lecture tour of Professor Miller. He spent a few minutes extolling the wonders of biotechnology. This was to be the great industrial revolution, opportunities were being created and it would all be wonderfully exciting. He then started to read out the CV, the biography, of Professor Miller. His academic posts, his numerous published scientific papers and books, his involvement with government advisory and international regulatory bodies, and his role in setting up and consulting to fledgling industrial companies was outlined.

While this was going on Louise pondered which was the great man. Perhaps, just perhaps, he was not on the platform yet. Would he enter from the side door or was there a trap door so he could pop up?

"And now I call upon Professor Miller to speak to you," said dark suit with a final flourish of his hand at 'Old Father Time'.

Louise felt her heart sink. All this build-up had been for some doddering old grandfather. She felt cheated. Max was already drawing rude cartoons on a piece of paper on the writing surface in front of him.

The old man got to his feet, put his walking stick on the table and walked to the lectern. He seemed to get steadier and taller with each stride. His suit now seemed to fit him. Had he grown during those footsteps? As he turned to face the audience Louise felt that two bright eyes under the white hair were engaging her directly.

"Good morning, future biotechnologists," said Professor Miller in clear steady tones. Then he flicked a couple of switches on the lectern control panel. The room lights dimmed and the three screens behind the Professor were illuminated, the centre with the Professor's name and his academic affiliation, the one on the right showed a picture of a crusty loaf of bread, while on the left there was a pint glass of foaming beer. Food and drink are always a good opening gambit for any student audience.

Louise had intended to take notes during the lecture but she found herself mesmerised by the torrent of information. She was swamped by the facts and figures. The stream of slides and words took her from the pre-historic uses of yeast to make bread and wine, to the development of antibiotics. Then they spun on to the discovery of the genetic code and how it was used to develop new crops, breed animals and understand human disease.

If Louise had glanced round the lecture theatre she would have seen every face was focused on the elderly professor and his slides. Even Max had abandoned his cartooning.

Although Louise had been aware of many of the uses of biotechnology described, she now saw them in a different light. A kind and clean technology could change the world, offer hope for future generations.

The lecturer moved on to the subject of cleaning polluted land and oil slicks at sea. Was there no end to the wonders that could be performed? They were swept into a future in which computers would be based on ideas and parts taken from biology.

Max leant forward, "Small, fast, good."

Louise was struggling to hold on to the flood of facts. Would there be nothing that biotechnology could not do? Would all the old technologies be swept aside under this tide of biotechnology?

Louise felt on a high, so many new ideas, so many facts, and such a sense of optimism.

"That was great. I thought it was going to be really boring when I saw the old man, but he was fantastic," said Louise as they came out of the university building to look for their bus.

"Yes, I liked the way he used the three screens at once. Clever how he made ideas move across between the screens," acknowledged Max, who had an intense fascination with visual effects.

"Um, his description about the future treatment of diabetes was interesting," was Ann's first comment. She was thinking about her aunt who had to prick her finger to take blood samples, then inject insulin to control diabetes. In spite of doing all this her aunt collapsed from time to time and had to be rushed into hospital.

"It all sounds so exciting. I had no idea that biotechnology was going to be used in so many ways." Louise had changed a lot in the last two years. Then she never considered the future, it would not have occurred to her that she could influence events. Now she was a very mature confident student. She wanted to have a hand in her own destiny.

"It's all a long way in the future; may never happen. Not like computers and IT; that's here now," said Max as he got onto the bus and led the three friends to the back seat.

"All the work on new drugs was interesting. Would be good if better drugs could be made for a lot of diseases, but it's all so expensive." Ann was taking world poverty issues to heart these days. She always watched the television programmes which dealt with Third World issues. She thought the drug companies should use some of their profits to help people in the poorer countries but she did not think they would.

"There should be lots of interesting jobs by the time we have finished at university." Again Louise had her eye on the future.

"I don't want to wait that long. Two more years at school to do A-levels then me and Jake, my cousin, are going to set up our own business designing computer games." Jake had already talked to a company who said they were interested. Max was confident that they were going to be millionaires by the time they were twenty-five.

Louise knew Jake. He was a couple of years older than her but such a pale skinny guy that Louise could not imagine him succeeding at anything. Jake and entrepreneurial millionaire were two images she could not merge in her mind.

"I'm not interested in the money. I want to be able to help people." Ann knew she would need to go to Medical School until she was about twenty-five, but then she would be able to fulfil her need for dedication by working with children in the Third World, in Africa, perhaps.

As the bus rumbled through the countryside Louise thought about her life ahead. Her aspirations were more modest, and perhaps more attainable, than those of Max. Enough money to be able to have a nice life, a decent house, a car, perhaps to be able to travel, would suit her. Having her own business, she wasn't sure. People always say they want to make a million, but they don't do it. The work has got to be interesting

"Something in research would be good."

"Research! That means staying at university for about six years, that's too long," Max was impatient with life.

"Medicine is that long, but you start to work in the hospital before you qualify, so I will start helping patients while I'm still training." Ann's sense of the dedicated life drove her on.

"I'm going to look at what A-levels and what grades I'll need to get for courses for biotechnology. Professor Miller said biochemistry, genetics, microbiology. Things like that would be good."

"You'll just end up owing lots of money if you go to university. That's crazy. I want to have a sports car and go on great holidays skiing, California. I don't want to wait."

Louise felt excited and certain in her mind that biotechnology could offer her everything she wanted. She would be able to travel and go to interesting places when she left university and might even be able to visit places while she was still a student. There might be field courses or meetings in other countries.

Perhaps it is the certainty of youth that can lead an individual to a life-shaping decision after a single one-hour lecture.

Chapter 9

During Louise's last two years at school the head teacher noted with pleasure the change in attitude and performance of his pupil. The biology teacher was one of the chorus who agreed that Louise had become one of the top students. Her attention in class was excellent, her homework was always done and she was mixing with the most ambitious and competitive in the year. The expectation for her exam results was high and she outperformed even this target.

Louise was narrowing down the list of universities offering the courses which interested her. There was support from the school as she sent off her applications and eventually there was the breathless excitement of hearing that she had secured a place at the university which had become her first choice.

The summer before she left home seemed a whirl. What would she need as she started her new life? What would be necessary for her to take to her room in the hall of residence? She had already seen how small the rooms were and how basic the accommodation was when she had visited the university on an open day. Now it would be a reality and there were decisions to be made.

Of course, life was different at university. Initially there was the adjustment to living in the hall of residence with strangers, some of whom Louise found intimidating. They had arrived with a sophisticated array of computers, TVs, suitcases of clothes and crates of cooking equipment; far too much to fit into the cramped living space. They talked about having spent time working in a summer camp in Canada or having had a job in London. Everyone seemed to have had so much experience and appeared better prepared for university.

To counter these feelings of inadequacy Louise threw herself into academic work. Every evening she wrote up her lecture notes neatly, she read extensively and was generally regarded as a swot! She restricted her time spent in the communal areas of the residence, preferring the privacy of her own room. Party and pub time was restricted to Saturday evenings. Louise desperately wanted to catch up with her better informed classmates. Preparation for the first set of exams was thorough.

To Louise's amazement and delight the hard work paid off. Her exam results were excellent and she had comfortably outperformed most of her classmates. She felt the self-confidence of someone who knows they can succeed. The surge of self-assurance allowed Louise to relax into university life and enjoy a whole range of activities during the next term. She was no longer the swot who isolated herself in her room.

It was the first day that Louise was home for Easter when the news spread through the village. Emma's mother had died. The same conversation was held in nearly every house: too young to go, terrible illness, perhaps relief from pain, daughter's problems contributed to the suffering.

Louise felt sad. Although she and Emma had pursued very different paths in the last few years she could remember the time when they were constantly in and out of each other's houses. She had regarded Emma's parents as family. Their house and routine was almost as familiar as that of her own home. She knew where the crockery went in the kitchen cupboards, what biscuits they usually ate, and where the spare rolls of toilet paper were kept.

She decided she would attend the funeral. It would be an act of respect for the dead and, perhaps, a gesture of support for Emma.

The crematorium was on the edge of the closest town, a bus ride away. As fate would have it, the bus was late that day. Louise looked at her watch as she found a seat. She would be a few minutes late arriving, perhaps the start would be delayed and she would make it in time. She had only been to one funeral before, that of her grandfather, and she was not sure of the procedure.

Eventually the bus reached the stop outside the crematorium and she stepped off into warm spring sunshine. She walked as fast as she could through the cemetery to the chapel. It would not have been appropriate to run, but, on the other hand, she did not wish to arrive even later by taking time to enjoy the pleasant weather.

As she slipped quietly into the chapel the service was just beginning. What a contrast to the pleasant atmosphere outside. The chapel was dark, little sunshine penetrated the narrow windows and that which did was swallowed by the dark stone and woodwork. The warmth of the sun did nothing to warm this place. Only the flowers on the coffin offered any contrast to the sober scene.

There were about twenty people in the pews at the front but Louise decided to cause the least disturbance by sitting at the back. It was difficult to recognise many of the people huddled in their dark clothes with their heads bent, but she saw Emma and her father in the front pew, close to the wreath-bedecked coffin. Emma was holding a baby in her arms and next to her was her three-year old son, just visible, standing facing the back of the chapel. The child was dressed in a bright red football shirt; such a contrast to the drab outfits worn by everyone else. An elderly church minister was shuffling some papers and then began to speak in such a low, quiet voice that Louise could hardly hear what was said.

The red shirted youngster was getting restless. He climbed onto the seat between his mother and grandfather. As everyone rose to sing the hymn 'Abide with me' the child moved along the seat, squeezing behind his mother, to the end next to the aisle. His mother appeared not to notice this as she was attending to the crying baby in her arms. The little boy got down into the aisle and began to make his way to the coffin. No-one tried to stop him. Louise felt that there was potential for disaster, she knew how unruly this child could be. She thought back to a visit she had made last summer to see Emma in a flat she was sharing with the latest boyfriend.

The flat had been above a local shop and was approached up a dark narrow staircase at the back of the building. There was a single room with some rudimentary kitchen facilities and somewhere there was a bathroom but Louise was spared the need to enter this. The main room was bad enough. There was a double bed on which Emma's boyfriend was sprawled drinking beer from a bottle and smoking a cigarette. Louise and the pregnant Emma sat on the only two chairs in the room. They had once been comfortable armchairs but now they were dirty and the springs had gone. Louise felt ill at ease and avoided putting her arms and hands on the grimy upholstery.

When Louise had arrived the child was sitting, in the middle of the floor, on a potty surrounded by plastic toys. He was systematically picking up each plastic component and throwing it as far as his little arms could manage.

"Stop that," was Emma's maternal intervention to control the situation.

When the heap of toys within arm's reach was exhausted the child got up from the potty and toddled, naked from the waist down, to a collection of empty drink cans and bottles at the bottom of the bed. He started to shake and bang these together to make the maximum amount of noise. Somewhere in this process he discovered that there was some beer left in the bottom of one of the cans. He emptied this over his head and proceeded to methodically examine the rest of the cans in order to repeat the experience.

Emma seemed oblivious to this activity going on less than one yard from where she was sitting, smoking a cigarette. Then suddenly, in a burst of activity, she grabbed a can from the child. “Eh stop that, give over, I’ve told yer.”

The child dodged away from his mother and continued the meticulous search for traces of drink in the bottles and cans.

At the time Louise had admired the curiosity and physical coordination of this two-year old, but had felt desperate about his future. Now, in the chapel, she saw the same curiosity in the child’s face as he approached the coffin and grabbed a wreath, a daffodil in each little hand. The previously inert congregation erupted into action. Women hurried out of each pew and about six of them appeared to collide in the dash to control the boy. He, in the meantime, dodged round the coffin and started to run down the side aisle towards the door at the back of the chapel. Louise was perfectly positioned to head him off. She stepped into his path and scooped him up in her arms before he had a chance to plan another escape route.

Louise carried the child to the front pew and sat down next to Emma as the final strains of ‘Abide with me’ died away.

The rest of the service continued uneventfully. It seemed very short and Louise had the distinct impression that the minister knew no more than the name of the woman whose last mortal remains lay in the wooden box before him.

As they emerged from the chapel into the sweet air and smell of spring, Emma thanked Louise for the rescue and child care help. “We’re going to the pub across the road. Can yer come?”

“Well there’s a bus in ten minutes,” began Louise looking for a way out.

"Louise isn't it?" came a voice from behind.

Louise spun round to see the smiling face of Sally beneath the brim of a very smart black hat.

"Emma has told me how well things are going for you. Microbiology isn't it? Tell me about it at the pub."

Louise immediately changed her mind and strolled down the drive through the cemetery, across the road and into the pub with Sally. Louise felt her spirits lift as she passed the flower beds bright with the sunshine faces of daffodils and narcissi. The presence of Sally who was dressed immaculately in a fitted black suit, grey silk blouse, black stockings and simple black shoes helped restore a sense of optimism. The rest of the funeral party looked shabby but Sally made the clothes of mourning look elegant.

Over plates of indifferent sandwiches, sausage rolls and pork pie, washed down with gin and tonic, they exchanged brief condolences over the departed, then got down to the real business of investigating how much Louise had changed in the past few years. Sally had the impression of a confident young woman full of enthusiasm for student life and excited about future prospects.

"What are your plans for the summer? Got a job lined up?" Sally seized the initiative.

"Nothing settled yet, but must make some money."

"Interested in helping us at a conference we're running?"

Before the last drops of the gin and tonics had been drained it had been decided Louise would spend the summer working at PSW, preparing for, then helping, at a conference to be held in September, just five months away.

CHAPTER 10

The summer term at university passed happily for Louise. She was quietly confident that her exam results would be good. She was mixing with some of the brightest students in a range of subjects. They were all looking forward to successful future careers. Louise mentioned her plans for the summer and the job with PSW. She thought about Sally. Sally had not left university after her first degree but had continued her studies and gained further qualifications. Louise wondered if she could, should follow a similar path. Student friends encouraged the idea.

By the end of her first year Louise had established a good academic record and developed ambitious plans for her future. She was to spend a week at home with her parents, then off to PSW for two months work. There would be two weeks for a holiday before university started again.

Her first day at home was spent catching up on all the news and gossip from the village.

Since the death of her mother, Emma, with her two children, had moved in with her father. She appeared to have changed a lot, settled down, become a responsible mother and daughter.

There was some vague news about Ann. Her last two years at school had not gone well. She found she could not keep up with the work. This had surprised Louise who had always looked up to Ann as the clever one, the brainbox. When they left school Ann's examination results had been very poor. There was no hope of her getting into medical school. The story, according to Louise's mother, was that Ann had become involved in some charity which was helping to establish schools and health clinics in developing countries.

"Oh yes, the organisation sends young people out to these poor countries to work as volunteers."

"That should suit Ann. Always wanted to do something good." Louise thought back to schoolday conversations when Ann had wanted a career that helped people rather than generated personal wealth. Now medicine was denied to her, work with deprived children in some poor country would fulfil her needs.

Max and Jake were doing very well with their company. An old farmhouse on the edge of the village had been bought. Max and his parents lived in the house, while the outbuildings had been converted into offices, studios and workshops. The conversion included a flat for Jake.

The success had amazed everyone. Max had not survived the last two years at school. He had quit halfway through amidst clamours of "That's foolish. You will regret it. You need qualifications."

Louise felt very pleased for Max. She thought it would be nice to see him and get all the good news at first hand.

It was Max's mother who answered the phone. "Louise, yes, Louise. Of course I remember you. Do come over and see us. Just come to the office in the old farm yard. You'll find us there."

The walk through the village to the farm on the outskirts proved interesting. The buds of prosperity were beginning to gradually open; a derelict old house done up there, new windows in a row of terraced cottages here, a face lift for a village shop. Even the local pub had had a coat of paint, a new sign and its garden, which used to resemble a scrap yard, boasted tables, chairs, bright parasols, flowers and, Louise could hardly believe her eyes, a small children's play area. Who went there? What was it like inside? Louise had never been in. It had always looked so uninviting she had never wished to enter.

Louise found Max's place very easily. The old farm yard had very little "old" or "farm" about it now. The buildings had been smartened up, new roofs, new windows. The stone farmhouse stood on one side, while two other sides of the yard were occupied by buildings which once housed farm animals, perhaps horses. The yard was an immaculate paved area with several old horse-troughs filled with displays of plants in full bloom. It was also the parking space for several vehicles including a top of the range Range Rover and a very smart red sports car. Max and Jake had accomplished all this. Louise was amazed.

She found the door marked office and walked in. Max was standing beside a desk, telephone in hand. He beckoned to her.

As Max finished the phone conversation Louise took in her surroundings and her old school friend. The office was neat, tidy and bright with the sunlight of a summer afternoon. In contrast Max was a mess. His jeans were crumpled; the T-shirt looked as if it had been slept in. His hair was all over the place and the face was pale and puffy. Was he not properly awake or was he hung-over?

"Hi, great to see you. Sorry I am a mess. Just woken up. Mum said you were coming. Worked through until 5 o'clock this morning. Didn't get to bed until seven. Come on through."

Max led her through a doorway at the back of the office into a long room full of computer equipment. The work surfaces, which ran round the walls and formed an island up the middle of the room, seemed to be cluttered with screens, keyboards, joysticks, consoles and mice. Three young men were earnestly gazing at one of the screens and there was a cry of "Yes, got it, great!" as Max and Louise entered the workshop.

As they approached the group one of them turned round and Louise recognise Max's cousin Jake. "You did it! You got it to look right. When did you finish? Your Mum said you were just getting to bed as she got up."

Max explained it was about 5 a.m. by the time he was satisfied with his work.

Louise looked at Jake. He had changed in the couple of years since they last met. She remembered him as the skinny, puny geek. He had always appeared pale and thin, and his hair seemed to hang down over his face obscuring his eyes. Now he appeared taller, had filled out and had an attractive golden suntan. The hair was still quite long but brushed back off his face; also it was lighter in colour as if it had been bleached by the sun.

The enthusiasm of the young men was palpable. It was difficult to decide if this was work or play. They were designing and writing the computer games but it was also their role to test them thoroughly. It was their job but they clearly enjoyed trying out the new software.

"This is our latest educational game. It shows how geology works, the movement of tectonic plates. As you play you can move the continents around and see what happens on the surface of the planet. It's meant to be fun but it also helps kids understand the processes. You can see where the volcanoes are, where there will be earthquakes, where the land will rise or sink, all sorts of effects," Jake explained.

Louise was given a demonstration of the prototype of the game. It was fun to play. She could see the educational value, but the greatest impression was the passion of Max and Jake to get their product correct. They were constantly involved in constructive criticism. New ideas were being sparked.

A full tour of the workshop and the room next door, which doubled as an office and conference room, was given. A long

Immediately the trio, which had set out for the pub, was increased to a quartet or, perhaps, two couples, Max and Beth, Jake and Louise.

As they cradled glasses of beer Jake asked Louise about university. Was student life all it was cracked up to be? Was the social life that good? They moved on to discuss what Louise might do when she finished her degree. Louise had the impression that, in spite of his obvious success, Jake felt he might have missed out on something special by not continuing his education through to university. However, before she could explore this thought with him, she became aware that it was time she should leave and go home. Her mother would be preparing a meal and Louise did not want to upset her mother by being late. After all she was home only for a few days. As she got up to leave, Jake followed her to the pub door. Would Louise like to see a film tomorrow? There was something good on in the cinema in the nearest town.

They arranged to meet at the pub the next evening.

Chapter 11

"What's up with you?"

"Nothing. Why?"

"You look a bit pink. Not getting a cold? Not got a temperature?"

"No, Mum, I feel fine."

"Sure?"

"Yes, Mum. Oh, I'll be out tomorrow evening. Going to see that new film."

"How will you get back? The last bus is too early."

"Jake's got a car."

"Jake, Max's cousin?"

Was the conversation when Louise got home.

Yes, Louise did feel a bit pink; it was not due to infection; it was the prospect of a date with a skinny nerd, Jake. Louise tried to tell herself not to be so stupid but then her mind raced on to what to wear.

By the next afternoon she had decided. She would not wear anything too special, just jeans and a plain T-shirt. After all there was no point in trying to impress, she had known Jake for years. Also she did not want to try to compete with Beth, Max's blond goddess with the cleavage. She would just be her normal self but why did she feel so nervous and excited.

She got to the King's Arms at the appointed time and went in through the front door. It was empty except for two older men at the bar and that smell of stale beer and tobacco smoke which haunts every old pub as the ghost of long dispersed drinkers. Little had been done to refurbish this area, perhaps a coat of paint, but still an odd collection of tables, chairs and stools. The pictures and wall hangings spoke more of an earlier taste than anything modern or themed. She walked past the two silent drinkers into a room at the back which was a lounge bar and small restaurant. Still there was no Jake. A door opened into the garden, perhaps Jake was waiting for her in the sunshine. Still there was no-one. Evidentially early Tuesday evening was not a time for commercial success at the King's Arms.

Had she been stood up? Had she left Jake with the impression that she did not wish to go out with him? Was this the right day? She decided to wait ten minutes. Then should she walk up to the old farm to look for him or should she go round and see if Emma was at home? A great tide of indecision swept over her. Perhaps she had misunderstood Jake the previous afternoon. Although her self confidence had improved during the year at university she did not like a sudden change of plan or a disappointment.

She walked to the front of the pub garden adjacent to the road. There was not much traffic, just a few people returning home after working late in nearby towns. Then, as she looked towards the old farm, she saw a red open-topped sports car. In a dramatic change of mood her poise returned and she greeted Jake with a smile. "Thought you had got lost," as he stopped outside the pub.

"Sorry I'm late. Al from California rang just as I was coming out. Managed to sort out the problems over those specs but meant I was running a bit late, sorry," Jake apologised as he leant over to open the car door for Louise.

A ride in an open-topped car was a new experience for Louise. It was great fun but she was surprised by the pressure of the wind on her face. Any suggestion of neat hair went and her eyes started to water. In films the female star always looks immaculate after being exposed to the elements in a high speed drive. She soon learnt that this was a respect in which the celluloid world was less than truthful.

As they drove into the town Jake explained that he would park the car at his uncle's house and they would have a five minute walk to the cinema. He was worried about vandalism if he left the car in the public car park.

"The insurance is bad enough without having any claims. Bloody insurance companies really rip off the young. Just because I'm under 25."

They drove into the quiet residential street and Jake swung the car into the short drive of his uncle's house. A face appeared in the front window, and Jake and an older woman exchanged waves. That must be his aunt thought Louise.

By this time they were a bit late for the film so Jake grabbed Louise's hand with a "Lets run." They made it just in time but had to settle for seats near the front as they each clutched a tub of popcorn.

The film was good. The story had been well published, and thus held no surprises, but it was funny with carefully spaced moments of tension and pathos. When they emerged into the pleasant summer evening Jake and Louise were both laughing. They strolled slowly back to the car looking in the windows of the shops they passed. One selling camping and climbing gear had posters showing magnificent mountain scenes.

"Fantastic views. I'd like to go somewhere like that," Louise commented.

"Yes, last time I was in America I saw some of the mountains. They had a big snowstorm late in the season so Al suggested skiing. We went to Snowbird in Utah. It was great. All that powder snow. I had tried skiing in Scotland once before. That was icy and cold and wet, but Snowbird was dry and the sun was hot. I got burnt, didn't realise that the sun was so strong," Jake touched his face in remembrance.

As they gazed at the posters Louise began to feel envious of Jake's ability to travel.

"I want to travel when I leave uni, when I have the money."

"If you like mountains Yosemite is wonderful. It's a National Park in California, high cliff faces, beautiful waterfalls and there's this mountain, Half Dome. Looks as if someone came along with a knife and cut it in half."

By this time they had reached the car. Jake knocked on the front window of the house and gave his aunt a wave.

Conversation was difficult in an open car with the noise of the wind, but Jake managed to explain his enthusiasm for some of the wild American country Al had shown him. He described photographs taken by the American photographer Ansel Adams, who had done much to elevate photography to a respected art form. When they reached their home village Louise was keen to see some of this art work and get a taste of the spectacular mountain scenery.

They drove into the farmyard and Jake parked next to the Range Rover. His flat was above the conference room and the workshop. It was reached by its own entrance, a door on the end of the building and a steep flight of stairs leading directly into a large room. The immediate impression was one of light and space. The room, which served as living room and kitchen, was painted white and sparsely furnished. Everything looked newly decorated and, indeed, Louise caught a whiff of fresh paint as she walked in. The long window on one side gave an elevated view of the scene that had so impressed her in the conference room the previous day. By now the daylight was fading, but a full moon gave the hills an air of mystery and magic.

Louise stood in the middle of the room looking round.

"Sorry not much furniture yet. Place was only painted a couple of weeks ago; got to get a carpet and sort out the kitchen. Coffee or something else? Don't know what there is." Jake opened the door of the fridge which was in the midst of the partly finished kitchen.

Two bottles of lager were found and, as Louise sat on a cushion on the floor sipping her drink, Jake disappeared through the only door in the room. He appeared a moment later with a book and a rolled-up poster.

"I want to get this framed and put it up on the wall somewhere," he said as he handed the poster to Louise.

They sat next to each other and carefully unrolled the poster on the floor. It had been rolled tightly and refused to lie flat. Louise brushed against Jake as she leant forward to restrain the self-willed piece of paper. The gentle touch of their bodies made Louise very physically aware of Jake and she turned to look at him. Jake too seemed to have lost interest in the poster. The headstrong paper escaped from his grasp, coiled itself and rolled across the floor. He made no attempt to retrieve it but put his arms around Louise, drawing her to him. His kiss was warm and gentle. Louise found it very pleasant, in fact so pleasant that she wanted another, or several more.

The artistic photography of Ansel Adams was very quickly forgotten in favour of more tangible physical pleasures. As Louise put her arms around Jake she was surprised how firm and muscular his body felt, not as she would have expected for one whom, she thought, spent his life fingering a computer keyboard. Perhaps there was more to Jake than she realised. She was uncovering a previously undiscovered side of him.

As they lay on the cushions on the floor Louise allowed Jake's hands to roam over her body. The experience was so pleasurable that she began to return the compliment. She slide her hands up inside his T-shirt to get direct contact with this warm well-toned body.

"It would be more comfortable next-door," said Jake nodding towards the bedroom.

The bedroom followed the same lines as the living area, a large room painted white. One corner had been partitioned off to form a shower room. Piles of books, some computer equipment and heaps of clothes were scattered round the floor. The only furniture was a rowing machine and an unmade double bed. Louise was surprised by the size of the bed. Louise's previous sexual experience had been limited to cramped single beds in student accommodation. It had always been fun, if a rather hurried business, characterised by measures to ensure that neither partner fell out onto the floor.

Jake's love making was unhurried. Louise had not encountered such a competent lover before. The experience was thrilling but, like all good things, it had to come to an end. She felt it was her filial duty to return to her parents' house that night.

As Jake walked her home through the quiet night-time village they laughed at the lack of fulfilment of their intention to examine the photographic work of Ansel Adams. They decided to complete the appraisal the next evening. They would meet at the King's Arms and then go back to Jake's place.

This became the pattern for the rest of the week. A drink at the pub, then return to the hedonistic self-indulgent pleasure of Jake's double bed. His love making was all Louise could have wished for in a physical relationship, and the more he satisfied her the greater her appetite grew for his body.

Their intercourse was not restricted to matters sexual. They explored each other's views on life, and hopes and plans for the future.

Jake had some regrets about not attending university and having missed the chance of student life. However, business success was opening up other very exciting opportunities. He and Max had realistic views about their business futures. Their technology and current ideas would have a limited shelf-life and they would need to move on. They did not wish to grow the company too much as they did not want to have the responsibilities of employing a lot of people. Jake expected to have adequate money to give him freedom of action when it was time to move on.

"It's strange. It was Max who always said he would have the fast car and the ski holidays, but you seem to be the one who has these now," Louise remarked.

"Yes, it does seem a turn around. I used to think that I would do most of the workshop end and Max would be out dealing with the customers but things have gone the other way. Perhaps things always work out differently. I travel to America the whole time now I didn't expect that."

Louise had realised that to follow a career as a scientist a first degree was not enough she would need a Ph.D., a further three years at university. After that, perhaps she could have a job in industry doing research. Academe did not appeal, no money, too much political intrigue. There was a seed of an idea that she would like to establish her own company but this was very vague and unformulated. Perhaps her discussions with Jake were adding nutrition to this concept, but it was too early in her career for any germination or development of this seedling.

Between these various forms of communion, sexual and intellectual, they did take time to admire the work of Ansel Adams and his ability to catch the essence of Yosemite and the Face of Half Dome.

CHAPTER 12

The week at home went all too quickly. Louise had expected it to drag as she waited to go to PSW, but there had been an abrupt change in her life. This change was Jake.

Louise had no concerns about the summer. Sally had helped her find accommodation while she worked at PSW in a flat that was within walking distance of the office. Two friends had shared the flat, but one had left to live with her boyfriend, leaving the other with a place she could not afford on her own. She urgently needed a flatmate for a couple of months. The arrangement was ideal for Louise. Although she had not met her co-tenant it did not matter. The arrangement was short-term.

Louise had planned to travel south by bus. It would be a long and tedious journey, but was the least expensive way of going. However, Jake said he would drive her there. It would take less than three hours and she could easily bring all the things she needed.

The motorway was surprisingly quiet and when they turned on to the country roads through the villages there was little traffic to spoil the journey. Louise thought back to the last time she had followed this route five years previously. She felt much more worldly wise now and enjoyed the pleasure of looking at the rural scene which, at least in her imagination, had changed little in the past five hundred years.

They found the flat with ease. It was not in the smart, prosperous area of town where Sally and Paul lived, but in an older area close to the railway station. The cul-de-sac of terraced houses had been built, about one hundred years previously, of a solid red brick. They had been made to last and had succeeded in achieving this. The street gave the impression that the inhabitants were neat and responsible, if not wealthy. The flat was on the ground floor and consisted of two rooms with a kitchen and small bathroom. Louise was to have the back room which was small, clean and furnished minimally with a bed, a small chest of drawers, a tiny table with a single white chair and a small easy chair. There was no wardrobe but a large hook on one wall could be used to hang clothes.

The flatmate was small, pale and slim. Her jeans and T-shirt could have been bought from a children's department to fit such a tiny frame. Her feet were bare.

"Hi, I'm Jennifer, but everyone calls me Jenny," were her few words of greeting.

Jenny showed Louise which were to be her shelves in the fridge and the kitchen cupboard. It was clear that the relationship was to be that of ships that pass in the night. Their lives in the flat would be completely independent. Jenny was not going to suggest joint meal preparation or even cosy shared cups of coffee. The arrangement sat easily with Louise. To her it was an inexpensive place to stay while she spent the next couple of months accumulating work experience and some money to help fund the next year at university.

Jake maintained a low profile during the tour of the flat but then found a role as a porter carrying Louise's various bags and boxes into her room. He suggested a visit to the closest supermarket to buy in basic supplies.

Pizza followed by strawberries and cream, they decided, would make an excellent last supper before Jake had to leave to drive north. A bottle of wine? Yes. A Californian red Zinfandel was Jake's choice. He lifted it off the shelf and laid it carefully in the shopping trolley. Jake would only have one glass as he had to drive but Louise would be able to enjoy its rich flavour after he had left.

The meal preparation was quick and easy. Then they retreated from the kitchen to Louise's room to eat. Louise watched as Jake poured wine into two tumblers as they could not find any wine glasses.

"Doubt I'll get home during the summer. Don't want to spend money on travelling." She took her first sip of the rich red liquid which tasted quite harsh without food. "Would you like to come down sometime, a weekend, perhaps?" She nibbled at the pizza crust and immediately the harsh feel of the wine mellowed.

"Yes, that would be good. I have to go to America again soon. This is not that far from Heathrow. We could get together."

Louise felt very warm and comfortable. Perhaps it was the wine, or perhaps it was Jake. He was showing such concern over her. He had made the journey easy, he had ensured that all her luggage was in the flat, and he had suggested the trip to the supermarket. He cared for her. Perhaps this was the beginning of love.

The strawberries were shared from a single bowl and they ate with their fingers. It was a messy business but pleasurable as they fed each other with the fruits of summer.

Louise would have liked the pleasure to have attained its ultimate level, but the austere room, the narrow bed and the awareness of the ghost-like presence of Jenny around the flat, somehow dampened their ardour. Also Jake wanted to get home. He was concerned about the level of traffic. It might be a long slow journey and he had a busy time planned for the next few days.

Jake's farewell kisses and caresses were warm and gentle. Louise, although sad to see him leave, was confident that this affair had a future.

The next morning Louise walked the short distance to PSW, arriving in what she thought would be very good time, only to discover that most people were in, already busy with the day's work.

The company had expanded in the past five years and now occupied a whole floor of the building. The main office was much the same as before. The front desk was no longer occupied by Trudy but by an equally smart young woman called Suzy. Apparently Trudy had met a very charming young French Canadian at the conference in Montreal and was now living in Quebec City with her husband and two young children. They were running an antiques business in the old area of the city.

Louise was taken to a smaller side office which had the appearance of a warehouse after a tornado had struck. There were disorganised heaps of boxes and bags and, in the middle, a desk. Here she was introduced to Stewart who looked almost as untidy as the room. His jeans and T-shirt were stained and dusty. His mop of curly dark hair had never been combed, but his smile was very friendly.

"Sorry about this lot, but we've got to get everything out this week to go to a conference in Birmingham next week."

Louise was given a small table and chair in one corner of the room.

There followed a week of fairly mundane tasks such as preparing name badges, sorting event tickets and checking lists. For Louise it felt as if she were the tranquil centre of a whirlwind. The rest of the room was the scene of chaos and panic. The telephone went continuously, the computer printer ran nonstop, people hurried in and out of the room with armfuls of boxes and bags, instructions were given and countermanded. Louise could not see any logic within the operations and considered the organisation to be in a complete state of collapse. She managed to work conscientiously at her intellectually unchallenging job and to remain as a spectator, not a participant, in the frenzied activity.

It was clear that the amount of work could not be done within the normal working hours but most people seemed prepared to work on into the evening. Food was ordered in for those who stayed at their tasks. These arrangements suited Louise. She had no plans for her evenings and no home responsibility.

It was on the Thursday evening that a transformation seemed to spread over the operation. It became apparent that the packs and timetables for each conference delegate were ready, information for speakers had been distributed, conference hall and exhibitor arrangements were in hand and catering requirements had been finalised.

On the Friday morning Stewart appeared at work looking immaculate in a dark suit, highly polished shoes, a fresh looking white shirt and a sober tie. Even the dark curls had been tamed and organised. Everything was ready to be transported to the conference venue and by lunchtime the carriers had cleared the room. Louise was left alone tidying up a few empty boxes, scraps of wrapping paper, bits of tape and escaped paper clips. The printer was silent and even the telephone lay dormant. Everything had been finished on time in spite of the confusion and bedlam. Perhaps there had been some underlying organisation after all.

Louise found the silence strange. She was already missing the hustle and bustle, the constant noise and interruptions as people rushed into the room. Everything seemed empty, her ears searched for sound but found nothing. Her eyes sought action but there was no movement. Louise felt sad. She was beginning to realize that she enjoyed life at a frantic pace.

At that moment Sally and Paul came into the room. "Sorry we have hardly had time to see you this week. Hope it's not been too bad."

Louise made reassuring signs that everything was alright. "It's been a bit crazy but I enjoyed it."

"Well, next week we'll get you working on the next conference. That's at a much earlier stage so you'll be able to get more involved in the organisation," Paul reassured her.

"Is the flat OK?" asked Sally.

"Yes, fine. Jenny's quiet, but OK."

"We're having a barbecue on Saturday. Just some friends and neighbours coming round. You free? Like to come?"

Chapter 13

Louise's previous experience of barbecues was limited. She had always anticipated the idea of a barbecue with pleasure but had found the reality a bit disappointing. The food was always late because an age was spent trying to persuade charcoal to burn. Eventually burnt sausages and burgers would be served in damp bread rolls. Now she felt apprehensive about an evening where everyone except the host and hostess would be strangers. Should she take something to the party? She could not really afford wine and felt beer was not appropriate.

She need not have worried. It was clear, when she arrived at the house, that Paul and Sally expected nothing from her as there was more than enough food and drink provided. There were about thirty people attending the party, mostly couples with their teenage children. Louise was introduced by Sally and it was explained that she was a student working at PSW for the summer. Although everyone was friendly and made polite inquiries about her enjoyment of the work experience or her course of study, it was clear that she had little in common with most of the other guests. She drifted over to where a group of teenagers had gathered. They were standing in a circle all dressed in the fashionable designer logo jeans and T-shirts. Their conversation seemed to be a round of one-up-manship for who had the most exotic plans for the summer.

"I'm going to a sports camp for two weeks to improve my tennis and then a cruise with Mum and Dad."

"We're going to the cottage in Cornwall. I just love the surfing. Got lots of friends who are really good."

"My uncle in Italy has his own business. I'm going to work there for a bit then go up into the mountains with my cousins."

Louise wondered what they would think of a week's summer holiday in a caravan somewhere in Wales.

By now the food was being cooked. Paul was expertly tending a gas-fired barbecue. No need to wait for ages for charcoal to reach the appropriate state of smoulder. A selection of steak, chicken, fish and vegetables were sizzling away without a trace of the burnt sausages which Louise associated with barbecues. Sally was bringing out bowls of salad. Louise went into the kitchen to offer help and quickly found a role carrying out baskets of different breads, and trays of pickles and relishes. It was all beautifully arranged and looked perfect.

When Louise had piled her plate with a selection from the feast she looked round for somewhere to sit. There was a group of empty chairs in the shade of a tree and as Louise sat down an older lady followed her.

"May I join you? Is this chair free? It is pleasant in the shade."

As they started to eat, her older companion continued, "Wonderful food. I don't know how Sally does it. A responsible demanding job, then entertains at the weekend. She has so much energy."

"Ah, there you are," an older man approached them. Louise thought he looked familiar. "Louise isn't it? Yes, I heard you were here for the summer. I don't suppose you remember me; we met when you visited PSW all those years ago. My name's John."

"Yes, I remember. You were the one who really set me thinking about my future."

"Have you introduced yourselves? This is my wife, Anna. I hear you are at university now. Sally said microbiology. Enjoying it?"

"It's great."

"Microbiology, of course most of that is the medical stuff but I remember looking at the environmental side many years ago. The water industry had a problem. A contaminated stream, somewhere in Yorkshire, all those dead fish."

Louise stopped eating and looked at the piece of salmon on her fork.

"Wonder how close we really are to killing people that way. I thought we could develop our technology to help spot a problem but the water authority people were not interested. They said their water treatment processes were adequate to keep drinking water safe."

Louise felt reassuring as she sipped her glass of flavoured mineral water.

"Of course the water industry is rather traditional in nature. They do things the way they have always done them for years. I wonder if they fully understand how their methods work. We now know there are bacteria which thrive in some strange places like hot springs, volcanoes, environments poisoned with metals, acids, things like that."

Louise was due to do a course on these organisms, extremophiles, during her next term at university.

"I wonder if these would be removed or killed during the water treatment process," mused John. "Still, they are unlikely to cause illness, so it's not really a problem. Is it?"

The conversation with John and Anna meandered on to other topics. Louise told them how much she was enjoying the social life at university and the companionship of the other students. After a year in residence she was moving into a house with friends. John and Anna agreed this was the usual desirable pattern of student life.

As Sally started to bring out bowls of strawberries, raspberries, other exotic fruit and cream, the conversation drifted on to John and Anna's granddaughter. Louise remembered that John had said she was interested in international business. Yes, she was studying business and languages, and was just about to start the third year of her course. This year was to be spent at an Italian university studying Italian and European business law. She had taken a gap year and spent most of it in India. No, not helping some impoverished village improve their conditions, but had worked in a high-powered marketing company in Bombay.

John finished his glass of wine as he consumed his remaining strawberries and cream.

"We should not monopolise your time," butted in Anna. "You should be meeting other young people here."

"It's interesting hearing your thoughts and news of your granddaughter. Next week, at work, I'm getting involved with organising the next conference so I'll meet lots of people then."

So it was that Louise spent the evening with quiet relaxed people before becoming fully involved in the team organising the conference to be held in two months time.

Her days were spent arranging timetables, taking bookings from delegates, sorting out seminar groups and what seemed like an unending round of contacting speakers to obtain summaries of their presentations and information needed to make the conference run smoothly. It fell to her to read and check the material sent in.

Louise began to wonder at the complexity of setting up a business. She had always thought it was a matter of having a good idea, then making it. She had learnt from Max and Jake that it was necessary to have someone to arrange business contracts and to look after the accounts. Now, in the literature she was collecting and checking, she was reading about patenting, technology transfer, getting ideas from researchers and inventors to commercial companies. Then there was financing, who would provide the money to set up the business. Then there were legal and regulatory issues. It was all much more complex than Louise had thought but she also found it exciting and stimulating to try to grasp all the factors which went into starting and growing a company.

Her days at work were busy and interesting. There were frustrations, mainly related to the inability of people to get promised documents to her on time or slow responses to her emails and telephone calls. However, as this was just a summer job, she did not feel the pressure of being responsible for the ultimate success or failure of the conference. Others around her were feeling these pressures and their frayed nerves got the better of them from time to time.

The volume of work to be done meant she frequently stayed late at work. Afterwards she would join others for a drink at a local pub. The pub served inexpensive food and she allowed herself the indulgence of eating an evening meal there.

This meant she spent little time in the flat with the ghost-like Jenny. Even when she had an evening in it was apparent that Jenny was fully occupied. She was working hard on a course which caused her to spend her time pouring over books and finishing assignments. During these academic activities she supported herself on an endless round of large mugs of coffee, cheese sandwiches and biscuits. Nothing, it seemed, would or could interrupt her striving for qualification.

The weekends were potential voids in Louise's life but opportunities seemed always to arise for entertainment or diversion. Louise found a friend in Suzy, the company's bubbly receptionist. Suzy lived at home in a large old house occupied by various members of an extended family from Hong Kong. Louise felt welcome in the house even if she did not understand the majority of the conversation which was conducted in Chinese. She found the noisy busy household such a contrast to her own small quiet family home. Suzy was a happy carefree companion with inexhaustible energy when it came to meeting people and acting as the hostess.

During this time Louise stayed in contact with Jake. Although she missed his tender caresses and passionate love-making she had no doubts about his affection and the future of their relationship. They shared the same interests and humour. Jake was very busy at work trying to meet deadlines. Max had gone on holiday leaving him with all the aggro and pressure. He would have liked to visit Louise one weekend, but things were too hectic.

Then came a suggestion. Jake needed to fly to New York. He could come down to Heathrow on the Friday and stay for the Saturday before flying out on the Sunday. Louise was delighted with the idea. Her only concern was where Jake would stay. Her tiny room in the flat and the spectral presence of Jenny offered limited facilities for entertaining the man she was falling in love with.

However Jake reassured her. He would take a room at a hotel and she could join him there. He would charge much of it to expenses as he was meeting people on business on the Friday.

It was arranged that Louise would meet him at the hotel on the Friday evening. She would catch a train into London after work.

"We can have some fun, perhaps go up to the West End," suggested Jake.

Chapter 14

Louise's sense of anticipation grew as the weekend approached. She spent a whole evening trying to decide which clothes, from her meagre student wardrobe, she should take. She confided, in Suzy, her excitement about the visit. Suzy was clearly impressed with the image of this handsome, successful, wealthy young man that was Louise's boyfriend.

"He sounds a gorgeous hunk. Doesn't he have lots of girls chasing him?" she joked.

"He's always been a bit quiet and now he is so busy at work." Louise had never stopped to wonder why Jake did not seek to exploit his attractiveness by surrounding himself with a crowd of glamorous girls. Perhaps he was shy. There was no shyness between Jake and herself, but they had known each other for a long time, even if the relationship had become close and intimate only recently. Jake's ability as a lover suggested that there had been other girl friends, perhaps quite a few. No, Jake could not be shy where girls were concerned. Louise contented herself with the thought that he was a hard working guy who was interested in a long-standing loving relationship, rather than a series of one-night stands with the glamorous types.

Louise left work promptly on the Friday afternoon and caught a London-bound train. She found the hotel with ease. It would have been difficult to miss it. The huge modern white building, topped off with the symbol of an international hotel chain, shouted its presence and its opulence. Louise had never been into such an impressive place. Once through the large revolving door she was isolated from the real world in a Valhalla of polished marble floor, soft music and plush sofas. She felt deeply uncomfortable and out of place. She hesitated for a moment and thought of bolting back to the tiny room in the small flat. Why had Jake suggested this place populated with immaculate people in sober business clothes? She drew a deep breath and mustered all her courage to cross to the reception desk. Then, with a bravado born out of panic, she asked if Jake Morrison was staying at the hotel.

The receptionist confirmed he had checked in and told Louise his room number. Jake was just coming out of the bathroom when he answered Louise's knock. His only clothing was a towel wrapped around his waist. His shoulders were glistening with drops of water which were running down his neck from a mop of wet lank hair which hung over his face partly obscured his eyes. For a second Louise was reminded of the puny geek that was Max's cousin when they were at school. Then she looked at the broad shoulders. The ugly duckling had grown up into the swan.

"Sorry, just caught me in the shower," Jake's kisses were passionate and demanding. He had missed her and she found the moist body that smelt pleasantly of shampoo was irresistible. They indulged their physical pleasures on the huge bed.

"You hungry?"

"Yes, only had a sandwich for lunch and that was a long time ago."

"Do you want to go down or, I have a better idea, let's have room service."

"Room service?"

"Yes, the menu is somewhere here," said Jake as he flipped the pages of the glossy hotel brochure. "What do you fancy?"

Louise looked aghast at the prices of the offerings with their Italian or French names.

"How about that?" Jake said pointing to something which he thought must be seafood in some sort of exotic sauce.

"Yes, fine, yes," at this stage Louise would have agreed to anything. She felt much too far out of her depth to offer any suggestion.

As Louise went into the bathroom Jake picked up the phone and asked for room service. While she splashed her face with cold water she marvelled at Jake's self confidence, his knowledge of what to do in this posh hotel. She felt daunted by the whole environment, but he acted as if living in this atmosphere was normal. Was it just business success that gave him this poise?

"It'll be here in about ten minutes. Fancy watching the film?" said Jake nodding at the TV. It was the opening titles of a recent film, a tear jerking story of tragic family life.

"Yes, great," she said giving Jake a quick kiss.

They settled themselves lying side by side on the bed, dressed in just towelling robes and became engrossed in the film which, so far, depicted the ideal family of a young couple with two small children. However, the storyline was already hinting that this myth of domestic bliss was about to the shattered.

Then there was a knock at the door and Jake opened it to admit a waiter pushing a loaded trolley. Louise had been hungry before but the smell of the food made her realise that she was ravenous.

Jake took the covers off two dishes to reveal beautifully presented concoctions of rice, vegetables and seafood in a steaming sauce. Then, from the lower shelf of the trolley, he produced a wine bottle.

"Oh, champagne."

"No, it's a Californian sparkling white wine. I prefer it to the French stuff."

Louise did not mind which continent it came from. The whole thing was wonderful and luxurious. It seemed like the ultimate enjoyment, lying on this huge bed beside Jake, eating and drinking a delicious meal and watching a sad TV movie. Life could not get much better.

The next morning they lay wrapped in each other's arms with that comfortable feeling that the day ahead was one for self-indulgence. They could do whatever took their fancy. There was no work that had to be done, no deadlines to be met.

"Let's be tourists and go to see Buckingham Palace," Jake suggested.

"That sounds fun. I went all round those places on a school trip but I can't remember much. Let's be tourists."

"I want to go to a book shop but after that let's just go wherever looks good."

The tube train journey into the centre of London was easy, if longer than Louise had expected. The first call was a book shop. Jake knew exactly which book he wanted. It was a newly published volume of wonderful photographs of the wilder parts of Britain.

"I know it may not be quite Ansel Adams standard," Jake explained, "but I have been trying to tell people in California that we have got some wild places here."

Louise flipped through the pages. There were shots of the Peak District not far from her home. The photographer had done justice to the scenery. Then she came to a section on Wales. She particularly admired a photograph taken from the peak of Snowdon. The foreground was rugged rocks and scree, the uninhabitable product of storm and the scouring ice. Then there was the forested valley with its lake. Human life could cling to an existence here in thick-walled, fortress-like cottages with tiny windows to protect against the wind and rain. Some of these dwellings were visible in the mid-ground of the picture. You would need to be independent and self-sufficient to eke out a living there. Beyond that, in the furthest reach of the frame, there was a glint of sea and the green fertile landscape of the Isle of Anglesey. Louise particularly admired the composition of the picture. The photographer had avoided the usual image of the green and pleasant foreground with the craggy mountainous background. Instead, he had reversed the normal view and looked at things from a different perspective. Louise noted that things looked very different from this alternative view point.

"I hope they like the pictures, come and visit, more American tourists," she laughed as they left the bookshop to continue their day as sightseers.

By the time they reached Whitehall the guard had been changed so they joined other visitors on the stroll up The Mall to Buckingham Palace. The open space and trees impressed Louise. She associated the centre of towns and cities with claustrophobia.

At the Palace they peered through the railings and speculated which bit the queen actually lived in. The place seemed much too large for a small lady.

They decided to continue their tour of the attractions by walking to Westminster Abbey and the Houses of Parliament. However, just as they reached Victoria Street the whole air became filled with the sound of emergency sirens. Then police cars, fire engines and ambulances rushed past them. They hesitated for a moment. Should they follow the stream of vehicles in order to satisfy their innate curiosity and be the bystanders at some disaster scene?

Before either could voice an opinion they were confronted with police telling them to stay away and the road was shut off with barriers and tape.

Obediently they beat a retreat into the nearby St. James's Park and sat down on a park bench next to an older man. They were unsure about where to go and what to do next. What was happening? Why were there so many emergency vehicles? Was it something really dangerous?

At this point their older companion joined the conversation. "Probably a terrorist threat."

"Terrorist threat?"

"Shooting or worse."

"Worse?"

"Chemical or biological."

"Chemical?"

"Yes, we could have the sort of thing they had in Japan. That gas attack," said this modern day Jeremiah, "Killed people in the Tokyo underground."

Louise began to feel alarmed. She had never felt at risk of terrorist attack. That sort of thing did not happen in the village where she had spent most of her life, but here in London was she part of the target?

"How awful to be caught in a terrorist attack, to be killed by a gunman or by poison gas."

"It would be terrible to be killed by anything."

"Yes, but if it was an accident that would be different from a deliberate terrorist thing."

"But you are just as dead afterwards, Lou."

Louise became aware that she was holding Jake's hand tightly, their fingers interlocking. They seemed to have moved closer together on the bench.

"I know that but I still think it would be worse to be killed deliberately by someone. If I got a terrible illness and died that would be different." Louise looked at a pigeon pecking at the ground beside her foot. "If that pigeon suddenly dropped dead, bird heart attack or something like that, I would feel sad. If someone kicked it to death I would feel angry."

They all watched the pigeon.

"But you would still feel sorry for the pigeon and angry at the person who kicked it."

The pigeon appeared not to like the conversation and flew off.

"Yes, I suppose you are right."

"What if the kick was an accident and the person who did it was full of remorse?" the older companion added to the complexity.

"That's different."

Two more pigeons had arrived to follow the conversation.

"But what if the person killed the pigeon because his child had died of an illness spread by pigeons?" Jake started to build up the scenario.

"You have to examine the motive to decide if a killing is justified. If it is to protect your own life. But what about revenge? Terrorism is quite often an act of revenge for something that happened in the past."

"I can understand attacking someone who has killed or hurt someone you love, but you should be able to go to the police to get them to deal with it with an arrest or something."

"But suppose you feel the need to revenge something that happened years ago in another country?"

Louise and Jake wanted each other's touch, not for physical pleasure but for security. Their bodies and minds were suffused with feelings of insecurity and vulnerability. These were new sensations to them.

"Come on, let's find somewhere else to go." Jake broke into their thoughts.

After saying goodbye to their older companion, they wandered across the park to The Mall and then embarked on an ill-defined walk through the streets and squares of Mayfair. It was an area of such obvious wealth and affluence that Louise could only wonder who could afford the goods in the shops and the cars in the streets. The immaculately dressed women were a different race from those who had previously entered her life. She felt like an alien in a strange world as she watched a Rolls Royce drive past. Who were these people? How did they gain their apparent wealth, poise, self confidence?

It was not until they reached Oxford Street that she felt she had re-entered the world of people with whom she shared a common experience.

By this time their feelings of personal security had returned and after a quick lunch they decided to go to the Tower of London. That proved a futile attempt when they saw the crowds of tourists. So they contented themselves with an afternoon of laughter, ice cream and exploration of St. Catherine's Dock. By now there were newspaper headlines telling of a false alarm over some poorly defined emergency in Westminster. The account was brief as the event was seen as having much less significant than the latest sexual indiscretion of a politician.

Jake and Louise intended to have a romantic meal in a little Italian restaurant. The reality was good Italian food but in a place so overcrowded and noisy that any degree of mutual intimacy was difficult to maintain.

Their return to the hotel room offered the complete opposite to the day. They shut the door on the outside world and entered a realm of mutual pleasure.

The next morning was separation time, Jake on a plane to New York and Louise by train back to the flat and Jenny. Yes, it was sad, very sad, but there was the consoling feeling that it had been a happy weekend spent together and there would be plenty more of these in the future. The future looked good, very good.

Chapter 15

Louise grew in confidence as she gained a better understanding of all the components necessary to organize a successful conference. She had become a full member of the team at work. She looked at the programme of events and lectures with interest. The titles of some of the talks seemed like a foreign language – 'Commercialisation of intellectual property', 'Technology transfer', 'Licensing routes'. What did all this mean? As she read through the material sent in by the speakers she began to feel the veil of confusion and unfamiliarity lifting. When someone made a discovery or invention, they needed to patent the idea to make sure there was evidence that they owned that idea. It was just like owning a piece of land. There had to be documents to prove ownership.

Then it was necessary to find out if people would buy the thing produced from the new idea. Would there be sufficient people willing to pay enough money to make it worthwhile? Would someone lend the money to get a business up and running, and would that person just take all the profit that was made?

As Louise read the papers she felt as if she was unrolling a map that showed the path to developing a business. She looked at the charts, diagrams and cartoons which were to be part of the speakers' presentations. These helped her to follow the course of events which would be necessary to establish a business, which she would have to follow to join this entrepreneurial business community.

Then Louise studied the biographical histories of the speakers. Could she follow their successful paths? They all had degrees and then further qualifications, often a Ph.D. which increased their scientific kudos. Many had qualifications in other business areas such as the law, accountancy or marketing. Most had worked within big multi-national companies before going on to smaller companies and setting up their own businesses.

In amongst all this information Louise found one speaker who had developed an idea while still a student and had gone on to set up his own very successful business. Louise felt she would like to adopt him as a role model.

"Could I go to this talk?" she asked Sally the next day.

"You can go to any session you want provided the front desk is covered and not too busy. I'll leave it up to you and Suzy to organise that, but make sure we have cover at all times so the conference delegates are looked after properly," Sally replied helpfully.

Although Louise felt sure they had organized everything thoroughly and properly, and everything was under control, she became aware of an under-current of chaos causing turbulence in the stream of the arrangements. As the event approached so the channels of communication became busier. A local print shop had made errors and time was running out to get the job redone. A principal speaker had to drop out and finding a replacement was proving difficult.

Louise felt the developing tensions in the team as the pressure increased to fit tasks into a diminishing time slot.

"No, that's impossible. If we have coffee in the exhibition area we will not be able to get people back to the seminar rooms in time."

"But the f...ing exhibitors need the people in their hall!"

"Can't we move that talk forward five minutes?"

"No, the bloody programmes have been printed. It's too late now!"

"Oh hell! Why didn't this get sorted out earlier?"

The language got stronger and tempers became more frayed. Although Louise was prepared to work long hours she began to feel frustrated. Team cohesion had gone; everyone started to follow their own agendas. Any sense of smooth organisation had disappeared. She began to sense she was on a ship which had no captain and was being engulfed by a major storm. Plus the actual weather was not helping the mood. It was hot and humid.

The conference was going to be an organisational disaster. Would she share the blame? No, she was just doing a summer job but she became aware of increasing levels of unhappiness. She considered quitting and returning home. No, that would be defeatism. She would stay and see how the whole thing turned out, even if she now viewed events with a degree of detachment, not her responsibility.

Just as the whole situation seemed to be reaching melt down Sally called a meeting of the conference team. In the course of two hours they went through the progress of the organisation, identified the problems, resolved many of them with a few minutes quiet discussion or assigned members of the team to work on specific issues.

The week before the conference was marked by hard work, long hours and there now seemed to be the cohesion that comes when the whole team pulls in the same direction. By the Thursday afternoon all the timetables were finalised, all the bookings confirmed. Everything was ready to be transported to the conference venue, a large hotel and conference facility on the edge of town.

Louise left work promptly and went back to the flat for an evening of self indulgence, grooming and self attention. She had had a feeling of self neglect but now she busied herself with laundry, a shampoo, a manicure and making a vegetarian meal of pasta and salad which, she was sure, would be more healthy then her recent diet of pizza and chips.

By bed-time she had that feeling of self-righteousness that comes from surveying a neat pile of freshly laundered clothes while enjoying the feeling of running her neatly manicured fingers through her freshly shampooed hair. By morning, after a good undisturbed night's sleep, she felt she would be able to take on the world. She would tackle any and every problem that was thrown at her during today's last minute briefing or during the week that was to come.

It came as no surprise to her that everyone arrived at work well groomed with a new level of energy and enthusiasm. The air of optimism was maintained through the day as things were finalised for arrival at the conference hotel by midday on the Sunday. Everything was ready for the registration of the delegates on the Sunday evening. Louise even managed to send a quick message to Jake to confirm that he would help her move out of the flat, back home, after the conference.

If Louise had been asked to describe her time at the conference she would have had difficulty, there was so much. The hotel was of a similar standard to the one she had enjoyed with Jake. Oh, the luxury of her own spotlessly clean en-suite bathroom. The registration desk where she was to spend most of her time was a whirl of activity on the first evening as the delegates arrived. Most people quickly found their badges and participant bags. There were some moments of confusion when names had been misspelt, badges lost and last minute substitutes made. However, Suzy dealt with these problems quickly and efficiently. At one stage during the evening a tall distinguished-looking man approached the registration desk with the confidence that he would be recognized immediately without the need for an introduction. For a moment Louise felt inadequate. Who was this man? Should she know him?

"Lovely to see you Professor Evans," said Sally appearing out of the crowd. "Here's your badge. Please come this way."

Professor Evans was one of the principal speakers at the conference. Everyone had been excited when he agreed to attend. Louise made sure she would recognise his face again if their paths should cross. She would be able to greet him properly. She would make a good impression. Impressions mattered, didn't they?

Louise did get to some of the lectures and did find the opportunity to talk to some of the delegates, most of whom were only too anxious to discuss their developments, companies or the services they offered.

By the final day Louise felt that the student who had embarked on a summer job was a young woman with confidence and ambitions. When she got back to university she would be much more focussed. Before that she was looking forward to seeing Jake and spending a week at home.

She wondered if Jenny had a flatmate organised, however, as she came in through the front door of the flat Louise could hear voices and laughter coming from the kitchen. She paused for a moment. Jenny never had visitors, her conversation was always minimal and as for laughter, that had seemed out of her repertoire. Louise closed the front door quietly. When she turned back to face the kitchen door Jenny was standing framed in the doorway. She was wearing a very pretty pale blue dress that fitted closely showing off her dainty figure. Her hair was nicely arranged and held in position by a coloured clip. She was the picture of loveliness, behind her stood a young man. He was tall, blond-haired, blue-eyed and with the sort of strong jaw bone that is reserved for film stars.

"Oh," was all Louise could think of saying.

"Didn't hear you come in. This is Guy, my fiancé."

"Fiancé! I didn't know..."

"We're just having a coffee, fancy one?" Guy's first welcoming intervention.

Louise was lost for words as she went into the kitchen and watched Guy prepare the mug of coffee.

"You never mentioned you were engaged."

"Well Guy has been away for a year. He has been..." Jenny's voice drained away.

"I've been in prison," Guy stepped into the breach. "Don't worry, I am not about to attack you or anything. My crime was to do with money. I worked in the City and was very ambitious. Got involved with a group of other fellows in a money-making scam. I was very foolish and paid the price."

Louise was stunned, this handsome man, a criminal, Jenny engaged to someone in prison. She found no words to express her feelings of amazement.

"I'm lucky Jenny and my family have stuck by me. My brother has offered me a job. He has a small printing company."

"We're getting married in two weeks and will get things sorted out for the future," Jenny declared. The tone of determination in her voice was something new to Louise. Jenny had always seemed such a quiet mouse-like creature but Louise was realising that things are not always the way they appear to be.

Chapter 16

Louise's last day in the flat dawned fine and warm. She had packed most of her stuff the night before so could afford to take her time this morning.

She joined Jenny and Guy in the kitchen for breakfast of coffee and toast. The conversation drifted through the plans for the next two weeks. In one week's time Jenny and Guy were to get married.

"Everything's OK," Jenny said as she sipped her coffee. "It was much easier to organize than the big church do. Just the registry office, then down to the pub for drinks and a meal. There will only be twelve of us so no big hassle."

"Afterwards we're coming back here so no posh honeymoon holiday to sort out, none of that expense." Guy buttered his second piece of toast.

"I've got to get everything sorted out for next term. There's some reading I am supposed to have done over the summer ready for my next course." Louise was beginning to think about her return to university in one week's time. "I'm going into a house with friends. I'll need more stuff than last year when I was in hall."

After breakfast Louise finished her packing and moved her bags close to the front door. She opened the door and sat on the front step in the pleasant September sun. This seat offered a good view down the road so she could look out for Jake's red sports car.

Sitting in the warm sunshine she picked a loose blade of grass from between the concrete slabs. Twisting the green foliage between her fingers she contemplated the summer. Yes, it had been a success. She had managed to save some money. Sally had been a generous employer. But more, much more than that, new horizons had opened up. She had found the idea of setting up a business exciting. The people she had met had been energetic and enthusiastic. The people back home, her school teachers and the university staff, seemed stuffy by comparison. Of course, Jake and Max and their company were the exceptions. They had this energy level, she smiled to herself.

Louise made a decision, one from which there would be no turning. She would finish her degree, go on to do a Ph.D., get some business knowhow, then set up her own business. She would be her own boss.

Could she do all this? She had seen people who were doing it and they seemed quite ordinary. Some of them had seemed very nervous before their presentations at the conference but if they had managed do it then she could do it, perhaps.

By this time the grass was so tightly wound round her finger it was cutting off the blood supply. It is amazing how strong a piece of grass is. As Louise struggle to release the tourniquet she did not notice Jake's car turn into the street.

Louise greeted him with the usual hug and kiss, "You OK?"

"Yes, fine, but have you heard about Ann?"

"Ann? You mean the Ann from school?"

"Yes. She's dead."

"Dead!"

"Max heard yesterday."

"What happened? I thought she had joined a charity to help with children or something."

"Yes, she did. They sent her to some remote islands somewhere as a volunteer in a village there. It seems she caught an illness and was dead in a couple of days, cholera or something like that."

"That's terrible. So fast."

Louise was numbed by the thought that someone her age, a school friend, could have died so suddenly. All the plans for her own future slid into second place in her mind.

During the journey home they had the top of the car down so the noise of the wind made conversation impossible. This gave Louise time to contemplate the fate of Ann. Of course the university studies had included courses on deadly infectious diseases, but this was the first time that the reality had struck home.

Chapter 17

The house which had been turned into student accommodation was instantly recognisable as the epitome of neglect and this house was no exception. It was part of a terrace of Georgian houses. The double frontage and flight of six steps, leading to a wide doorway, said it had once been the home of a prosperous family. A family that maintained a position in society. But that was then. Now two of the steps were broken, the low walls on either side of the steps had lost some of their bricks. The fabric of the house appeared to have a crack which ran down the wall above one of the bay windows.

Inside there was always a smell of stale curry, dust and cannabis. The hallway was dark, cluttered with broken chairs, a pile of cardboard boxes and there was a table littered with uncollected letters and junk mail.

This was to be home for Louise for the rest of her undergraduate life and she seized the opportunity to create her own space.

For Jake this was a place where he could experience the student life which, in spite of his business success, he felt he had missed. He would spend two or three weekends each term with Louise, visiting the student pubs and enjoying the student parties. He would enter into the late night discussions on how the young student population could run the country, in fact the world, so much better than the present world leaders.

As a visitor Jake could enjoy the freedom that comes from the ability to explore ideas without the ultimate responsibility for implementation. For him it seemed a carefree existence but he was sheltered from the immediate problems of student debt and examinations.

For Louise it was a happy relaxed relationship in which she lived for the day. She did not question their future together. She assumed it would continue and adjust as her situation changed. It was the constant in her life which, she knew, would involve great shifts as she moved from undergraduate, to post-graduate student, then on to business woman.

"Jake coming this weekend?" asked one of her house-mates. "That new film is on. I thought I might go. Do you want to come?"

"No, I don't think he will be over. He's just had a couple of weeks in California so will have a lot to catch up on, I expect."

But Louise had a phone call that Friday evening.

"OK if I come over tomorrow morning?"

"Yes, of course. The others are getting tickets for that new film. I'll ask them to get tickets for us."

"Eh, well, perhaps not for tomorrow."

After putting the phone away Louise thought about Jake's hesitation. Usually he was keen to join the rest of the student group, but today he sounded unwilling. He must be tired.

Louise settled down to complete an assignment. Then there was a knock at the door and three of her house-mates burst in.

"Coming for a drink?"

"No, want to finish this. Jake's coming in the morning. Need to get this done tonight." Louise was contemplating a work and study-free weekend.

"What about that film?"

"No, Jake doesn't want to."

"Perhaps he's seen it already. It's been out in America for some time."

Louise had not considered that option.

The next morning Jake arrived earlier than Louise expected. The front door of the house was ajar so he pushed it and went in. At the top of the first flight of stairs he found the door with a large number five painted on it in white. Louise was sitting sipping coffee, while flipping through a student magazine, when Jake pushed open the door.

"Hi, want a drink," she said as she gave him a quick kiss.

"It's OK; I'll fix it, no problem."

The room was a contrast to the hall and stairway. The sun was shining in through a large window and the light was reflected off white walls. Some bright red curtains gave a warm inviting feeling. Although the proportions of the room were inappropriate, the ceiling was too high for its size, it was pleasantly furnished with a desk and filing cabinet on one side, a small dining table with three chairs was beside the window and easy chairs were either side of a low coffee table. The furniture was not of the highest quality and not new but had it been cared for. The window sill was home to several healthy looking house plants and the walls were decorated with bright travel posters. Coffee was the odour which dominated this flat with perhaps a suggestion of a pleasant shower gel. Everything in the room suggested order and care. Louise had taken control of her own space.

"Good trip to California? When did you get back?"

"Wednesday. Eh, fine, yes, OK."

"Hungry?"

"No, no." Jake stood stiffly in the middle of the room clutching the coffee mug to his chest.

"We need some more milk. Shall we go round to the supermarket to get some bits?" The practical side of Louise' nature came to the fore.

"Yes, we could walk across the park."

Jake usually drove everywhere. The suggestion of a walk through a park on a fine March morning surprised Louise, but appealed to her.

The daffodils were just coming out, the trees were beginning to show green and the birds were conducting a lyrical battle to establish their territorial preferences. Louise ran a few steps ahead and jumped in a vain attempt to touch the branch of a beech tree. Laughing she turned to face Jake. He was standing looking at her, a tense expression on his face.

"What's the matter?" Louise could not understand that anyone could be less than delighted with life on this beautiful spring morning.

"Al's coming to work in England."

"Oh that'll be good. Save you going to California the whole time." Louise picked up a pebble and tossed it into a small puddle watching the ripples flood outward. "First time he's been to England?"

"He's a she. Al's a girl, Alexandra."

Louise froze, Al a girl. The ski trips, the meetings in New York all took on a different significance. "She's just coming over for a few months?" Louise was clutching at straws.

"Well, you see, Al and I ..." Jake's courage failed him. He sat down on a park bench, elbows on knees, head in hands. "Lou, oh, Lou I have not been fair with you. Al and I are more than business partners. We're an item. We're going to get married."

The end of the affair came as a terrible shock, a devastating blow to Louise. There were days of tears, anger and despair, but then the post mortem started. She had always made the assumption that she was the only woman in his life and that was the way things would continue.

Quite how events would unfold she had not contemplated. Would they eventually find a place together, marry? All these were to have been future considerations. They had lived for the present, he had his business and she had her studies. They had each other as sources of intimate pleasure, both physical and intellectual.

She started to think back. He had never said anything about her being the only one, his undying love, but then, she did not remember saying anything to him about her underlying feelings. She had just taken it for granted, built up her own expectations. These were the unspoken assumptions.

Why had she not had suspicions? She remembered a friend commenting that such a handsome, successful, wealthy, young man must have a bevy of glamorous girls chasing him. She had dismissed the idea. His shyness or his desire to have a quiet uncomplicated love-life, compared to his frantic business world, meant there was no fan club. She recalled thinking that there must have been previous girlfriends. He could not have been such a wonderful lover without previous experience. However, she had decided that these were all past relationships and she did not wish to hear or know about past events. After all, he was not the first man in her life, but he was the only one now and she had no desire for another.

Why had she not picked up some clues? The frequent business trips to America which usually involved some sight-seeing or excursions into the mountains. Now, as she looked back, she saw the hints, the descriptions of shared delight for the wild mountain scenery of the Rockies and, especially, Yosemite. She had assumed his travelling companions were just like-minded business contacts. Why should she suspect that one was a beautiful woman who had captured his heart and body?

Her mind ran back searching for other clues, other fragments of evidence. The bottles of wine; he always chose something from California. His choice was very precise. He knew exactly what he wanted from California.

Through the intense feeling of loss she tried to remember the happy times together. She wanted to hang on to something. He had helped her move into the flat with Jenny when she had the summer job at PSW. He had been so concerned for her, helping her to find the supermarket and get in the first few essentials. These were the acts of someone who cared and she had interpreted them as acts of love. Why his regular visits to her at university? If he had just wanted a date for the night there were plenty of girls at home. No, he had travelled to be with her, to share her student life.

There were the lengthy discussions about their future ambitions. Perhaps that was where the clues lay. There had been no strategies to dovetail their plans so that they could be together.

On the day of the break-up Jake had told her something about Al. She was the daughter of a wealthy, successful business man. Initially Jake had thought that this affluent American girl was beyond his reach, but as he attained his goals in business it enabled him to have access to and success in other aspects of life. The more he gained, the more he could gain.

It seemed for a time that Louise, the wronged lover, was acting as the father confessor to the sinner. She had sat beside him on the park bench, in the warm spring sum, with her heart turning to ice, while he tried to explain, perhaps rationalise his behaviour to her.

Her house-mates offered unending support. Each took it in turn to supply coffee and a metaphorical shoulder to cry on, but Louise had changed. Initially the change was subtle. Her trust in the actions and motives of others had gone. There was a growing realisation that her own future was her own matter, that she could, and would, control her own life. If business and financial achievements led to empowerment she would follow that course. She had changed from an easy going, somewhat ambitious, young student to a focused adult. No one, no man would distract her from achieving her short or long-term goals. She would need to overcome her self doubts by hard focussed work.

Chapter 18

The decision about where to continue her studies was beginning to occupy Louise. She did not want to stay at her present university for a whole range of reasons. The research projects available were not of great interest to her. There was no Business School to offer her access to the training, information and support she would need. But, perhaps, the most important driving reason was that the spectre of her affair with Jake still inhabited the environment. She needed to escape fully, not so much from Jake but from the feelings of her own failure. The stupidity and naivety had led her to think that she was the one and only in Jake's love life.

There was plenty of information about studentships at other universities but Louise felt it would be useful to discuss the options with the lecturer whose opinion she most respected, Dr. Jim White.

"Come up and see me in my office on Friday afternoon, about three." His willing reply when she asked for his help.

She arrived on time.

"I'll be with you in a second. Take a seat."

Louise looked round for a seat to take. Every surface in the small office was cluttered with books, papers and bags.

"Sorry, sorry, I need to tidy up a bit," he said as he removed a bag from one of the three chairs.

As Dr. White moved some piles of student assignment papers across his desk Louise gazed out of the window. The view through the dirty panes was a blank brick wall a few yards away.

"Now Louise, you want to continue on to do a Ph.D., but not here."

"Yes."

"Well, it will be a shame to lose you, but your marks have been very good and providing you continue that way there should be no problem finding a studentship. You should have a good choice of opportunities but what do you want to do in the long run? That must influence your decision."

"I don't think I want to teach or stay in university research."

The more Louise saw of this small chaotic office with its grim outlook, the more she felt that her future did not lie in a career which depended only upon successful research outcomes and the publication of scientific papers. "I am interested in using scientific research and ideas to set up a small company, my own business."

"Going out on your own is difficult, challenging and lacks security. Would you consider working for one of the large companies, medical, food, water, even brewing? There's plenty of choice out there."

"I really want to try to set up my own business." Louise was thinking back to the role model she had adopted at the conference and to the proof given to her by Max and Jake, that it could be done.

"OK, if you are sure then it is worth spending some time analysing the skills you will need and what area you want to do your research in. Have you thought about which sector you want to be in?"

"Microbiology."

"Yes, but applied to what? Medicine, food, environment? This could influence where you go. You need to set up the right contacts, to learn about the industry, its market demands, regulatory environment."

Louise looked at the balding, bearded academic. He seemed to know and understand much more about the commercial world than she expected.

"The medical area, increasing healthcare needs ...," Louise' voice trailed off as she had not considered this question.

"Medical area can be difficult for a one-man, I mean woman, band. There are a lot of regulations about what can be done and the whole business is dominated by a few big multi-national companies. Makes it difficult for a small newcomer."

"What about water or environment?"

"Yes, those may offer more possibilities. I looked at those a few years ago and did quite a bit of market research. You see I was thinking along the same lines as you, but then I was offered this lectureship and my wife was pregnant." He pointed to a photograph of two young children and a baby. "I guess my priorities changed. All the demands of family life and the sleepless nights meant I probably would not have had the stamina to run a small company. There are also the risks." Louise thought he looked rather sad. "Perhaps it's an idea I will get back to when the family is older."

Louise moved uncomfortably, running her hands along the arms of the chair. The conversation was focusing on life's disappointments for Jim White, rather than the future prospects for Louise.

"Still, what about your future?" The smile had returned amongst the beard. "If you are interested in something in the water or environmental area, and want a place with a good Business School and a helpful attitude to the possibility of a scientist going into business, then I am giving a lecture at the right place, next week. I'll ask them what studentships are coming up and what you could apply for. I think Sillfield University should be high on your list of possibilities."

CHAPTER 19

The journey to Sillfield University was awkward and tedious, two trains, followed by a bus. Louise began to wonder if she was going to the right place. The literature and travel instructions had described the location as being on the edge of a small town, but she was beginning to think that the back of beyond would have been a truer statement. The letter from the Professor's secretary had advised her to allow plenty of time for the journey and she was glad she had taken that advice.

Just as Louise was beginning to doubt that she would reach her destination the bus slowed down and stopped opposite a wide drive flanked with majestic trees. At the entrance to the drive there was a large green notice board bearing, in gold lettering, the crest and name 'Sillfield University'.

As Louise stood on the side of the road the bus pulled away to revealed the view up the drive to a large red-brick house, Victoriana in its full glory.

Louise had read the history of the university. Following the Second World War the owner had left this house, its grounds and a sizable fortune for the establishment of a university which would equip young people for work in industry. Apparently he felt that the nation needed a better supply of good engineers, scientists and business oriented people, rather than an excess of lawyers and politicians, as he saw it.

The university had followed its benefactor's wishes by concentrating on engineering and the physical sciences, then adding biotechnology and a business school as these seemed appropriate for the changing needs of industry. Sillfield

University prided itself on its close ties with industrial companies.

Louise stood for a moment and gazed up the drive. Through the trees she could see there were other, more modern buildings, but much of this was obscured to the casual viewer. Louise took a deep breath, straightened her skirt, flicked her hair back, hoisted her small rucksack onto one shoulder and started her self-conscious walk up the drive.

Everything was clearly signposted so she found the School of Biotechnology without any trouble. Outside was the obligatory green notice board with gold lettering stating 'Reception and Professor's Office' and an arrow pointing to a door in the corner of the building.

Louise felt her pulse rate increase. Up until then she had had no real concerns about the interview, but now, faced with the reality, panic was surging up. She paused for a moment trying to convince herself not to be so silly. Dr. White had assured her that her academic standards were totally adequate; she had done her homework and studied plenty of information about the activities of the School. She was dressed appropriately in a smart skirt and simple white blouse. She had taken care with her hair and applied just a little makeup. If Sillfield University did not like her that would be just too bad, she had done her best and there would be other options, she rationalised.

Thus mentally fortified she opened the door and walked in head held high, mustering all her limited acting abilities to appear as self confident and relaxed as possible.

Louise had heard about totally efficient secretaries. The dragons who guard their bosses' lairs, but up until now she had never met one.

Mrs. Baker sat at her pristine desk, telephone, keyboard and screen to one side. The manicure on each pink nail was immaculate and exactly matched the colour of the creaseless silk blouse. Even the lipstick was perfectly colour coordinated. This vision of administrative perfection was flanked on one side by a battalion of matching and aligned filing cabinets, while the opposite wall displayed neat panels with photographs of the School's academic and research staff. Other panels showed some of the more photogenic aspects of the School's work.

Louise stood there. All her preparation and the cloak of self-confidence left her.

"Miss Browning, Miss Louise Browning?"

"Yes, yes, but think I am a few minutes early."

"That's all right. Professor Able will be free to see you in ten minutes. Can I get you a coffee or something else to drink?"

"No, thank you, that's fine. I had one a few minutes ago," Louise lied.

Louise sat down and looked at the door to the Professor's office. If there was a dragon outside what lay beyond? She could hear muffled voices from inside the room but everything was too indistinct to understand the words or catch the mood. Ten minutes was beginning to seem like a life-time as she sat listening to the secretary's high speed, unerring use of the keyboard. Louise ran her fingers along the zip of her rucksack. She had brought a summary of exam and assignment marks. Should she get that out ready to convince the Professor that she would reach the required standard? Before she could put her thoughts into action a tall slim man came into the office.

"I need to see Prof as soon as possible."

"Well he is very busy," the secretary tapped on the keyboard and scrutinized the screen. "He's leaving today as soon as he has interviewed Miss Browning. He's out all day tomorrow, BBC interview in the morning, meeting a government minister in the afternoon, then a Research Council dinner in the evening," the secretary was savouring the importance of each of her boss's diary entries. "The next day he's in Brussels, but I expect him in between eight and nine that morning before he goes to the airport. I could fit you in between eight ten and eight thirty. Would that be OK?

"I supposed so."

Louise was feeling amazed that a person as busy as this Professor had time for her. Should she feel important or very humble? Before she could answer this question the door to the Professor's office opened to reveal a balding man in faded jeans and a misshapen T-shirt.

"If you can get the information I'll speak to him."

"I should be able to get that in Brussels, "came another voice and the Professor stepped into view.

If Mrs. Baker was at the pinnacle of smart business woman Professor Able was her male counterpart, dark suit, striped shirt and neat tie. Student Louise was out of her depth, but in one of the quickest transitions of her life, future business woman Miss Browning was making a right connection.

"Could you sign these? I need to get them in the post," the secretary put her own priorities first, then, "This is Miss Browning."

Without waiting for further explanation the Professor turned to Louise and offered his hand. "Jim White told me a lot about you." The handshake was firm and warm. "Come through." He waved a hand towards the office. "Will you bring us both a coffee and I am expecting a call from Japan so please put it through, even if I am still busy talking to Miss Browning." The Professor was in complete control of the situation.

Louise thought Professor Able reminded her of someone she had seen or met before, but she could not place the connection.

The Professor's office was like a conference room, a long table up the centre with a large desk forming the top of the T. The walls were busy with framed certificates and photographs of the Professor shaking hands with a collection of the international good and great.

"Now, Jim White said you might be interested in continuing your studies here. Why do you want to come to Sillfield?"

Louise had expected questions about her fitness for Sillfield not the suitability of Sillfield for her; however her brain was working fast and adapted to the unexpected line of the enquiry. "I want to go on to set up my own business. I am looking for a university where I can get the appropriate research training and experience, and somewhere where I can learn more about going into business. Also, if I can come up with a suitable idea for a new business, while I am doing my Ph.D., I want somewhere that will give me the freedom and help to realise my ambition. Everything I have heard and read about Sillfield suggests it is the right place for me."

The coffee arrived at the end of Louise's opening statement. She had not realised how dry her mouth and how thirsty she was until the liquid touched her lips.

The Professor seemed pleased with Louise's opening gambit. "Yes, I am sure we offer the appropriate support for students who see their future in a commercial and business environment." He went on to described how the Business School offered a course which could be taken by the engineering and science students at the University. He explained it did involve a lot of extra hard work and sacrifice on the part of the students as they had to run their business studies alongside their scientific and research training.

Louise assured the Professor that she thought this short term sacrifice would be worth the long term gain.

The Professor went on to describe the measures that the University went to in order to protect the interests of a student in any discoveries they might make. It would not just be a question of publishing good scientific papers, although that was very important. The University had to maintain its academic reputation by publishing in peer-reviewed journals. There was the patenting of ideas too.

"How much do you know about the patenting process?"

"I spent a summer working for a company, PSW, and helping organise a conference. There was a paper presented there that explained it all."

"PSW, yes, good people, I'd been to some of their conferences."

Louise was sure she had gone up one more step in establishing her credibility in the eyes of the Professor.

Just at that moment the telephone rang. Louise jumped. The conversation with the Professor had totally absorbed all her senses. She had shut out everything else.

"Excuse me. This will be a call from a colleague in Japan."

Louise realised that she was sitting forward on her chair, shoulders hunched with the effort of total concentration. She allowed herself to relax back as Professor Able picked up the telephone.

"Yes, I was expecting your call. Have they agreed to it?... Two of yours and two of ours."

Louise looked out of the window. The view was dominated by a huge solitary cedar tree.

"What about the funding? Will they cover the travel as well?"

The cedar tree must have been planted by the owner of the house at a time when it was expected that it would remain the family residence in the future, a confident view of what lay ahead.

"Well we have some discretionary resources we can use for that. What about the projects? Can the students do what I suggested?"

Louise had time to examine the contents of the office. Antique scientific instruments were displayed in a tall glass cabinet with a large brass microscope occupying pride of place.

"We can sign the agreement when we are both at that conference in San Francisco." The telephone conversation seemed to be coming to an end. No time was to be spent on unnecessary small talk. "Good, I'll look forward to seeing you there."

The receiver was put down and he turned back to Louise. "We arrange student exchanges with universities in other countries. I try to select universities which are doing the most exciting innovative research in a range of topics. By sending our students there we hear about the new ideas before they are even published. You cannot afford to miss any chance these days."

Louise was sure Professor Able did not miss chances.

"Now, is there anything you want to ask me about the business training and opportunities for commercial exploitation of ideas? Then we'll discuss the studentships which are coming up and see if they are in areas of technology and science that interest you and for which you will be equipped."

Louise thought everything had been explained very well and it all exceeded her expectations.

"As you know we deal with a wide range of scientific issues and opportunities. We are helping the chemical industry improve their production, reduce costs and reduce pollution. Other project areas are in the medical and pharmaceutical sectors where we are assisting in the development of a new generation of drugs and medicines. We are, of course, doing some work in the genetic manipulation of crops, particularly for tropical countries. We are very keen to help reduce crop losses to pests in the third world. I know genetic engineering in plants is controversial in this country, but improved diet could make such a difference to parts of Asia and Africa."

Louise was impressed by all this but did not quite see what it had to do with her background in microbiology and her expressed desire to work on a project in the areas of water or environment. She did not think there were business opportunities for a small start-up company in the areas dominated by the huge chemical and pharmaceutical companies. Although she thought it was a desirable aspiration, she did not imagine herself feeding the starving millions of Africa. Perhaps Sillfield would not have an opening for her.

"Perhaps our most exciting and advanced work is in the field of biochips, the use of biological molecules as part of a future generation of computers. These will be much faster and have much greater storage capacity than current technology."

Louise shrank back in her chair and looked down at her hands. Her expectations and excitement seemed to be draining into a sea of lost hopes.

"Then we are also working with companies, at lower technology levels, on cleaning up old industrial sites using microorganisms. One of the water companies are partly funding some students to study how some bacteria can live in, what we think of as, hostile environments. It is fundamental research into how life can exist in very cold or hot environments and where there are a lot of poisons. There are some people in the water industry who think, in the long run, it may help them improve their water purification processes. Of course, our students do the pure research, not the applied stuff. We must maintain our academic standards. These will not be compromised for commercial considerations."

Louise looked at the expensively furnished office and wondered if there had been some commercial, or at least financial, compromises to achieve this in what was presented as an academic institution. Her present university did not run to such decor.

CHAPTER 20

"It sounds as if the water company studentship might be the appropriate one to consider in your case. I think we should get Dr. Charles to talk to you before you leave today."

Professor Able seemed about to bring the interview to an end and Louise was beginning to doubt that she had made the correct impression. The initial discussion concerning the business studies opportunities appeared to have gone well, but had she disappointed the great man when she had not been enthusiastic about advances in the pharmaceutical and computer industries? Should she say something to try to bolster her image in the eyes of the Professor? Her decision was reached quickly. She wanted to be her own boss, to dictate her own future. If Sillfield did not offer her what she wanted there would be somewhere else that did. She would not compromise her ambitions.

By the time she had reset her mental determination the Professor was explaining that Mrs Baker would have arranged for one of the students to take her on a tour of the laboratories and she would have a chance to meet some of the other students.

"Thank you for coming today. I hope you have found it useful."

"Yes, very, thank you."

The farewell handshake was again firm and warm as Professor Able ushered Louise out of his office exactly half an hour after she had entered. Everything was precisely according to the diary structured by Mrs Baker.

Rhian Thomas was the student assigned to take Louise on the tour of the laboratories. Small, dark, pale dressed in torn jeans and T-shirt, she did not look old enough to be an undergraduate let alone a final year Ph.D. student.

"Hi, I'm supposed to show you round the place," was the soft Welsh-accented greeting.

Rhian led her through the side door of the office into a wide corridor flanked with laboratories. They both put on the white coats with high, close-fitting collars and snug-fitting cuffs.

"This is one of the main laboratories in which most of our students work," Rhian said as they went through the double doors.

One of the first impressions was the high level of light. Not only did the laboratory have large windows down one side but all the lights were on. The other immediate impact was the smell, the very distinctive musty smell, of the culture media used to grow microorganisms. This was the signature smell of a microbiology laboratory and Louise felt at home with the atmosphere.

The laboratory benches were pale grey while the cupboards below the benches and the shelves above were white. A long counter down one side of the laboratory housed three microscopes and various other instruments. White coated students were busy at work surrounded by piles of Petri dishes, reagent bottles, Bunsen burners and an array of laboratory plastic and glassware.

"All Charlie's students work here. Charlie, Dr Charles, he does the water and environmental contracts. Some of the others are working for different supervisors on chemical transformation and pharmaceutical projects."

A group of students was standing talking and laughing by the open door to a smaller room. Louise could see shelves filled with bottles of chemicals and assorted laboratory glassware.

"That's the media and reagent preparation room. Most of the chemicals are stored there." Several notices on the walls implored the users to tidy up, return chemicals to the correct places, check instrument calibration and generally to keep the place clean.

Next to this room were two stout windowless doors.

"Those are temperature controlled rooms used in the culture of microorganisms. There are fermenters for larger scale culture in a room further down the building." As they came out of the laboratory Rhian continued her commentary, "There are other smaller laboratories which have restricted access and are fitted with appropriate equipment for different levels of containment. These are to be used if you are working with organisms or processes which could give rise to a biological hazard. We won't go into those laboratories but you'll be given specific instructions on their use if, and when, you need to use them."

"I'm going to take Louise over to the bar for some food when I've finished showing her round," said Rhian as they passed a group of white coated students studying a notice board.

"Huh, the food will put her off this place."

"D'you want to come so she can ask questions about working here? See you in half an hour."

Rhian guided her visitor into a small laboratory. "This is where I work."

The room seemed to be full of computers and bits of electronic instrumentation.

"I'm doing a project on biochips, using biological molecules in the next generation of computers."

Louise looked round the room. The instruments were unfamiliar to her. She looked in vain for evidence of biology.

"I'm working on trying to put single molecules onto silicon surfaces in exactly the right place and keep the things working. It's difficult to do; some Russians say they have done it, but I doubt they have really got it to work." Rhian picked up a tiny shiny grey disc from the lab bench. "Who put this bloody thing in my area?" The unexpected petulant outburst was to no one in particular. Then she returned to quiet controlled tones, "I've only started to get some decent results in the last couple of months, after over two years of work, but I'm beginning to write up my thesis."

Louise watched Rhian's eyes scan the laboratory. Nothing in this environment was going to pass her attention.

"Who're you hoping to work for?" she asked Louise.

"Well Dr. Charles was mentioned but it's not certain."

"I'll show you the office and lecture room area upstairs. That's the lab used by the short course students." Rhian waved her hand at the open door leading to an empty laboratory. "No one's there this week, they come and go. Some of the courses are very short, a week or two. Others are longer, up to two years. Students from all over the place. Good money spinner. The non-Europeans pay a hell of a lot." Rhian was beginning to undo her white coat. "That's where the plant people work. GM and all that." Little was visible through the small window in the door. "We can leave our coats here." She indicated a row of hooks.

The tour of the offices focused on the cramped nature of the office space for the students. It appeared, however, that kudos was gained by achieving the best desk site.

"We'll go across to the Money Maker. It's a student bar where we can get some food. Cheap, but OK. Some of the others are coming so you can ask questions; find out more about being a student here."

When they reached the bar Louise recognised some of the students she had seen in the laboratory and the corridor.

They were queuing for food. She looked at the menu on the wall. The prices looked very reasonable.

"This place should be done under the trades description act. Meat and potato pie - there's no meat. The veggie lasagne is OK."

Louise took the food recommendation of lasagne and decided on a coffee. She was concerned that anything alcoholic might reduce her concentration during her meeting with Dr Charles.

"Did Prof give you the 'biotechnology as saviour of the world and future of mankind' speech'?" one of the students asked, "He's very good at that. We are going to be feeding the starving millions, make perfect medicines and revolutionise the computer industry. And all that in the first half of next week!"

"We've all heard the gospel according to Prof," another added.

"So has every conference audience, every government minister and every Research Council."

Louise suddenly had a flashback to the lecture she had attended while at school. Professor Don Miller had described some of the applications of biotechnology past, present and future. Here she was now with the people who seemed to be making the future possible.

"His name is not Able for nothing. He's able to do everything!"

"Then for an encore he walks on water!"

"But he does get the money, the funding for the lab."

"But he expects us to deliver research results which just cannot be done in that time scale."

"Well, you just have to ignore him and get on with your own thing."

"That's all very well unless he's your supervisor and you have to see him from time to time."

"But he's hardly ever here to see you."

"Yer. He's out of the way most of the time. That can be a nuisance when you need to discuss your work with someone."

"He's not the best supervisor when you first start and need help planning your research and at the end when you need someone to discuss writing up your work."

"He's fine in the middle when you just want to get on with your own stuff."

"Dr. Charles is the best supervisor. Charlie's there when you want help but stays out of the way when you don't need him."

"But his research area is not so exciting, all that business for the water people. No real future, not like the biochip area. That'll be big. Good, well paid jobs."

"But some of Charlie's students do get good field trips, Iceland, Mexico."

"I think he has got all the samples from the ice fields and volcanoes he needs. I expect future students will just be working on something from Wales."

"Great if you like rain and sheep!"

"I've heard that one of Charlie's students will be working on water samples from my home area," said Rhian as they left the Money Maker. "There are some old copper mines which have pools of very acid water. Some microorganisms grow there but not much."

When they got back to the laboratory Louise immediately recognised Dr. Charles as the man who had been in Professor Able's office prior to her interview. Now he was dressed in the ubiquitous white coat, standing with a student, in front of a complex collection of laboratory glassware and tubing.

"We're trying to set up an environment to simulate the growth conditions for microorganisms in a hot vent in

Iceland," explained Dr Charles, "Difficult to control the temperature and pressure."

"Every time I increase the pressure one of the joints blows apart during the night," the frustrated student explained as he carefully poured a liquid into one end of the tubing.

Louise looked at the crude structure of the apparatus. "Where does that tube go? What does it do?" Louise wondered if things could be simplified. Within moments she was involved in the discussion concerning the redesign of the apparatus.

"What happens if you bubble the gas up rather than passing it over the top?"

"What conditions are you going to change?" Louise moved round the laboratory bench to get a different view of the equipment."Is that where you can take samples?" she said pointing at part of the structure, "How can you be certain that the sample will show the reaction of the whole population?"

The research supervisor was impressed by the searching nature of the questions. The candidate was interested in the design of the experiment, making sure the results were valid and meaningful.

"Able said you might be interested in our extremophile work. Jim White suggested you might like to work here?"

Louise nodded in affirmation.

"You want to do the business course and try to set up something of your own." Dr Charles was well briefed. "Lot of hard work to do a Ph.D. and study business at the same time."

"Yes, I realise that but I really want to do it."

"Setting up in business on your own needs dedication and patience to accept the setbacks and frustrations."

"I have friends who have managed it and they have gone through difficult times and explained to me some of the pitfalls. It is something I have thought about and wanted for some time. I understand that research and business can be full of frustrations. It won't be easy."

Dr Charles moved slowly away from the laboratory bench. "Our work is funded by a water company. They allow us to do pure research with no short term expectations of a commercial application in mind. Of course our students meet the water people, visit their labs and plant, get an understanding of their operations, but rarely work directly with their problems and processes."

"But if I came up with research findings that could lead to an application?"

"Every situation is looked at individually but all my students are expected to devote themselves to research projects of sufficient depth and integrity to justify the award of a higher degree."

Chapter 21

Louise's self belief was in contrast to the emotions of those around her. Most of her student friends were in a general state of panic about late or incomplete assignments, incomprehensible concepts and, for many, the future seemed a threatening haze. There was the challenge of finding a suitable job, the realisation that the mountain of debt accumulated as a student would need repaying. Often there was the trauma of the probable separation from one's lover. Would their relationship end with the passing of student life or would it add to the difficulty of finding a career by imposing a requirement that a couple had to stay geographically close?

Louise was not troubled in this respect. Since the break with Jake she had not allowed any man to cross the emotional fence she had built as self protection. Her heart was locked away in a safe, the key to which she had buried in the deepest recesses of her psyche. Romantically she was an iceberg and wished to remain that way.

These feelings became unflinching since the one time she had seen Jake after the break-up. It had been both unexpected and traumatic but she had managed to conceal the inner maelstrom of emotions.

Louise had gone home for the weekend.

"I'm short of potatoes. Can you pop round to the shop and get a small bag? Oh, and while you're there could you get some milk. I forgot I'd need extra as you were home," her mother's request in the early afternoon."Don't be long, don't get chatting. I need the potatoes for this evening."

Louise had no intention of chatting to anyone. There was no one she wanted to chat to.

"OK if I take your coat? Mine's upstairs."

"Yes, fine."

Although Louise and her mother were similar in size their taste in clothes could not have been further apart. Louise hesitated about taking the lazy option as she put on the shapeless, maroon, woollen garment. Should she change her mind and get her own fleece? No, no one would see her.

As she was passing the King's Arms clutching her purchases she literally ran into them. Jake and Al were just coming out of the pub.

"Oh, Louise!"

"Jake!"

In a single moment Louise took in the vision of Californian youth and fashion, and regretted her own maroon wool.

The introduction was brief, Al's smile open and friendly. Did she have any idea of the previous relationship between Jake and herself? If she did, she did not show it.

"How's business?" Louise sought safer waters away from the inner tempest of her feelings.

"Fine, fine. I'm moving to California and Max is going to continue running things here."

Louise felt she had moved into calmer water, then the tidal wave hit.

Al smiled showing the pearly white perfection which was the product of expensive dentistry. "We're going back to California in a month's time. Then will have a month to get ready for the wedding."

The dagger had been unwittingly thrust into Louise's heart.

A heavy lorry roared through the narrow village street forcing the trio to step back to the shelter of the pub wall.

The noise interrupted the conversation. Louise was offered the physical and temporal opportunity to escape and she took it.

"I'm sure I will see you again before you go," she lied. "Can't stop now; Mum needs these things."

The tears that flooded down Louise's cheeks were hot with rage at herself. How could she be caught so poorly prepared, at such a disadvantage? How could she ever have thought that Jake's love and body were her exclusive property? How could she have been so stupid, so stupid, so stupid?

Chapter 22

During the last few months of undergraduate study Louise grew in the confidence that she was in control of her future. To add to this feeling Louise's marks were excellent. She was well on her way to a first class honours degree. She was content that if she could keep a cool head she would achieve this short-term goal. Nothing would be allowed to distract her.

The letter offering her a provisional studentship to study for a Ph.D. at Sillfield arrived two months after her interview, but in the interim she had already spoken with Dr. Charles to confirm that she would like to conduct research into the chemistry of organisms which live in extreme conditions of acidity and toxic metals. She would be contributing to the understanding of how some life could exist in environments which would be fatal to other life forms.

The degree was first class, as predicted. The place and scholarship at Sillfield were confirmed. The scholarship, although modest, would offer her more financial freedom than she had enjoyed as an undergraduate.

Louise's parents were embarrassingly proud of their daughter but rather confused by the meaning of the success and the source of her ambition. No one in the family had been to university before; no one had had a career; they just had jobs.

A congratulatory card arrived from Sally. 'Knew you would do it. Keep up the good fight'. Acknowledgment and encouragement from her role model was the best support she could wish for.

Riding this wave of success and the prospect of slightly increased affluence, Louise changed her hair style. The shoulder length hair was cut back to an easily-managed short style. She bought some new clothes including a couple of tops which showed off her trim figure. Subconsciously, or was it consciously, she realised that her gender, usually regarded as a disadvantage in business, could be used to buy her attention.

Dr Charles (or Charlie as he was known) was an attentive supervisor of his entourage of research students. He was keen that they should get off to a good start at the beginning of their three-year course. Later they would be left to work independently and proceed at their own pace.

"Well, Lou," he usually developed his own title for each student and used it with or without their consent. "You need to meet the water company people, or at least their Research Director. Nominally he is supposed to be involved in helping supervise your work as he is the Research Director but, don't worry, he will leave that to me."

Louise was not worried. There had been research students at Louise's previous university but they had always seemed like creatures who inhabited an alternative universe. The undergraduates did not use the laboratories inhabited by these strange beings. Louise realised she knew little or nothing about the research being followed by this elite and the equipment which was available for their use.

The whole Ph.D. course was so new to her that she had not formed any opinions about the method of supervision. Now she was much too busy trying to settle into the house she was sharing with three other students, finding her way round the campus and learning the names of all the new people she was meeting. Then there was the range of equipment and facilities she might have access to. At times she was bewildered and, if she was truthful, she was scared.

"Dan Norton will be a useful person if, and when, you need to know about the workings and requirements of the water industry. As Research Director he is very knowledgeable about his own company with its reservoirs in the mountains of Wales, but also he knows about other water companies and their systems. Although his title is Research Director he doesn't really do any research. He is involved in making sure that the water company is using the up-to-date procedures and that safety is maintained. He looks at research on water quality but does not do it himself."

"Dan Norton, old hot hands Norton, you need to watch him. Norton by name and 'nought on' is the way he likes his female staff and students," the comment from one of the second-year research students.

"You'll need some suitable samples to start your work. It's a new line for us working with extremophiles from acid areas which are contaminated with metals such as lead, copper and zinc. No one has worked on these. You will need to collect your own samples." Charlie was keen that Louise had an understanding of where these organisms survived. She should collect the samples for her own work and see exactly where they came from.

"There's a field trip going up to North Wales to study the rocky coastal environment, but they will be passing an area of old mining sites, copper mines. You could go with them and should be able to get plenty of useful material to get started," Charlie suggested.

It was all arranged. A minibus was to take the research group to North Wales and they were to stay in local student accommodation.

The motorway journey was long and tedious but just as the light was fading they had their first views of the coastline and out to sea they could see rows of windmills. Of course Louise was aware of the use of wind but this was her first sight of the reality of harnessing that form of energy offshore. The avenues of huge windmills stretched out beyond the horizon.

The overnight accommodation was adequate, just adequate, the following morning any discomfort of the previous evening was compensated for by a beautiful view of mountains. Then, as they drove to their final destination, the view of the mountains was augmented by the sight of the coastline, sandy beaches and rocky coves. The countryside was almost completely dedicated to sheep farming. The fields were bounded by dry-stone walls which looked as if they had stood for centuries marking out the territory of each farm. There were farm buildings and cottages scattered across the countryside and occasional small villages but no towns or signs of industry other than sheep rearing. Louise idly wondered what was the ratio of sheep to humans in this place. Could it be one hundred to one? Just as Louise was pondering this question the mini bus pulled off the road onto a track and stopped. Louise had reached her destination for extremophile collection.

It was the landscaped garden of hell, a flat expanse of mining waste, an area of grey rocks streaked with brown and red seams. The only interruptions on the rock-strewn plateau were pools of dark apparently lifeless water coloured grey to complement the dreary surroundings. Even the hardy weeds, which usually eke out an existence on abandoned industrial sites, failed to inhabit this. There were no splashes of green and pink relief. There was nothing to lift the spirit, no glimmer of hope or optimism.

Beyond this lunar landscape rose a small hill, or the remains of a hill. The side gouged by long-gone industry. Left like some unloved ragged orphan to fend for itself in a cold climate; no hand had attempted to regenerate or beautify this scar of industrial pillage.

No smell reached the nostrils. Dead earth has nothing to decay, nothing to act as the catalyst for rebirth. The cold wind encouraged Louise to hide her face inside the fleece lining of her jacket.

Even the sky colluded in this atmosphere of desolation. The cloud cover was a uniform dark grey. A pair of jackdaws circled high above, their black and grey plumage coordinating perfectly with the landscape. It appeared that even these birds could find nothing of interest in this place as they flew off.

What a miserable outlook, could anything useful come out of this? Then Louise thought back to the time when the ore was being taken from the hill. The copper had been used to clad the hulls of ships. Cladding reduced fouling and kept the hull smooth. It had helped Nelson's fleet to be faster than that of the enemy. Someone had seen the potential of the technology. The smelting and ship-building industries had benefited from these developments. Some people had made money, a lot of money.

Here, now, Louise would search for life; life that could tolerate the extreme environment; life that may represent the last remaining survivors of the early forms which inhabited earth. The bacteria which can thrive in harsh acid water deriving their energy from the oxidation of sulphides.

She needed to find these survivors, take them back to the laboratory and then get them to grow under the conditions she could find in the laboratory. These might not be easy tasks.

Chapter 23

"Dan's coming today. I'll make sure you meet him sometime," was the limit of Charlie's early warning of this significant event.

Louise did not have a chance to prepare for this first encounter with Dr Dan Norton. However, this morning she had taken more care with her appearance as she was among a group of friends who had decided to go out for a lunchtime drink to celebrate a birthday. Normally she wore old jeans and T-shirt for a day in the laboratory.

She looked down at the top she was wearing. It was one of the new ones that showed her figure off to its best advantage. If first impressions really do count Louise felt prepared to give the right initial impact. She then recalled the comments about 'hot hands Dan' and 'nought on'. Should she worry? No, this was a business meeting, the first encounter between student and the funding organisation. There would be no question of anyone getting the wrong signal; she was just looking smart. Also, she would be wearing a lab coat the whole time.

Louise spotted him the minute he came into the laboratory; tall, slim, dark with rather pointed features, younger than she had expected. Eventually he made his way up to the bench where Louise was sorting out some of the bottles of water and gravel samples she had collected in Wales. Charlie introduced her.

"While I'm here today perhaps we could have a chat about the plans for your work. I know it's early days but I like to have some idea of where the research is going and any findings that can be put to a practical use." Dan Norton's approach seemed entirely professional. "You are hoping to culture something interesting from these?" Dan Norton leant over the laboratory bench and picked up one of the sample bottles. He read the label, then, as he replaced the bottle his hand brushed against Louise's arm.

"I'm trying to set up culture conditions which will encourage growth of the extremophiles without allowing other organisms to take over."

"I'd be interested to hear more about your experimental design. Could we get together later today?"

"Yes."

"I'll arrange it."

With that Dan Norton was ushered out of the laboratory by Charlie who was clearly anxious that they should not be late for some prearranged meeting.

Her next encounter with Dan was when she returned from the favourite student drinking hole, 'The Money Maker'. As she came back he was standing, by himself, looking at a notice board outside the laboratory.

"Ah, Louise," his eyes wandered over her figure stopping momentarily at her cleavage. On their initial encounter she had been concealed under a shapeless all-enveloping lab coat. "Perhaps we could discuss your work this evening."

"This evening?"

"I've got meetings all afternoon but there is some time early this evening before I have to leave."

"Yes, OK, fine."

"All right, we can go through your plans during dinner."

Louise assumed that the evening meal was an extension of the working day for this busy man and that other people, such as Dr Charles and even Professor Able, would be involved. Maybe some of her fellow students would be going along.

"I'll see you here at six, an early dinner."

Louise did not feel in any position to query the arrangements made by this representative of the organisation that supported her financially. In fact, her main priority was to finish her work in the laboratory then prepare some notes for the evening's discussion. Her overwhelming anxiety was to create the impression of a competent student with a well thought-out programme of research.

There was no time to go back to the house to change but her outfit was smart, although she did wish the neck line of her top was a little higher.

At five to six Louise was standing outside the laboratory, hair combed, waiting to be joined by the other diners. However, there were no other students there. She looked through the glass panel in the laboratory door. There were some people finishing off the day's work but it appeared that most had left already.

"You ready? Let's go." Dan appeared on his own, no Dr Charles, no Professor Able."We'll just go to the 'Full Tum'. They'll do a reasonable meal this early."

Louise had seen the 'Full Tum'. The food had a very good reputation, the menu chalked up on a board by the entrance looked enticing, but the prices were out of her range.

"Is anyone else coming?" Louise enquired.

"No, no, I've got through the rest of the day's meetings."

There were few other diners as they entered the restaurant. It was too early in the evening for most people. In spite of the widely available choice of tables, they were shown to, or did Dr Norton select, a small table tucked away in a corner and partly hidden from view by a potted fern.

"This will give us privacy to discuss business."

Louise did not consider their business that private. She slid her small rucksack off her arm and put it between the chair and the wall confident that the notes she had prepared during the afternoon would be close at hand if she needed them.

"May I take your coat?" Dan touched her shoulder.

"No, it's fine. It can go over the back of the chair." Louise was aware of his eyes moving to her neck line as soon as she removed her fleece. Perhaps she should have gone back to the house to change, but it was too late now.

"What would you like to drink? Gin, rum, wine?"

"A glass of white wine would be fine, thank you."

Dan ordered a non-alcoholic tonic for himself. "I've a long drive home."

They looked at the menu. Louise had come a long way from that meal in the hotel with Jake, where the prices had shocked her. She chose a dish of chicken in a wine sauce to be served with pasta. It seemed a safe choice.

Dan selected steak and salad. The steak was to be served rare with no covering sauces or garnish.

"Now let's run through the plans for your work. I saw you have some samples already.

The drinks arrived and Louise took a small sip of the wine.

"Yes, I'm setting up culture conditions to grow the extremophiles. I must be very careful to make sure that the culture conditions do not allow the other microorganisms, those that grow in better environments, to grow and swamp out the extremophiles."

"Have you got the culture medium sorted out yet?"

"Yes, Charlie, I mean Dr Charles, has helped me with that."

More people were beginning to drift into be restaurant but none chose to sit close to the intimate table for two.

"When the cultures have grown I intend to harvest them and start extracting the proteins, the enzymes, the lipids to try to find out how they differ from those in similar organisms grown in better environments."

"That seems an interesting piece of work. Tell me how do you intend to look for these differences?"

Louise started on a detailed explanation of the plans for her future experiments. She did not need to refer to her notes. She knew what she wanted to do.

"How long will it be?" Dan asked the passing waiter.

"Sorry sir, the chef was a bit behind, but I'll be bringing your order in a couple of minutes."

"Another wine and a tonic, please."

Louise was so intent on explaining her work she had hardly noticed that she had finished her first glass of wine."Although we know a great deal about the microorganisms in our environment, it is surprising how little is known about why some conditions and chemicals kill some life but other organisms can survive."

The couple of minutes to the arrival of the food was an under estimation but the drinks arrived quickly.

"Yes," agreed Dan, "in the water industry we are good at producing safe water, no dangerous live bacteria in the stuff we drink, but sometimes we do not understand the exact effect of the chemicals we use."

Eventually the food did arrive and Louise found herself drinking her third glass of wine.

The conversation was flowing freely over the nature of the water industry. It was a conservative industry which tended to do things in tried and tested ways. There were also the restraints imposed by government.

"That does not mean that we are not looking for new and better ways of doing things," assured Dan.

"If a researcher came up with a useful discovery?" enquired Louise.

"Yes, there would be a market for something that was safe, reliable and cut costs."

Louise was feeling very relaxed and open about her ideas for the future. "I would eventually like to go into business, set up my own company. Perhaps, if I can, develop something for the water industry."

"If you are thinking along those lines you will need to know a lot about what we do, an intimate knowledge of our operations."

"I will need a wider understanding of your needs."

"A visit to our plant, see some of our reservoirs, would be a good start. I could arrange for you to visit us."

"I would like that."

"The next few weeks are busy for me but after that..."

"Yes, I want to get my research really underway. Then I am starting the course on business for scientists and engineers. In three or four month's time I should be in a better position to get the most out of a visit. Get a better feeling for things."

Dan Norton smiled and leant across the table, "OK, in four months time we will get together. I will arrange everything, a place for you to stay. Everything will be fixed."

Louise looked across the table at the sharp features. There was something that reminded her of a rat, but she should not let her prejudice about a person's appearance get in the way of the useful business contact.

"I think I had better start the drive home."

"It will be late by the time you get back. Your wife may be worried."

"I'm not married, still single and fancy free," the rodent-like face had that smile again. "Can I give you a lift back to your place?"

"No, thank you, I'll walk. It'll do me good to get some fresh air after all that good food."

As Louise walked back to the house the cool evening air sharpened her thoughts. She knew she had created the appropriate impression of the good student, but had she, unfortunately, left Dr Dan Norton with other expectations. If that had happened she would need to give the correct signals in the future. She was interested in an academic and business relationship, not a romantic or sexual one, especially not with Dan Norton.

Chapter 24

Flint returned to his university town and took a modest job working as a laboratory technician for a company which imported food. The job involved bacteriology as the produce which had been imported was checked to make sure it was not contaminated with anything dangerous. The pay was poor, the level of responsibility nil, and the job requirements formed a poor fit with his qualifications. However the advantage of this job meant Flint had time to think and to plan. His evenings were free to do what he wanted. He still had access to the university libraries so he could read about possible ways of preserving bacteria. He knew bacteria remained viable, alive when frozen. They could be thawed out and would start to grow again but he could not get them to England in a frozen state. That could not work.

The other ways of preservation included freeze drying and then putting the dry pellets of bacteria into a sealed vial. This sounded ideal but Flint did not have access to the laboratory equipment which would be needed. There was also the problem of how he could get the vials, little bottles, of bacteria into England. If they were found in his luggage how could he explain what was in them? What if someone wanted to open them?

Flint felt frustrated. His life seemed to be going nowhere. Poor job, no idea of when he might be going to England and he did not know how his goal could be achieved in England even if he got there. He could not even discuss these problems with his friends.

He was so frustrated that after work one evening he did not go into the library or even to a nearby beach. Instead he wandered aimlessly down a stream which ran behind some old houses. As he ambled along he looked at the polluted water and he started to think about how bacteria were preserved in nature. He had read that sometimes bacteria could survive for long periods of time in dry mud. He decided he would do an experiment.

The next evening he took some sheets of paper when he went down to the stream. He selected a place where there was a patch of mud covered in a green slime. He picked up a nearby leaf and used it to smear some mud onto the sheets of paper. He folded the paper carefully to enclose the mud. Then he went back to the house where he was living. In his room he spread out the sheets of paper on a shelf and left them to dry for a few days. Then at work, he put some of the tubes containing the culture broth that was used to grow bacteria into his pocket. That evening he cut up the mud smeared paper and put the slithers of paper into the broth. Over the next few days the contents of some of the tubes became increasingly cloudy. Something was growing. Something had been dried then come back to life again.

Would the same happen with the cholera bacteria? He had no way of checking. However he would spend time improving this method of preserving bacteria so they would not be spotted as he entered England. Also he needed to refine his method so it was just the cholera bacteria which would go to England, not the full range of bacteria which were growing in the mud of his native islands.

He needed to do a lot of careful work but he told himself that it could be done.

On occasion when Flint met university friends they were astonished at his lack of progress.

"But he was one of the best in the class."

"Has he had a breakdown or something?"

"Is there some other opportunity he is waiting for?"

"Perhaps he's working on some other idea and just not saying anything yet."

Friends found it impossible that he had lost his drive, his ambition.

By this time it was almost too late to apply for the course at Sillfield University. Would he have to wait another year or would a decision never be made?

Things might have drifted on like this if it had not been for the terminal illness of one of the remaining members of the community. He was the last one who had experienced the massacre at first hand.

As the old man lay on his deathbed he expressed his disappointment that he would not live long enough to see the deaths revenged. "It was my wish to see the English pay the price. I had hoped Flint might be the one to have achieved that."

"But his ideas might not succeed."

"If we leave it much longer there will be none of us left who were there. We will have all gone without the price being paid."

The old man was so pale and thin he was almost transparent, then with the last gasp of energy from his body, "It is my dying wish that Flint be supported in his plan. If he is not allowed to carry the torch, to attempt the deed, the determination, the desire, will perish. The next generation will be too far away. There will be no one left to stoke the fire to provide the drive to reap our just revenge."

The group of elders surrounding the deathbed hung their heads. Why had it been necessary for this old man to use his last breath to goad the community into action while they had sought refuge behind a cloud of indecision? If they did not act the principal goal of the community would be left unattained. The strength of the desire passed from the dying man into the hearts and minds of the surrounding group.

It was the unanimous decision that Flint should be given total support.

Chapter 25

Growing extremophiles in the laboratory proved more difficult and frustrating than Louise had expected. When she thought back to her first discussion with Dan Norton she felt she had been stupidly overconfident. There were days when she felt the idea of doing a Ph.D. was foolish. She did not have the tenacity to complete the project.

One evening Louise sat on her bed and cried, the tears rolling down her face. She was an utter failure. Her ambition was in shatters. Charlie had suggested she should take a rest, a day off and do something like a walk in the countryside. He had said she was tired and overstressed. She took it to mean she was not up to it. He was beginning to suggest she should drop out. She collapsed on her pillows in sobs. She had never felt so depressed in her life.

However, the next morning she did take Charlie's advice. She walked along a country lane. Initially her pace was brisk but gradually she slowed down. She heard a high pitched birdsong and stopped to see if she could spot its origin. Then, briefly, she saw a wren. What a delight to spot the tiny bird! By now she could hear the bees and she watched one as it busily went from flower to flower. She smiled, sat down on a grassy bank and listened to the noise of the cows munching on the grass. The countryside was so pleasant; she must take time to enjoy it. She took a deep breath and decided to do this walk regularly. She would be able sit at this spot and adjust her priorities. She would plan her week's work in the laboratory. She would schedule her management course studies and assignments. She would take control of her life.

That night Louise slept well.

The next morning she sat at her desk reviewing the culture conditions she had tried for the extremophiles. Had she had done something wrong, had she missed something obvious or was it something obscure that was hindering their growth? Although she had looked at some research papers her examination of published articles had not been exhaustive. She opened her laptop and started a new search. Yes, she had not seen all these papers before. She sat and stared at the wall, concentrating on a small crack in the plaster, contemplating if it would ever open wider and the whole building would fall in two, revealing the outside world. Then, with a jolt, she suddenly thought of modifying the words she was searching under. Several new papers came up. Most were not very relevant but there was one by a Russian group. The computer translation made her smile but it appeared they had done what she was trying to do. She was doing the same as them, apart from one ingredient they had put into the culture mixture. It was as if all the lights went on and all the bells rang in Louise's mind. She could not wait to try this out. However, before she did that she made a record of the reference which would have to be quoted in her thesis. Then she sat and made is a list of what she should do next. The work would be much more systematic that it had been previously. She showed the plan to Charlie. He said nothing but smiled.

She contacted her tutor in the management school. The tutor suggested a face-to-face meeting to review the situation.

"I cannot keep up with all the work that needs to be done," started Louise with a flood of words which were about to continue to admit her failure.

Dr. Susan Williams held up her hand, "Before we go any further I have been reviewing your work so far. Your marks have been adequate but looking at the assignments you have handed in they start off very well then they become rather incomplete as you ran out of time." She stopped and looked at Louise who nodded in agreement. "You have too much on your plate." Louise thought here it comes, the drop out message, but Dr. Williams continued, "You know you can defer part of the course until next year or even to the final year of your Ph.D., although I do not recommend that. Shall we go through the units and decide which you will complete this year and which will be deferred?"

Louise felt a huge load sliding off her shoulders. Here was someone who understood and could help.

The formalities were completed quickly and Louise left the Management School feeling as if she was walking two inches off the ground. She was beginning take control of her life. She knew what her short term goals were.

Shortly after this crisis the first pure cultures of the extremophiles started to grow. The work was scaled up and eventually Louise had enough material to begin investigating their biochemistry in order to find what made these extremophiles so special. She needed to know how they could grow in conditions which would kill other life forms.

In spite of this success Louise had doubts about her future. The initial work had taken so much time. She would not have enough results to constitute a thesis. Again Charlie came to the rescue. He assured her that her negative results could be scientifically interesting and important.

Gradually, very gradually, Louise's self confidence returned. When Charlie suggested that she should publish a short paper on some of her work Louise experienced a huge boost in morale. There would be her name, as an author, in print, in the scientific journal.

She began to look at a wider picture. If she understood why these bacteria could live in such hostile conditions she began to ask if they could pass through the chemical processes used by the water industry. She would discuss the ideas with Dan Norton.

Louise had made several visits to the water treatment plant with other students, never alone. She was always aware of Dan Norton looking at her, his eyes roaming over her body. During discussions he would move too close. There would be the touch of hands, arms and even legs, perhaps accidental, perhaps not. Louise thought of his reputation, 'hot hands Dan'. Was she over reacting to Dan Norton's approach? He was certainly very knowledgeable and would be a useful contact but should she try to distance herself from him physically. No, she decided that would not be the sensible reaction. She should continue seeking his help and advice unless something overt happened. She was an adult who could deal with any situation that might arise.

It was in this atmosphere of assurance that Louise began to look at the processes used by the water industry. Could there be a better, less expensive way of ensuring the safety of the water supply? An idea began to grow in her mind. Was this something that should be patented? Could this be the basis of a business? Perhaps, just perhaps, she could be running her own company in a few years. Could she emulate Max and Jake?

On a recent visit home Louise had walked over to the converted farm which was still the headquarters of Max and Jake's business. She had fully recovered from the break up with Jake and was delighted to hear that he was the father of a young child and was living in Colorado, in the mountains near Denver. Yes, she remembered Jake's enthusiasm for the Rockies. It sounded as if he was living his dream.

The other surprise was that Emma was working for Max. She was doing some of the graphic design for the company. Louise thought back to their first visit to PSW when Emma said she wanted to be an artist. So it had not been such a hollow statement and Emma had managed to turn her life round. She had completed a graphic art course at college. Her two young children were entering their school years and Emma was enjoying the start of her career.

Louise and Emma sat in what had been the old farmyard discussing their various school friends.

"Max is out," said Emma.

"Yes, I would have liked to have seen him," said Louise.

"No, I mean he has come out. He is much happier these days," explained Emma.

So that platinum blond goddess, Beth, had only been a passing fancy, perhaps just a status symbol.

Part Three

Chapter 26

Flint was constantly scanning the scientific literature for anything which might be of interest when he saw a paper by L. M. Browning and R. F. Charles of Sillfield University. The research findings on extremophiles looked encouraging to him, very encouraging. Flint noted the names of the authors and decided he must get direct access to this work as soon as he could. He would need to find out exactly how far their research had gone and decide if it could be used to promote his cause.

Flint had already identified the programme at Sillfield University which interested him, so the decision was taken immediately. Of course there was the realization that the course might already be full and he would not be able to get a place. To his relief he got a quick response asking him for full details of his educational background, references from his tutors and evidence that he would be able to pay his fees and support himself financially.

The provision of details of his university qualifications was easy. When he had contacted two of his university tutors they were very happy to provide references. They were both very interested to hear what he would be doing in England and offered good wishes for his continuing studies.

Next there was the issue of providing evidence that he had enough money to pay for the course and cover his cost of living. A number of emails went back and forth between himself and Sillfield University. Eventually it was agreed that he would be offered a provisional place subject to the University receiving payment of the fees and evidence that Flint had adequate money in his own bank account.

Flint showed the emails to the elders and suddenly he had doubts about their resolve to support him.

"It is a lot of money," commented one.

"But I did tell you what it would cost," replied Flint.

"That's just the fees and then there is the money to cover your living costs," chimed in another.

"Yes, England is expensive," defended Flint.

"How certain are you that you can get your ideas to work?" asked a third.

"I have done everything that I can to find a way of getting the bacteria to England safely and so they won't be detected at the airport," Flint started to feel frustrated and this frustration built through the evening as doubts and objections were raised. Then suddenly the whole issue was resolved. It was agreed that the fees would be paid, a bank account set up in Flint's name and this would contain enough money to cover his costs.

As Flint left the meeting he was not sure what had turned the tide in everyone's attitude but suddenly everyone was positive and offering their best wishes for success in the mission.

One of the elders had agreed that he would handle the financial arrangements. To Flint's surprise things started to move very quickly. Within a few days he heard that there had been a money transfer to Sillfield to pay the fees and a special bank account had been set up in his name with half the money which he would need while he was in England. Evidence of this account was sent to Sillfield University along with assurance that the rest of the money required would be put into the account after three months and six months.

Flint received an e-mail with an official offer for him to enrol on the one year course in the School of Biotechnology, Sillfield University.

"Look, look I've got a place," he said in great excitement to his mother and sister.

"Yes, good. How wonderful! But now you will need to get things organised. When does the course start? How will you get there? What flights will you need to book?" his mother started to discuss the practical side of her son's move.

"You'll need warm clothes there," joined in his sister. She was always very sensible but since her marriage and the recent announcement of her pregnancy she seemed to have become even more concerned about the welfare of others.

That evening one of the elders came to Flint's family home. "I've looked at flights and this seems the best way of getting there. You will fly into London and Sillfield has a bus transfer to the University for overseas students." At that point the elder turned to Flint's mother, "if that is all right I will book it."

Flint began to feel that he was being treated as a child as the arrangements were discussed with his mother but he did not care as he was about to be on his way.

Flint wandered down to the beach. He sat on a wooden box that had been washed up in the recent storm. So he was going to England. England, a faraway country about which he realised he knew surprisingly little. He had been told about the cruelty of the English many years earlier but what about now? What was the country like? He had seen London on the news and in films, the tall buildings and narrow streets. He tried to imagine what it would be like to be in a place like that. One of his university lecturers had studied in Manchester. He had said he enjoyed the university life with the students from all round the world. However, he said, the climate was terrible, cold, wet and dark. It was particularly the lack of sunshine that he had found difficult. Initially Flint could not understand this lack of light until he looked at a globe and realised how far north he would be going. Almost to the Arctic Circle he thought.

How could humans, originally a tropical species, have adapted to that climate?

Flint walked to the water's edge and let the warm ocean wash over his feet. If England was such a cold, dark, foggy place what was the countryside like? He had seen images of fields of green grass. He had seen pictures of the various trees such as the oak and the elm but he did not feel that he knew what they looked like in reality, what they smelt like, what noise they made in the wind, what they would feel like to touch. He had been told that all the leaves fell off the trees in winter and grew back in the spring. The spring, what was the spring?

For all his upbringing and concentration on wreaking revenge on the English he felt that in reality he knew very little about the people and their country. Now, in a few weeks' time, he would be boarding an aircraft to begin the long journey.

He determined that he would spend as much time as possible, before his departure, gaining information about England and the English.

The other imperative work was to prepare the cholera samples for the journey. The bacteria would have to survive until he could get them into the laboratory at Sillfield University. The means of transporting them would not have to arouse any suspicion as he entered England. He had been warned about the searches which were conducted at the airports.

Flint returned to his university and went up to the laboratory under the pretext of telling his former colleagues about his exciting news. His familiarity with the people allowed him freedom to wander around the laboratory. He took two test tubes containing the deadly bacteria from their place of safekeeping.

The next day Flint collected some sludge from a local pond and put it through the heating process which he had developed to kill all the bacteria and other forms of life which might be in the paste. He had rehearsed the process several times over the previous months and had a reasonable level of confidence that this method of sterilisation would work every time. However, ultimately he had to trust that he had done it correctly on this important occasion. He had no way of checking before he added the cholera bacteria to the paste.

Next he took the two test tubes containing the cholera bacteria and poured the deadly culture into the sludge. After mixing it thoroughly he carefully smeared his preparation onto pages taken from a notebook. When everything was dry he reassembled the book. Yes, it looked as if the book had simply got dirty during fieldwork.

He put the book into a plastic bag with other notes and papers about his studies and about Sillfield. The precious package was ready for its journey.

Before starting the procedure Flint had built and lit a small fire. Now he dropped the laboratory test tubes, his blue protective gloves and all the other items which might have been contaminated by the bacteria into the fire. He stirred the embers to make sure everything was burnt or at least sterilised. He needed to ensure there was no risk to his home island.

Later in the evening he returned to rake the cold ashes into the sea. No trace was left as a telltale signature of his activities.

The following day the mission would start. Would this mean realisation of his ambition or would his ideas, research and planning turn into a great failure? For the first time in his life Flint felt the dry throat and tight chest of nervous apprehension.

CHAPTER 27

The captain's voice came over the intercom. "We are just coming over the coast of Kent and will be passing over the centre of London before landing at Heathrow, ten minutes before our scheduled arrival time. The weather in London is overcast with a light rain. The temperature is 15 degrees Celsius. I hope you have enjoyed your flight and on behalf of myself, the flight crew and cabin crew I wish you a happy stay in the United Kingdom".

Up until this moment Flint had been dozing, only half aware of the activity in the aircraft cabin and oblivious to the view outside but suddenly he was wide awake and every sense in his body was heightened. Like a hunter, poised for the initial sight of the prey, Flint peered at the clouds below hoping to get his first view of London, the imperial city, the seat of colonial power. He knew the landmarks to look for. The Houses of Parliament, St Paul's Cathedral, Buckingham Palace, the river Thames with its various bridges should all be visible from the aircraft. Still, all he could see was a layer of grey cloud like a mat of dirty cotton wool.

Flint considered that the most successful act of revenge, the one that received the most publicity, had been flying aircraft into buildings but he had questioned whether he could replicate this. He would have had to learn to fly, get a plane and then fly it to an appropriate building. The more he had examined this idea the more barriers he had found. That would have been a suicide mission. Was he prepared for that? Flint was no Kamikaze pilot. He was prepared to be a soldier who would risk death for the Cause, but to deliberately undertake a venture which would certainly end in his own demise. He was young, bright, and healthy. He was aware that he could have a full, rewarding life ahead. He wanted a chance to live this life to the full.

Now, as he looked out he realised that he would not even have managed to find the appropriate building in this cloud. Or was it fog?

As they approached Heathrow airport the passengers were told to bring their seats to the upright position, fasten seat belts and remain seated until the plane was stationary at the airport terminal. The cabin crew hurried up and down the aisle checking that everyone had obeyed the directions.

At that moment the plane entered the cloud layer. Soon they would pass through the veil and all would be revealed.

The undercarriage went down with a bump and the plane shook due to some turbulence. We will reach the bottom of this cloud and I will see it all, thought Flint, as he strained his eyes to discern some recognisable shapes through the murk.

The first thing he saw, as they made their final approach, was the roofs of houses and warehouses. He had passed over central London and not caught a single sight of his quarry. His sense of disappointment was palpable.

He looked out at the grey, wet scene. So this was England. The sight was so dismal that the thought crossed his mind that some higher power had already wreaked revenge on a nation with such an unforgivable past.

Entry into England through passport control posed no problem. All the paperwork concerning his acceptance to study at Sillfield University was in perfect order. He had appropriate evidence of his ability to maintain himself financially during his time at the university. His well practiced ability to construct a Chinese Wall between the student and the terrorist did not let him down. There was no perceptible change in his pulse or breathing rate as he answered the few questions put to him.

Any casual observer watching the arriving passengers clustered around the carousel waiting for their luggage might have seen the relaxed young man casually scanning his surroundings as he waited for his bags. He was noting that most people passed through the customs hall without being stopped.

Flint's bags were some of the last to arrive. As he walked towards the exit a woman just ahead was intercepted by a customs official and lead away. Flint had seen her on the plane. She looked like many of the other passengers. So why had she been stopped?

"Put your bags here."

Flint started at the command. He had been unaware of the official's approach.

"Open that bag."

Flint fumbled with the lock while his inner voice was telling him not to panic, to concentrate and breathe normally.

Flint was asked to move some of the contents of the bag and that revealed a transparent folder. A booklet containing information for students at Sillfield University was visible from the front and a rather worn, stained notebook, perhaps containing records of laboratory or field work, was visible at the back of the folder. The official told Flint to repack the bag.

"Enjoy your studies."

Flint nodded his thanks. A nodded acknowledgement was safer than saying anything. His voice might have given away the anxiety he was feeling.

Flint stood in the arrivals area of the airport. So he was in England. What emotion should he feel? He did not know. There were so many feelings racing through his mind.

The instructions from the university said there would be a special bus waiting to take new overseas arrivals to their destination. Flint looked round and saw a man holding a sign saying Sillfield University.

"What's your name?" the man asked as Flint approached. The driver checked his list, "Yes, you're the last one. Been waiting for you."

"They wanted to check my bags," apologised Flint.

"OK, come this way," said the driver and lead Flint out of the arrivals hall to a mini bus. There was one unoccupied seat at the rear of the bus. As Flint past the other passengers there were some faint nods but no one spoke. Everyone looked tired.

The bus journey was along a motorway away from central London. Flint did not get a chance to see any internationally famous buildings.

The countryside was a mixture of woodland and fields. Flint liked the trees, their foliage looked lush. Some of the fields had been freshly ploughed giving the vista a patchwork effect. The variation was accentuated by the pale sunshine, so different from the cloud cover and drizzle which had obscured London. Flint found himself admiring the view. He had heard people refer to England as a green and pleasant land, and he was beginning to understand why, but he must not allow himself to be lulled into any sense of ease. He was here on a mission. He must remember the suffering of his people.

Flint looked at the instructions he had been given. He would be taken to the student hall which would be his home for his time at the university. Everything was as described and the welcome was friendly. That evening Flint sat quietly in his student room. He had decided that he would start early the next day with an exploration of the university campus. Then, he was due to go into the School of Biotechnology to meet the staff who would be his mentors and the students who would be his companions for the next year.

For now he would refresh his thoughts about how to use this academic institution to further his objectives. He read some of the literature which was on the desk in his small room. The university had been established to educate people to work in industry. Initially the students had come, predominantly, from Britain but now an increasing proportion came from other countries. Flint felt reassured by this. He would quickly and easily merge in as just one of the many overseas students. He must in no way stand out from the crowd.

He picked up the booklet that dealt with the School of Biotechnology. Much of it outlined the research interests, the academic and commercial successes of Professor Able, however, there was a section that dealt with work on the clean-up of industrial sites and projects undertaken for the water industry. The name Dr Charles seemed to be associated with most of these projects. Yes, that was the name he had seen when he had trawled through the Internet looking for a suitable place in England to develop the technology to put the cholera bacteria to their ultimate use.

Tomorrow, Flint expected to get his first meeting with Dr Charles and some of the students who would, unwittingly, help his mission.

Chapter 28

Flint woke early the next morning. His biological clock was not set to this time zone. He drew back the curtains from the window in his small room. It was still dark outside and he could only distinguish the outline of the surrounding buildings and trees.

He lay on the bed waiting for dawn. Gradually he could see some detail of his surroundings. It was possible to discern the contents of his room. The single cupboard which now held his clothes and the desk marked by the careless application of the pens by previous occupants. The chair at the desk was plastic and functional. The fabric of the seat and back of the other chair in the room was stained and frayed.

If people came to visit they would have to sit on the bed. Flint thought back to student days at home. He had enjoyed close friendships. They had sat late into the night discussing the future from a personal and international perspective. Flint had always been careful during these talks, but everyone had assumed he would have a bright successful future.

Flint pushed his mind into the present reality. There would be no visitors, no long discussions until dawn. He would need to focus all his efforts on the one objective. However, there was the thought that the qualification awarded at the end of this course would be held in high esteem internationally. It would open doors to good prestigious jobs. That was for the future; the successful completion of his mission had to be the target at this time.

The level of light outside had increased and now he could see the detail of a tree close to the window. Somewhere in the building he heard a sound; perhaps someone was out of bed preparing for the day. Flint decided he should get up and go outside. He could take a short walk before breakfast.

The air was cool and damp, but the smell of dew-covered foliage was pleasant. A pale sun was struggling to come through the mist. Perhaps the climate would not be too bad if he had the right clothing.

Flint walked across the quiet campus until he could see a group of women coming down the drive from the road. They were laughing and chatting. Domestic staff, cooks or cleaners, coming in to work, thought Flint. As they drew level with him they all turned and smiled.

"Nice morning, bit of sun. You OK, luv?" one of the women greeted him.

Flint found himself smiling back, "Yes, nice."

The women continued on their way, occupied in their gossip. Flint watched them. Could these friendly people be the descendants of the soldiers who committed the massacre? It was difficult to reconcile the image of an uncaring barbarous nation with the reality he was finding.

As Flint walked back for breakfast he pondered the dilemma posed by the discovery that England was a country populated by a friendly multiracial society, rather than uniform hard Anglo Saxons. Perhaps he was just meeting an unrepresentative section. He would find the true English as he explored the country further.

The rest of the morning and most of the afternoon was taken up with the formalities of registration for, and introduction to, the course. Flint found himself being shepherded round with the other new students, on a confusing timetable of visits to laboratories and form filling. There were so many new faces and the various accents made his mind spin. By mid afternoon he was sitting at a desk with the knowledge that this was to be his bit of space for the duration of the course. Already he was feeling tired as his body told him he should be asleep.

He tried to assess what he had achieved during the day. One thing was certain; he had not met Dr Charles. He had visited one large laboratory where he had been told that students were working for Ph.D.s and some were funded by the water industry. However, he did not know which of these people might be important to him.

Flint looked at his watch. It was ten minutes to four. The new arrivals had been told that at four o'clock there would be some sort of informal gathering to meet other members of the School. Perhaps Dr Charles would be at that event. Flint began to feel wide awake again.

When he arrived at the large lecture room he found Mrs Baker, the Professor's secretary, behind a table on which there were name badges. The badges were arranged in alphabet order. Yes, there was one for Dr Charles.

"Please help yourself to a drink," Mrs. Baker waved a hand, with bright red finger nails, at the table across the room. "Professor Able will be along shortly."

Flint collected a fruit juice then looked round the room. On one side there was a group of self-conscious new students who had gone through the day's initiating process with him. Most of them were standing silently clutching their drinks. There were two blonde women talking in loud voices and gesticulating wildly. He had tried to speak to one of them earlier in the day but could not understand her version of English. He gathered they were from somewhere in Eastern Europe but he did not know where.

Flint decided to avoid that linguistic barrier and wondered if he could, or should, try to talk to someone else.

At that moment an immaculately suited figure walked into the room. Mrs. Baker immediately approached the newcomer and leant forward in confidential conversation. Then the great man stepped into the middle of the room.

"Good afternoon, I am Professor Able for those new students whom I have not had the pleasure of meeting yet. I would like to welcome you to our postgraduate course, especially those of you from overseas. By choosing this course at Sillfield you have already acknowledged our position as world leaders in the research and development of biotechnology."

The next ten minutes were spent, by the Professor, extolling the strengths and virtues of biotechnology and particularly the version being produced at Sillfield. Flint looked round at the other faces in the room. Most appeared to support the views of this professor and share in his opinion that Sillfield was leading the crusade to change the world by using this science.

An arrogant approach thought Flint. His mind switched from the present to events over eighty years earlier. Yes, this was the sort of arrogant Englishman who would take a course of action regardless of the consequences and, it appeared looking at some of the faces in the room, others would follow. If, earlier in the day, Flint had doubts about his mission he now had no reservations.

The address over, the great man turned and left be room with Mrs Baker close on his heels.

"Always very impressive and inspiring," said a small, thin, pale woman.

Flint looked at her, took a sip of his drink, "Yes."

"You must be one of the new students. I am Mary Moore, librarian. If you need any help finding papers or information, or with searches, I may be able to help."

"Thank you," Flint remembered being shown the library earlier in the day and being told that the librarian, although out at that moment, was usually available to give advice and assistance.

Flint finished his drink and decided to leave.

As he made his way across the room a balding man, in faded jeans and a misshapen T-shirt, accompanied by an attractive young woman with dark shoulder-length hair, entered the room. They were in an intense conversation but as they reached the table with the name badges Flint stepped quickly to one side to get a better view. The man picked up two badges from the table, somewhere close to the beginning of the alphabet, and handed one to the young woman.

"There's yours."

He pinned the other badge onto his own T-shirt. Yes, this was Dr Charles.

"Bit late, but at least we can get a drink. As I was saying, if you are serious about getting a patent, you must delay any publication. Don't even present your ideas at a department seminar until the agent says it's OK."

"Yes, I know I have to be careful so I have arranged to speak to the patent agent next week," the young woman replied.

Flint suddenly decided he was still thirsty and returned to the table to get another fruit juice. The young woman, who had selected a glass of white wine, turned and smiled at him.

"You just started today?"

"Yes."

"Bit confusing meeting all new people and finding your way around."

"It is, but I am sure I will soon find everything I need."

"I'm Louise, Louise Browning. Doing a Ph.D. with Charlie, Dr. Charles.

"Flint."

CHAPTER 29

By the end of the first week at Sillfield Flint was feeling happy. He had a timetable of lectures and seminars dealing with the different areas of research which were being undertaken in the School. He had been assigned a laboratory bench, refrigerator and freezer space. Everything seemed to be well organized and Flint felt confident as he put some slips of dirty paper from a notebook into plastic vials, labelled them and placed them in the freezer.

Following a lecture on the use of genetic engineering in crops, to increase their resistance to tropical pests, Flint eagerly questioned the lecturer. He expressed his interest in learning the techniques involved. It was arranged that these studies would be a major component of his practical laboratory work.

In the meantime Flint saw a notice in the hall of residence describing a tour, for new students, of the university sports facilities. It was to happen the next evening so he decided to go and see what was available. Even if there would not be much time he might try some different activities here. He felt it would make him merge in and appear just like the other students. At home he had enjoyed swimming and football.

The first part of the tour took them to the gym. The climbing wall looked fascinating but Flint looked at the people who were using it and decided that their level of skill was much greater than his. He was used to climbing trees not rock faces. He did not want to stand out as a beginner.

Next they were taken to the swimming pool. Flint's first impression was the smell of the chemicals in the water. For him swimming was something you did in the warm sea of a lagoon protected from the ocean by a coral reef. The firm white sand, the shoals of brightly coloured fish made the experience wonderful. In contrast this lifeless pool offered no attraction. In fact it just made him long to slip into the water at home and swim out to admire the variety of wildlife. Flint decided the swimming pool could not and would not offer him any enjoyment.

The football pitches were pointed out during the tour but again the field looked foreign to Flint. It was muddy grass, so different from the firm ground he was used to.

Nothing appealed to Flint during this tour. Perhaps the university experience would consist of study with little recreation. This year would be very intense if he was to achieve his mission and complete his qualification. There would be little time to enjoy the lighter side of life. That would have to wait until later, until another time.

As the weeks went by Flint relaxed into student life. There was a lot of work but it was interesting. His fellow students were friendly and he enjoyed the intellectual stimulation.

However, for Flint, the English climate was proving difficult. He was adjusting to the cold and damp but the effect of the shortening of the day length was something he had not fully anticipated. He had been warned that this would get worse; however, he told himself that this was all part of the learning experience.

Yes, it was interesting to note the changes on campus since he had arrived. The trees, which had been covered in leaves, were stark, black skeletons now. He appreciated why the Americans call this part of the year the 'fall'.

One morning he awoke to see everything had turned white. Was this frost or snow? He had been told that these were different things. As he walked across to the laboratory Flint tried to pick up some of the white stuff which encrusted the grass. It melted immediately and he was left with cold wet fingers. Flint smiled to himself as he rubbed his fingers on his jacket.

He was close to the laboratory when he saw them; two police cars were parked outside the entrance to the School of Biotechnology. Flint felt completely unprepared. He must not panic, he must retain his composure, control his heart rate. What had the police discovered? Had he done something suspicious? The little slips of paper in the freezer, had they been found? He must walk quietly, normal pace, normal facial expression past the police cars, into the building.

As he began to go up to the laboratory he heard shouting. At the top of the stairs he was passed by one of the blonde students with a police officer on either side. She was screaming as they went down the stairs. Then she began to struggle.

Flint found himself part of an audience watching these happenings.

"What was all that about?" asked someone.

"Dunno," came an answer.

No one knew why it had happened.

Flint joined in the discussion and banter. He was just one of the students whose situation would not be affected by the events, in fact, there seemed to be a change in atmosphere. People were more relaxed and everyone was talking together.

Chapter 30

The first lecture of the day was postponed as the members of the School's staff were seen disappearing into Professor Able's office. A few moments later another police car arrived outside in the building and the normally unflappable Mrs. Baker was seen rushing out to the car gesticulating wildly to the police officers.

The sight of Mrs. Baker in disarray was enough to distract even Louise from her previously planned morning in the laboratory and she joined the group of onlookers at the window.

The student body began the speculation.

"What?"

"Who?"

"Why?"

The discussion moved on to what sort of crime could have being planned or committed.

Were they illegal immigrants? They seemed like genuine students. They appeared to have the appropriate background knowledge. They did not seem to hide themselves away in fact rather the opposite. This all suggested they were not in the country illegally.

However, Flint did wonder as they both seemed very clumsy when it came to laboratory work.

Were they smugglers, perhaps people smugglers? No evidence of this sort of business had been detected by any of the students.

Were they spies? If so what or whom were they spying on? National Security seemed unlikely but what about secret research? Was there something going on at the University which would be useful to another country?

At this point Louise joined in the speculation, “It could be something that would be commercially valuable. New research ideas are potentially valuable and a foreign country or company might want to steal them.”

Suddenly all eyes were turned on Louise.

“Your work, you hope to patent. Are they after your stuff?” came from someone in the crowd.

“My ideas are not going to be very valuable. I think they may be just useful,” said Louise thoughtfully.

“What other work in the School which would be worth stealing?”

“What about the biochip stuff?”

Flint had adopted a quiet unobtrusive appearance as the list of potential criminal actions of the women increased and spread. He could not afford to leave the group. Would the list include terrorism? If so could he be a casual listener? If someone asked his opinion could he give a relaxed answer? He must not give rise to any suspicion concerning himself. If they started to involve him in the conversation was he sure he could control his answers and appearance. There would be no increased heart rate or change of breathing pattern. He would just be one of the students speculating about the police actions but if some of his fellow students started to look for evidence. What if they looked in the fridges and freezers? What if his small tubes containing slips of paper were examined? Should he intervene and stop the examination? He had to stop the tubes being opened. There was the chance that cholera could spread through the laboratory.

By now Flint had stopped listening to the conversations around him. He was desperately trying to think of a way of protecting himself.

"You OK, Flint?" a voice suddenly brought him back to what was happening in his surroundings, "You look worried."

"Yes, I'm fine," Flint said becoming aware that his self control and mask were slipping, "I was just wondering what they might have done to get all these police here. It must have been something serious."

CHAPTER 31

By now six students had opened up their computers and were busy searching a variety of sites. Flint watched on in interest. Within half an hour the picture was complete. They were Russians who had gone to Australia to study the biotechnology. However, it was alleged that they had laundered a large quantity of money. The newspaper reports suggested they had bought a piece of land in New South Wales with money from a criminal source in Russia and they were in the act of selling the land so the proceeds of the sale would go into a bank and look like money that had been obtained legally when they had been arrested. But they had disappeared, fled from Australia before the court case.

"They are trying to do the same sort of thing here," declared the member of the group."No wonder the police are so interested."

Flint felt himself relax. He was not under suspicion. He was not going to launder any money. He could concentrate on his job in hand.

A few days later this friendly atmosphere moved events in the desired direction for Flint.

The weather was sunny so Louise bought a pork pie and a can of drink, then she decided to sit on the wall outside the School to enjoy the warmth. She smiled at the student who had joined her in the sun.

"Settled in OK?"

"Yes."

"Finding the course interesting?"

"Good, fine."

"Sorry, forgotten your name. I'm Louise."

"I'm Flint." The newcomer felt sufficiently welcome to sit next to Louise.

"I hope you don't think that business with the police happens every day here," started Louise.

"Students involved in money laundering does seem like a strange idea," commented Flint.

"I suppose being a student is good cover for that sort of thing. Students move around the world and no one thinks of them being anything but students. Being a student isn't usually a cover for anything except occasionally a sort of an illegal immigration if you want to stay in the country where you have been studying."

"I don't intend to stay on after I have finished here," joked Flint.

"I suppose where you come from biotechnology will be very useful, lots of applications."

"I'm sure I will be able to use it. You work for Dr. Charles, don't you?" Flint tried to nudge the conversation towards Louise's research.

"Yes, an extremophile project, but got a bit side-tracked onto water purification and sterilization."

"Extremophiles and water purification - what's the connection?"

The sun passed behind a cloud and Louise felt the sudden drop in temperature and perhaps she shivered slightly.

"It's given me a much better understanding of how and why our present methods for water safety work." Louise looked up to see where the cloud was and when the sun would appear again. "I have shown which biochemical steps, in bacteria, are knocked out by the chemicals used by the water industry."

"Interesting."

"Yes, very interesting. Some bacteria, extremophiles can survive this process. I've looked at their chemistry; why they are protected."

The light and heat level rose as the sun emerged from behind a cloud.

Flint gently moved a pebble with his foot. "Disease carrying bacteria never naturally have this protection?"

"It would be a disaster if they did. Could go through the system and infect people."

Louise turned and looked at Flint and as if a sudden memory had crossed her mind. "A school friend of mine went out to your part of the world. She died suddenly. Think it was a waterborne disease; a real shock."

"Our water's fine," Flint defended but he felt as if his heart missed a beat. He was totally unready for this revelation. He had to maintain his calm appearance so he continued as if vaguely remembering. "There was something a few years ago on one of the other islands. A sort of charity home, they had a problem. All a bit isolated but a few people died. I think they said there was a young person from England."

"That must have been Ann. Sad," Louise's voice trailed off.

They both sat in silence for a few minutes.

"Did they ever find out what it was in the water?" asked Louise.

Flint looked down to avoid Louise's gaze. "Some samples were taken to the university, I believe, but I don't think they did anything," then gently changing the line of conversation, "Water borne disease in a large English city would be terrible. You'll be giving a talk, a departmental seminar, on your work?"

"We all have to do that but I'm using some of my findings as part of a patent application so it has to be kept secret until that's sorted out. It will be some time before I give my seminar."

"I'll look forward to it," said Flint.

"You've come a long way to do a course here. Was there nothing at home or at least a bit closer?" Louise enquired.

"Nothing as broad as this course," Flint started to explain.

"Or did you just get this opportunity to travel?" suggested Louise.

"It is a good chance to travel, to experience a different country and environment but the course was the main attraction. It covers so much," said Flint trying to ensure that there was no hint of the single reason for coming to this particular university. The single reason was sitting next to him and her work had just been their topic of conversation.

A large black cloud passed over the sun. Louise shivered as the temperature returned to the November norm. She quickly ate the last piece of pork pie and finished the drink. "It's getting cold. I'll go in," she said and got up.

Louise had not thought about Ann for years but now her mind went back to the school days when Ann was so determined to study medicine. She had been concerned about health issues in poor countries. What had happened? Ann should have graduated as a doctor about now. All the ambitions which had not been met and then there was her death. How could everything have gone so badly, and so wrong? Louise considered how she was achieving her own ambition; what a contrast!

Flint followed Louise into the building. He paused in the corridor and looked at a notice board. His eyes followed Louise as she went into one of the offices and he noted which of the six desks she went to. Then he turned to go back to his own work.

"No good looking at that one, a bloody iceberg."

Flint had not realised that his actions had been watched.

"We were just talking, nothing more."

"Waste of a nice bit of arse. Won't go out with anyone, just wants to run a business and make money. Bloody ambitious."

"Perhaps she has a boyfriend somewhere else."

"No, just wants to get her stuff patented. Works the whole time. No fun, no good."

Flint laughed gently. He did agree that Louise may not be much fun but he disagreed about her not being much good. She seemed very good, very useful; she held the key to his future. There was a pleasing feeling of milestones having been achieved. He knew the person, the project, the geography of the information. The cholera bacteria were frozen safely. Now he had to bring all these things together. The marriage of the material and the technology would have to be handled with great care.

That night Louise lay in bed sleepless, something that was unusual for her. Her mind was too busy remembering school times and friends.

Ann, the one who had great ambitions but they had all come to nothing.

What about Max and Jake? At school Max was impatient, could be obstinate and, in retrospect, he was probably unsettled and unhappy. Louise remembered Max's cousin, Jake, as a pale skinny boy who was a couple of years older than her. He did not look as if he would have a great future. However Jake and Max had great ideas and plans. They had succeeded and realized their ambitions. Jake was already wealthy, married with two children and living the life he longed for in Colorado. Max was obviously fulfilling his goals and now that he had come out and found a wonderful partner, a classical musician, he seemed to be living his dream.

Then there was Emma. Of all Louise's friends she was the one who lacked ambition. She was the one who drifted into a pit of alcoholic squalor as a single the mother but she had turned her life round, a good job with Max. Her two bright children were well-cared for. Emma was even planning a trip to Colorado to visit Jake. She was taking the children with her. It was some sort of holiday which would include work. Or was it work which would include some holiday? Emma had somehow arranged things so the business would pay for everything. Emma had become a very astute woman. Perhaps she was someone Louise should emulate when she was growing a business. Louise smiled to herself as she thought of Emma as a role model.

Who would have thought things would have turned out like this for the people Louise remembered at school? The future, the outcome, was not predictable.

Louise drifted off to sleep pondering the uncertainty of things.

Chapter 32

Although there were regulations concerning the hours during which students and researchers could work in the laboratories, and the whole building was supposed to be vacated after a certain time, rules were frequently flouted. The message from above, from Professor Able, was that the only thing that really mattered was the generation of research publications and funding for future work. The means by which these were achieved was largely left to the individual. Results at any cost seemed to be an ethos which emanated from above.

Flint felt confident that he could remain in the building after everyone else had left. Access to Louise's research results - well, those would certainly be held at her desk. Flint thought about it. There was her computer and her filing cabinet which could hold her notes and records. He already knew which laboratory bench was hers. That could hold information.

He would need her password for the computer; that might be a problem. However, there would be laboratory notebooks. Perhaps there would be paper copies of the material used to prepare the patent. Yes, they would be locked in the filing cabinet, but that lock would not be a problem.

The ideal opportunity presented itself two weeks later. There was to be a graduation ceremony in the afternoon, followed by a dinner and ball in the evening. It had developed into a tradition that the University used this as the beginning of the Christmas season. The evening's entertainment would be well attended by the great and the good, the academic staff, the new graduates, their parents and the present students who wished to be seen in this elite company. The members of the community who felt ill-at-ease in this atmosphere would stay well away and the campus security staff would be totally preoccupied with the comings and goings for the big event.

Flint worked late in the laboratory. He was the last in his class to put his culture plates into the incubator. As he took off his laboratory coat he nodded to his class mates, "Just going to write up the day's work."

The exit from the laboratories and offices was earlier and more complete than the usual Friday pattern.

"Only one left at work?" asked the cleaner, whose meagre duties seemed to be emptying the waste-paper bins and cleaning the toilets.

"Just finishing," lied Flint.

"Aren't you going to the party?"

Flint ignored the question.

When the security officer came round checking that the buildings were empty he found no one. Flint had turned off the office light and hidden himself in a corner behind a cupboard.

The campus was quiet for two hours as the University congregation and the honoured guests consumed the dinner and endured the speeches.

Flint waited.

The change came with the slamming of car doors as some of the guests left. Then the music and dancing started.

No one noticed the faint torch light in the School of Biotechnology. No one heard the gentle sounds of drawers being opened.

To Flint's surprise Louise had left everything unlocked. There it was, all neatly filed, all labelled for quick easy access. There were folders dealing with marketing, business accounts, company law, copyright and patent issues. Louise's neat handwriting annotated the lecture notes for the whole curriculum of the business course.

The only files covering scientific subjects contained notes from seminars held in the School; the information easily available to any student in the School.

There were no laboratory notebooks, no research findings and the computer was not there.

Where were the records of Louise's laboratory work? Flint knew that researchers who wanted to take out patents had to keep meticulous records of their work. A notebook should be kept, records written in ink and the pages should be signed and dated by a third party. There had to be proof of who had made the discoveries. Louise must be keeping her notebooks somewhere, probably locked away.

Flint sat on the floor in the dark. How foolish, how naive to think that everything would be left out for him to find.

The marriage of Louise's findings and his bacteria was off, unless he could find the books. Where could they be?

Carefully Flint scanned the office with his torch. It was a plain room with just the desks and filing cabinets. It offered no secure locations. Where else in the building could they be? The laboratory was the obvious next choice. He made his way to the laboratory where Louise worked. He knew which bench to investigate. He opened the drawer under one side of the work surface. Yes, there was a notebook. Using the light of the torch he examined the pages. It was not a record of the work done but appeared to be a timetable of things to be done, no use. Then he noticed the January entries:

patent file date
submit publication
give seminar

Over the next few months there was a schedule of experimental work and instrument preparation. The last entry was for June and this was:

field trial with Dan.

Did this mean that he would have easy access to the results of Louise's research in a month's time?

Flint gazed out of the window. A few large flakes of snow were drifting down. He was frustrated with himself for thinking that the technology would all be there just waiting for his eyes, but now it appeared that Louise would be telling him and everyone else, in January.

There was still the question of should he wait until January or continue the present search. Flint told himself he should spend some time looking at the risks involved in the different approaches. In the morning he would consider what to do.

By the morning the world looked different, everything was white. This was snow! It was like a clean sheet and Flint felt it was an indication that he needed a mental clean sheet to plan the future and to get a clear idea in his head as to his next move.

Louise's notebook was probably locked in Charlie's office or she had taken it home. There would be no risk-free access to these places. If he waited until January there should still be time to complete what he needed to do. He considered a timetable that would mean everything would be ready by June.

The genetic engineering practical work had gone very well. He was ahead of most of his class mates. Surely he had time to consider the bigger picture but, before he did that, he wanted to experience snow.

He put on all his warm clothing and went out for a walk. He chose a country lane close to the University. The lane was clear but the hedgerows and verges were covered in snow. He picked up a handful and squeezed it. It formed a firm ice ball. He threw the ball against a tree trunk and laughed as its shattered into a spray of white. When he got home he would have to tell everyone about snow. Home? He had communicated with his mother from time to time. His sister had just had a baby so his mother's attention seemed to be directed to this new arrival. This meant that he was not subjected to many questions about his present and future plans.

The future, what would he do after June when this mission was complete? The lecture on the development of biochips has been very interesting. Next week there would be a chance to see some of the practical work. Perhaps, just perhaps, he could use the next month to find out more.

Could this be where his future lay? He would have a future after June.

Flint picked up another handful of snow, squeezed it, and threw it high into the air. He watched the snowball as it disappeared into a snow bank in the field.

Snow was fun, but cold!

Chapter 33

Louise lay in bed and smiled to herself. Everything seemed to be working out; it was all coming together. The research studies for her Ph.D. should be complete by early next summer. That gave her six months to finish off the practical laboratory work. Then, through the summer, she could write up the thesis. After that there would be the 'viva', the oral face-to-face exam. She had been told that this could be the most stressful experience of her life but surely they were exaggerating. A well prepared student should be alright in that situation; shouldn't she?

The business studies course had been completed successfully. Parts of it had been very interesting and parts not appropriate for her. However, as a result of taking the course Louisa felt she knew much more about how a research idea could be transformed into a commercial product. She had gained a more realistic understanding of the costs involved. Also Dan Norton had been very helpful with suggestions and encouragement.

Then, perhaps the crowning success was the patent. She had heard that by January it would have reached the stage where she could tell everyone about the invention. She could have a paper describing her findings published in a scientific journal. She had been given a date in January when she would give a seminar; she would tell the rest of the people in the School about her idea. It would be her idea. She would own the idea. She felt good.

Louise let her mind drift back to the day when she nearly gave up; when she thought she was not good enough. Charlie had saved the situation. He had told her to take a bit of time out, to go for a walk. Yes, he had been so right.

Then there was that bird, was it a wren that had brought her mind back to the real world. Her frustrations with growing extremophiles had become overwhelming but the song of the bird and the sight of the tiny creature had allowed her to get some sense of reality. Perhaps, when she wrote up her thesis, she should include that bird in the acknowledgements. Thanks to the wren for saving me. She liked the idea.

Yes, things were working out. She knew that her fellow students thought she was a boring swot who was obsessed with her studies. But it did not matter what they thought or what they said.

Of course some of the students seemed to appreciate what she was doing. There was that one, what was his name? Flint, that was it. He seemed particularly keen to attend her seminar.

As Louise drifted off to sleep she remembered his question about disease carrying bacteria getting the genes which would enable them to resist water purification systems. That would be disastrous. A whole population infected with a dangerous disease and the healthcare system overwhelmed. However, Louise's system for water purification could prevent such a disaster. She would save the healthcare system of the country, of the whole world, becoming overcome. Her achievement would be recognized internationally. She awoke just as she was about to step forward to receive her Nobel Laureate!

Louise savoured a wonderful feeling of success, even if it was all in her dream world. But this was a new day in the real world and she needed to get up and get going.

CHAPTER 34

There it was, pinned to the notice board, the timetable for the seminars to be held over the next three months. Louise would be the first to give one in January. Flint felt a huge rush of relief. He would have the information after that date. As he walked back to the hall of residence he started to plan his work for the new year. He would have to get hold of some of the extremophiles culture but that should not be a problem. It was easily accessible. After all, bacteria from an old mining site were not dangerous, no risk to human health. No reason for it to be held under locked isolation.

The difficult steps would come after that. Had the bacteria he brought from home survived? He hadn't done anything to them; the dirty slips of paper were still in the freezer. He would need to make sure they would grow. He would have to be careful, very careful. That sort of work should be carried out in special laboratory conditions to make sure that nothing escaped to infect people working in the area. Although the School had these special facilities Flint could not afford to ask to use them as too many questions would be asked.

Even after he had managed that dangerous work there would be the problem of doing the genetic engineering in the ordinary laboratory. Flint knew he was a very careful, capable scientist but this would take all his skill and, he had to admit to himself, some luck. Then, if and when he had achieved all this, he would have to culture enough of his modified bacteria to put them into the water supply in London.

In London! How stupid! He had given no thought at all to this ultimate target. The last time he thought about London was on the day he arrived in England and there had been all the disappointment when he could not see the centre of the city due to cloud cover.

He must plan ahead; he must gain first-hand knowledge of London. What about the water supply in London? He knew nothing. However, before that, he would have some time to be a tourist and see some of the sights in London. He would try and satisfy some of the interest which he had felt on the evening after Anna and Maria had been arrested when he had looked at the maps and images of European countries.

There were churches, cathedrals, palaces and museums. Before Flint could stop himself he was making a list – Buckingham Palace, Westminster Abbey, the Houses of Parliament, the Tower of London. How old was that? A thousand years? And that was where they kept the crown jewels. Jewels worth more money than he could imagine!

Then there were the modern buildings up to seventy floors high and looking as if they were made of glass windows the whole way up. He must actually see something like that, not just in pictures.

Yes, he would see London and experience the place just as any other tourist would do.

Flint realized he had stopped walking. He was standing still in the path as other students stepped past him. One or two gave him questioning looks. Fortunately no one asked if he was alright. He must walk on, usual pace, not to draw attention to himself. Self control was his mantra, normal walk, normal heart rate, normal breathing rate. He must not relax his guard.

Tomorrow would be Saturday. He knew there was a group of students from hall going to London to see the decorations and Christmas festivities. He would go with them. He would be on a sightseeing trip to the big city.

The excursion was arranged quickly and easily that evening. They would get a train to London first thing the next morning. There was some discussion about the timing of the return journey but as the group would split up when they reached London it was decided that they would each make their own way back to Sillfield.

A quiet student from Guyana asked Flint if it would be his first visit to London as it would hers. Bibi suggested to Flint that they could go sightseeing together and see the famous places. Flint agreed readily. He would just be a tourist in London for the day.

The added bonus was that his fellow tourist had to get back to Sillfield in good time. Flint could stay in London by himself after four o'clock. That would give some time to start exploring other sites of interest to him.

Flint had never visited a large city and found himself unprepared for the reality. The train seemed to travel through built up areas for ever, houses, industrial sites, shops. It went on and on. When he got off in London there was the turmoil of people, the noise and the smell, the exhaust fumes of vehicles.

Next, they had to negotiate the underground railway system. One of the party suggested that they should go to Charing Cross station. Again the experience was totally new to Flint and Bibi. There was the moving staircase that took them to the bowels of the earth. The passages to where? The rush of wind as the train entered the station. The crowd of people pushing to get onto the train.

Flint had studied the attack on the Tokyo underground in Japan as a model for his act of revenge. That attack by the Aum Shinrikyo sect involved the release of Sarin gas, a gas twenty six times as deadly as cyanide and almost odourless, not easy to detect. It had killed twelve people and left about five thousand injured. Now he understood fully why this attack had struck at the ordinary person. It had given rise to fear in the hearts of people around the world. An act like that did not go unnoticed. There were reports that precautions were being taken in the big cities globally. The London police had been put on guard against a chemical attack and had advised key installations on safeguards.

Flint recognised the terror that could arise in the enclosed underground space.

Even as they emerged at Charing Cross there was confusion. Where were they? Which way should they go? And the busy streets, cars, people everywhere.

Then Bibi saw the column and the statue of Admiral Lord Nelson, then there was the arch over the entrance to The Mall, soon they would see the home of royalty. Here, in London, Flint sensed the imperial power. This was where his act of revenge should take place. However, when he looked at the people surrounding them in the streets they were not the English. The skin colour and the dress styles spoke of family origins from around the world.

Bibi stood looking at the lions round Nelson's column, "I am going to get a picture of those to send home," she said. "Aren't they huge."

Flint had to admit they were large; in fact everything around them was large, but this did not prepare them for Buckingham palace.

Bibi peered through the railings. "I've been to Washington, seen the White House, but this is so much bigger."

Flint felt Bibi's sense of wonder but told himself this Palace was the product of the rape of other nations. He remembered that he had considered assassination. He had been told how the shooting of President John F. Kennedy had resounded round the whole world. At that time it was claimed that everyone could remember what they were doing when they heard the news. The assassination of Mrs. Indira Gandhi had been global news. But in both cases the reason for the act of assassination, the assassin's cause, seemed to have received little attention or was unknown. The world would need to understand why the act of revenge had taken place. Flint considered the punishment would have to fit the crime and the world would have to understand. The act of killing a single person, even if that person had a high profile, would not fit the crime of mass murder of the general population, of the innocent. If a member of the British royal family was killed it would merely be the death of a single individual.

Flint thought a prominent politician, or head of state, was an ephemeral creature who would be replaced when lost. The members of a family cannot be replaced. It would be the death of the ordinary man which would strike at the heart of the people.

Bibi suggested that they walk along Birdcage Walk, beside St James's Park, saying they would come out close to the Houses of Parliament.

As they strolled along they found their way barred by police. The Mounted Band of the Household Cavalry trotted in front of them.

"We can cut across the Park to avoid them," suggested Flint.

"I would like to watch them," said Bibi. "They look so splendid in their uniforms and look at those horses." As they paused Bibi commented to Flint, "You don't like all this grandeur, do you?"

Flint gave a noncommittal shrug.

"As I grew up I was told about Guyana's membership of the Commonwealth and was always aware of our connection with Britain. Our language is English and the architecture of some of our buildings was influenced by British styles, but they are built of wood and nothing so imposing as all this," Bibi waved her hand at the surrounding buildings.

Flint felt unable to contribute anything to the conversation. His upbringing had been the opposite to that of Bibi. He had been taught to hate the English but here was someone, who looked as if her ancestors had been taken as slaves from Africa, probably by the English But she did not hate them, rather the opposite. Yet again it was a time for complete self control. He would admire the buildings and the uniforms of the soldiers. At the same time he would scan for weak points in the defence. However, everywhere appeared so well protected. Armed police were all over the place. There was no sign of any construction work which would allow access to the water mains.

He would keep looking.

Chapter 35

Flint and Bibi did modify their route and went across Horse Guards Parade, then through the arch into Whitehall. As they walked Flint decided he must steer any conversation onto safe ground. The buildings and the famous landmarks were safe. He commented that Downing Street looked interesting but it was a pity that it was blocked off so they could not see where the Prime Minister lived. Parliament Square offered wonderful views of Westminster Abbey and the Houses of Parliament. However, privately, Flint noted how well everywhere was guarded by armed police.

As they approached a road crossing Bibi noticed the pedestrian lights had turned green.

"Come on, if we run we can get across," said Bibi grabbing Flint's hand. They reached the other side just as the lights turned red. For a moment they both stood and laughed.

Flint realized this had been the first spontaneous action he had undertaken in months. These days every move was planned and carried out carefully. How pleasant it was to do something without forethought. How pleasant it was to be touched by another human and by this young woman. Could Flint afford to let a friendship develop? Perhaps he could find out a bit more about Bibi; make sure he was on safe ground if they were to become friends, just friends.

They walked onto Westminster Bridge and stood looking at the view, the fine buildings and the huge wheel, the London Eye.

"It would be fun to go on that," said Bibi, "but there is not enough time today."

Flint agreed it would be fun but he also thought it would give him a better view of the city. From there it would be possible to see where there were areas of construction that might have exposed water pipes.

"There is so much I would like to see," continued Bibi, "the Tower of London, the museums."

"Which way would you like to go now?" asked Flint.

"I'm hungry," said Bibi, "let's find somewhere to eat."

They found a cafe and sat down to eat overpriced burgers; Flint's was beef; Bibi's was veggie.

"What are you doing at Sillfield?" asked Bibi.

Briefly Flint described his course at the School of Biotechnology. Then he moved conversation on to find out more about Bibi. She explained that she had studied computing and had become very interested in artificial intelligence. Sillfield offered a good course in advanced computing and she had been lucky enough to get on this. She said her other interest was climate change. She explained that humans were wrecking the planet but she thought artificial intelligence could be used to help solve some of the problems. After all, she said, humans always had their own interests in mind, while computers, artificial intelligence, can be completely objective. Bibi wanted to see what could be done to preserve the forests and wildlife of her native Guyana.

After they left the café they strolled along The Embankment and looked across the Thames at the Houses of Parliament, but their discussion was not about the London sites. Flint wanted to know more about Bibi's thoughts and ideas. She told him about Guyana and its varieties of forest, from the rainforest to the mangrove. She spoke of the wildlife with the abundance of plant and animal species. She laughed and assured him that there were jaguars in the forest but not in the towns. She explained that forestry was an important industry. It provided an income for the people but damaged Guyana's ability to protect against global climate change.

At this point Flint said he was starting to feel cold. They were exposed to the wind blowing along the river so he suggested they crossed the Thames at the next bridge and walk along the streets which would offer more shelter. They laughingly suggested that winter in London could benefit from some climate warming.

Flint began to probe Bibi's ideas about the use of artificial intelligence to solve some of the climate problems. While he acknowledged that computer modelling could help in understanding what was happening, ultimately it depended upon human behaviour. Flint had not engaged in such intense discussion since he left his home university. As they walked along he was largely oblivious to their surroundings. He was not looking for a vulnerable target. His mind was occupied with the ideas Bibi was putting forward.

"Where are we?" Bibi asked suddenly. "I've got to get back to Sillfield."

"Look, that's Buckingham Palace. We have walked round in a circle," Flint suddenly realised. "You OK to find your way back to the station?"

Bibi assured him she would be alright.

"Your ideas are great," said Flint. "We must talk some more when we are back in hall."

Bibi smiled, "Yes, I would like that. Humans are so destructive with their wars and ruining the environment. I want to do something constructive. It is my ambition that when they put me in my grave, they will say she did good for the world."

Flint wondered what his epitaph would be.

Chapter 36

After Bibi had left him in London Flint wandered on telling himself he was looking for any breaches in the water supply system to the city. However, he was feeling very disturbed and confused following the discussion with Bibi. It was the strength of her argument about doing good, doing something constructive not destructive. His mission was destructive. It was revengeful. He knew these things in his heart. He tried to balance this truth against the fact that he was *the chosen one* and this was his mission. How did he reconcile these opposing feelings? Could he reconcile them?

On the train back to Sillfield he thought about Bibi and their possible friendship. Yes, she could be a friend, a person with whom he could discuss ideas, but nothing more. Anything more would be too dangerous. There was also the reality that Flint had work to do. He needed to know more about how, and from where, London got its water supply.

He soon found out that historically cast iron piping had been used but this had been replaced using modern plastic which was less subject to cracks and leaks. However, from time to time, there were news reports of damage in London caused by leaking water mains. The system was not foolproof. Could he make use of these breaches?

Flint needed to identify the companies involved in supplying water to London. He had to find out the locations of the water treatment sites and where water was stored. He needed to know more about the treatment of drinking water to ensure his genetically modified cholera bacteria were added downstream from any purification steps which would remove them. There was a lot of work to be done. His evenings would be very busy.

Late one evening, while Flint was doing some work online, he heard a noise. It sounded like an argument. It was coming from the kitchen shared by the students on his floor in hall. When he got to the source of the commotion he found Bibi being berated by another student. This student was saying that her ideas for using artificial intelligence were a waste of time and computer power. He was accusing Bibi of being a stupid idealist. By the time Flint got to the kitchen Bibi was quietly explaining that humans seemed to have limited strategies for saving the situation with regard to the world's climate. Perhaps, unemotional software should be tried?

Bibi's accuser left the kitchen and returned to his own room.

"That guy was terrible, stupid. To attack your ideas like that," said Flint.

"Don't worry," replied Bibi, "he's had too much to drink. He is missing his wife and baby. They are back at home while he is here for over a year."

Flint wondered at Bibi's quiet temperament which allowed her to see the full situation, the bigger picture.

"Tomorrow I'm doing some cooking. Got some of the ingredients we use at home. Do you want to try it?" Bibi asked.

The next evening Flint and Bibi feasted on a meal of rice and peas with fried fish. Flint declared it was delicious, a taste of home.

After they had eaten they sat and talked. They talked about their studies and their experiences of coming to England. Bibi wondered whether they would ever see sunlight, proper sunshine, here. Flint assured her that by early June there would be plenty of sunlight, in fact, very little dark. But that was June; that was six months away.

June, thought Flint, that is not a long time away. He had a lot to do before that. His mind went back to his finding in Louise's note book, 'field trial with Dan'. That was scheduled for June. Would that mean that her research would be finished by then and her work could be tried out and put to the test?

The evening meetings of Bibi and Flint became a regular feature of their lives. Their discussions moved on from the present to the future. Flint had already explained that his course covered a wide range of biotechnology but he was focusing on genetic engineering. He vaguely mentioned the problems of pests attacking crops and suggested that genetic engineering was a technique which would be much faster than traditional methods of plant breeding to overcome crop infestation. Then he went on to describe the work on biochips which was being conducted in the School of Biotechnology. He talked about how biological molecules were being put onto silicon chips and the idea that they could be used to speed up computers and increase information storage.

Bibi was fascinated with the idea of biochips. She considered it would be the technology for the future. Soon their discussions were dominated by the development of these ideas and the amount of research which would be necessary to convert an idea to a usable reality.

Bibi suggested to Flint that he sounded more enthusiastic about biochip research than genetic engineering of crops. Could this be his area of work after he left Sillfield and went home?

After he had left Sillfield, when his mission in England was complete, what would he do? Flint had not considered the question. He was focused on one task. His future? Where did that lie? He did not know.

"Where are you going next? I cannot imagine there is anywhere in Guyana that is at the forefront of artificial intelligence," asked Flint.

Bibi smiled, "No, the first thing I'm going to do when I get home is get married."

"Married!" exclaimed Flint, "I didn't realize you were even engaged."

"Well, we decided to put off officially announcing our engagement until I get back home," explained Bibi, "After we are married we are off to Australia. We have both been offered posts there."

Was Flint jealous? After all he and the Bibi had been friends, just friends, nothing more. How could he be jealous? But he was. This beautiful, kind, intelligent young woman was going to marry someone else. How could this be?

Chapter 37

The news of the flooding in London was announced late on Christmas Day. By the next morning it had become clear that a water main had burst causing damage to houses and disrupting Christmas celebrations. Some families had been evacuated and others were left without a water supply. There were pictures of bottled water being handed out to angry residents. It was going to take several days to restore things to normality.

Flint noted the name of the affected area, then he looked at a map of the underground. Yes, there was a line that went to that region and there was a nearby station.

The next morning Flint went on his own sightseeing trip. The site of the problem should be easy to find, but it was some distance from the station. Flint came up to street level to a cold wet day. The drizzle was continuous, wetting the buildings and the streets. There was a steady flow of water in the gutters and it gurgled down into the drains. At one time the street must have been busy with shoppers but now most of the shops had shut. All that was left were some places selling drab second-hand clothes to raise money for various charities and there were the takeaways, fish and chips, Chinese and Indian. Did anyone cook at home, make their own food?

As Flint walked to his destination he looked down the side streets, row upon row of red brick terraced houses. The uniformity was strange and he found it depressing to think of living in one of these houses which lacked individuality and even lacked gardens where people could express their originality. How could young people, children grow up in this depressing environment?

Then Flint saw a group of youths standing at a road junction just ahead of him. They were leaning against the wall of a building which must have been a place of worship at some time. The uniformity of their dress was in keeping with the uniformity of their surroundings. They wore torn jeans and hoodies pulled down over their faces.

Who were they? Why did he feel nervous in their presence? He was just a visitor on his own business. Just keep walking at the same pace, normal breathing, normal heart rate, he told himself.

As he passed them Flint could feel their eyes following him. Nothing happened but he felt fear. Why? They were just a group of young men about his age. Perhaps it was because they were English; the people against whom he had to retaliate for the past wrongs to his people. They were still a threat.

A little further on he found the site of the water problem. Part of the road had been dug up to expose the broken water main and new piping was about to be laid. The work was being directed by a number of engineers wearing bright orange jackets with the logo of the water company on the back. Those involved in the work where clearly identifiable. There were several vans bearing the same logo parked in an adjoining street. The door of one of these vans was open and, just inside, Flint noticed a bright orange jacket bearing the water company logo.

He carried on walking, then turned into a side street and walked along passing the anonymous houses. He found an alleyway which connected the parallel streets and he doubled back to where the vans were parked. He slipped his student backpack off his shoulders and opened it as if to search for something. He waited until everyone's attention was held by a local resident who was shouting angrily at the water company officials on the repair site. Flint reached into the van, lifted out the jacket and quickly stuffed it into his backpack.

Passing the work site he walked on quietly, heart rate normal, breathing normal.

As he returned toward the underground station the rain stopped and a pale sun came out. The youths were still standing on the street corner but they had been joined by a couple of girls and they took no notice of Flint. He was someone just out on his own business.

CHAPTER 38

Louise looked at herself in the mirror. Normally she was not concerned with her appearance but today was different. Today she would be the centre of attention; today she had to make the right impression. Her audience would need to see her as a successful scientist and businesswoman. This would be the great transformation from the work obsessed swot which, at present, was her image to so many people.

Louise had modelled herself on Sally, simple smart clothes, neat hair style and minimum makeup. Yes, Emma's aunt was her example and it was Sally who had given her help and support during the last year as Louise went through the process of applying for a patent.

What would have happened without that meeting nearly ten years ago? Would any of this been possible? Would she have just left school and got a job, any job? Many of the girls who had been in her class were married with children already and that would be their lives for the foreseeable future. It was Sally who had opened Louise's eyes to other possibilities in life, to ambition. Then there was John Wild, the older man who worked part time for PSW. He had caused Louise to think about the longer term with his questions about her interests and her future. Talking to him she had realised that work, a career, could be interesting and rewarding.

Sally had asked to attend today's seminar. Louise could think of no greater praise.

The seminar to be given by Louise Browning was the source of unusual interest in the School of Biotechnology. Until now Louise had not discussed her findings and although others knew about her application for a patent they did not know the details. The student who awaited the seminar with the greatest interest was Flint.

Dan Norton and several of his colleagues decided to attend and the greatest accolade was that Professor Able would be present. Normally he was too busy to be involved in the seminars given by students but this particular student was fulfilling his idea of perfection. She was producing interesting research results and the patent would open the door to, hopefully, profitable commercial exploitation.

Louise had prepared the materials for the event in the greatest detail. Charlie suggested that she should give a talk lasting thirty minutes and that would allow another half hour for discussion. Louise had practiced everything to fit this timetable. She had memorised her presentation so there would be no need to read a script. She would engage with the audience the whole time. She had seen too many students mumble into their lecture notes so that their audience had trouble hearing what was being said. She would not fall into that trap.

A few minutes before the seminar was due to start Charlie came to find Louise. For a moment she hardly recognised him as he was wearing grey trousers and a shirt, rather than the usual old jeans and shapeless tee-shirt.

"You ready?" he smiled.

"Yes, quite ready," Louise smiled back. The confidence in her reply masked the feelings of nervous excitement.

The size of her audience delighted Louise. She could see Sally sitting at the back and they exchanged quick smiles.

Everything went as planned. Louise did not stumble or get confused as she gave her talk. The questions and discussion at the end were lively and constructive. Even after the seminar was over a lot of the audience stayed to continue the conversation. Louise found herself being congratulated by Professor Able, Charlie and Dan Norton. Then Sally came forward to join the group. Louise had to do the introductions and suddenly she felt she had the leading role in the gathering.

Professor Able, Charlie, Dan Norton and Sally were enthusing over the seminar, the research findings and the patent. There were discussions about where the work would be published. Sally suggested that it could be presented at a conference she was planning for the first week in July. She thought it would be a good example of academic research being turned into a commercial product. Dan Norton agreed with the idea as, by then, they would have undergone field trials of the technology.

Professor Able liked the idea. This would be the perfect example of a product of the School of Biotechnology, Sillfield University. Charlie commented that not only was the idea a product of Sillfield but the prototype was to be built in the on-site workshop at Sillfield. Professor Able smiled. Things were getting even better.

Louise saw Charlie smiling at her and she thought she saw a slight wink. She found herself being swept along on an enthusiastic tide.

Dan, who had been standing behind her, joined in the discussion about the prototype and as he did so he leant forward slightly. Louise became aware of the closeness of his body and a slight touch as he moved to enforce a point he was making. Louise decided it was nothing, just the random bodily contact of people in a close group.

She did not notice that some of her audience had moved on to other topics of their immediate interest. Dan Norton's colleagues were discussing the burst water main which had caused so much flooding in London on Christmas Day, the worst time to upset people's lives and to get the maximum wrong publicity in newspapers and television. They were glad they did not work for the company involved. It was agreed that there was a lot of work needed to prevent this sort of problem in the future. One of the group mentioned work that was going on to replace old piping. The new mains would serve an area of old houses and new blocks of apartments in London.

"Supposed to be finished by April but, knowing these things, it will be the end of June by the time it's ready and it will be well over budget," commented one of the group.

While most of the students had already left the seminar room a few remained discussing Louise's work and admiring what she had achieved. One student was writing up his notes from the presentation. He was close enough to hear the discussion about the burst water main. He listened to the comments about the future work, the location, the time scale and, most importantly, the water company involved. Flint thought about the jacket hidden away in his room in hall and he knew he had his target.

Chapter 39

"Is there anything else you need me to do today?" asked Mrs. Baker as she entered Professor Able's office.

"Oh, no, I don't think so," was Professor Able's vague response.

Mrs. Baker stood in the doorway for a moment looking at the professor. He had been sitting gazing out of the window and he seemed to be distracted.

"Are you alright?" she enquired.

"Yes, yes, I was just thinking about this afternoon, about Louise Browning," he said turning to look at Mrs. Baker, "bright, ambitious and very pleasant young woman."

"I gather she is doing very well," agreed Mrs. Baker.

"I think she will have a very good future," predicted the professor. Then turning back to his desk, "No, there is nothing more I need you to do today. I am ready for tomorrow's meeting with the vice chancellor, thank you."

After Mrs. Baker had left Alan Able had returned to his view through the window. He recalled what he knew about Louise Browning's background. He had gained a lot of information from Sally Walker. He knew Louise had come from a family with no academic ambitious background. She had grown up in a small town which had been left behind by changing industry. Although he did not know how much support Louise had had at home Sally had been the perfect role model and she had been in the background supporting and encouraging.

Without Sally, Louise's background could have been similar to his own. He had come from an environment which inspired and aspired to nothing.

His father's attitude had been summoned up in 'why do you want to stop on at school. You need to get a bloody job, not sit on your arse all day looking at books'. Then there was the version about university 'you don't want to waste all your time at some university. You need to get out and earn a decent wage like a real working man.'

Alan had tried to explain that people who went through university ended up getting good jobs and earning decent salaries. However his father believed that a man was not a man unless he earned his keep by the sweat of his brow.

Things became impossible at home so he moved out and for a time lived with his grandmother. She said she sympathized with him having ambition but her idea of success was to be a footballer or something on the telly, a celeb.

Alan got no support at home. At school he did not form any close friendships. Few people seemed to understand his drive to succeed. There had been a chemistry teacher who had understood, or at least sympathized with his ambition but the teacher had left for another job. Most of the rest of the staff had just seemed occupied with trying to keep order in the classes. At least that had been Alan's impression.

During his early university days Alan had measured his achievements against his fellow students. He always had to be the best.

He did well in academic life becoming a professor at an early age. He married and in everyone's eyes he was the image of success but he drove on to become head of a university department and to develop an international reputation.

Then there was the evening when his wife had said "Alan, you are very successful. We are financially well off, in fact quite wealthy, but you are not capable of love, showing love or even feeling sympathy."

His marriage failed completely.

Alan Able suddenly came out of his reverie. He had been staring out into a dark January evening. Nothing was visible except some faint lights along the campus paths. The scene was empty and quiet.

He had gone home to the expensive house in a nearby village, to a lonely meal in front of his computer screen.

His life had become an endless round of airports and four star hotels - Montreal, San Francisco, Sydney, Singapore, Berlin – they were all similar as he moved from one international conference to the next, one business meeting to the next, or to a round of discussions with government ministers. His evenings were spent with colleagues discussing the outcome of the day's proceedings. He never saw the sights of the exotic locations he visited.

If this was the outcome of ambition would he wish Louise success?

CHAPTER 40

Five months, that was the time left for Flint to make all his preparations. He thought about the little pieces of dirty paper in the freezer. Were the cholera bacteria still alive? If he got them out, let them thaw and put them in culture medium would they grow? Perhaps he should take two out of the freezer and try.

Getting hold of some of the extremophiles grown by Louise would be no problem as he knew where she kept them. He also knew how to culture them. He was confident he could replicate what she had done.

The next challenge would be the genetic engineering which would be necessary to allow the cholera bacteria to survive in the water supply to London. He knew the theory of what he needed to do but he had to prove that he could do it in practice using his limited experience of genetic engineering techniques.

Flint thought about the conversation he had overheard discussing the laying of new water mains. He would have to visit the area and plan ahead to find the ideal site and opportunity.

Running through these steps it seemed straight forward but there would be difficulties, unforeseen problems, to be overcome. Just five months, that was all the time left.

Firstly, he must check that the cholera bacteria were still alive. Flint knew the steps he needed to take but this involved handling very dangerous bacteria. If they got out in the laboratory there would be serious illness and possibly deaths. He would have to undertake the whole procedure with great care. Could he ask to use the special containment laboratories in the School? What story could he concoct?

Why did he need to take that level of precaution when he was just doing crop, plant, genetic engineering? If he said he was very concerned about the general environment and wanted to make sure his GM crop could not escape into the English countryside, could he convince the staff that he should use the School's special facilities? Yes, he would speak to his tutor about his concerns.

The tutor stated that she saw no risk involved in the work Flint would be doing but then he suggested that his future work, after he returned home, might be more risky. Therefore he would welcome the opportunity to learn and experience the special laboratory procedures which would be necessary. The tutor considered his argument. This was a very keen student who wished to learn as much as possible while he was still at Sillfield. She should not stand in his way but should encourage his enthusiasm. She consented to his request and said she would set aside space for him to conduct his work. Flint thanked her and decided to start work on his dirty pieces of paper as soon as the laboratory space had been arranged and he had been given instructions on how to use it safely.

Finding the exact location of the work on the water mains in London should not present a problem. Flint went online and quickly identified the roads which were closed. He decided to visit the area. He would go on Saturday so he could just mingle with people doing their shopping. He hoped he would be able to get a good impression of the total area so he would be able to monitor the progress of the work during the next few months. He needed an idea of the situation as it approached early summer, June.

Fortunately there was an underground station close to the area of interest. This time there was a cloudless sky as he emerged from the station. The sun was pale and gave little warmth but at least it gave a reasonable level of daylight.

Flint found himself in a street market with a bustling array of different colourful stalls. People were chatting and laughing as they bought fruit, vegetables, breads and cake. There were vans selling hot food, burgers, Indian and Chinese. The aromas were very tempting but Flint told himself he had work to do. That came first. Afterwards he would indulge himself.

He walked away from the market down a side street of the anonymous red brick houses until he could see where the construction work began. That must be the new apartment block he had heard about. Towards the end of the street he saw bright red barriers and a sign saying the road was closed. Another sign said the road would be closed for a month and there were arrows indicating a detour. A triangular sign showed an image of a man with a shovel. There seemed to be so many signs but, in amongst them, one stated that the way ahead was open to pedestrians.

Flint walked along beside the trench which had been excavated in the middle of the road. At the bottom he could see the freshly laid water pipes. This was the work he needed to monitor over the next few months.

At the end of the road there was another sign announcing that an adjacent road would be closed the following week. Flint found several subsequent notices about road closures so he could follow the plan and timescale of the work to be done. He walked on toward the apartment construction site. It was easy to see that the work was at an advanced stage. However, the whole area was surrounded by a solid, metal fence. Flint could not see the ground work to determine where the water main was laid. He walked along the fence until he came to a panel which had an image of the completed building and announced the apartments would be ready for rental in July. It was as if a whole schedule was laid out in front of him.

Flint turned and wandered through the streets of red brick houses. Would the new apartments allow more individuality for the inhabitants? He doubted it when he considered the uniformity and claustrophobia of city life. As he thought about the life of Londoners he smelled something pleasant and rounding a corner he found himself back in the street market. The smell got stronger. Was it coconut with cumin and garam masala? He could pick up pineapple as well. It smelled like a meal his mother would make.

An elderly woman was busy cooking while a young girl served the customers. Flint felt completely at home as he ordered his food. Should he ask the older woman where she came from? She looked so like his grandmother. No, he could not, must not get involved in a conversation. There might be questions about why he was there. All he could do was enjoy the taste of home and decide to visit this market every time he came to monitor the progress of the work on the water mains and the apartment building.

Chapter 41

On Monday morning Flint arrived at the special containment laboratory promptly. He was looking forward to finding his place and receiving the safety instructions. However, the tutor was not there. After a few enquiries he was told she was in a meeting with Professor Able. He had nothing to do but wait.

He decided to do something useful while he was waiting but when he got to his desk he was uncertain what would be the most useful thing to do. He had already done all the planning for the work he wanted to complete over the next few days. Perhaps he could do some reading about biochip research, after all that was a subject that interested him. Then he found he could not concentrate. His mind was occupied with one question. When would he have access to that special laboratory?

As Flint sat lost in his own thoughts one of the other students in his group ran into the office in a state of great excitement.

"Look what I've found! They have been deported to face the court over that money laundering charge!"

By now there was a crowd of people trying to see the news report on the student's phone.

"They should not have fled from Australia in the first place!"

"It's all a bit strange. They did not seem my idea of big money criminals."

"Wonder where the money came from originally."

"Was it really their money?"

"Perhaps they were just being used by someone else to move the money around. A couple of students studying abroad might not excite as much interest as a wealthy older person. A known rich Russian might be monitored while young woman students would be regarded as innocent parties."

Flint started to pay attention.

"I suppose if they got paid enough they might do it," was a suggestion.

"It might not just be the money. It could be that they were brought up to follow the ideas of their families and communities."

"What? Have the ideas instilled by their backgrounds?"

"Yes."

Flint listened carefully to the suggestions.

"But surely a bright intelligent young person is not going to be brainwashed by older people at home."

Flint considered whether it was possible for an intelligent young person to be persuaded to that extent.

"Most of us adopt the ethics and principles we grew up with," came a reply.

Flint thought about his own background and felt he agreed. Perhaps the vision of his grandmother's grief was one of the biggest influences in his life. Then there was the fact that his father had been drowned, had died when he was at a vulnerable age. The elders in the community had stepped in and taken the role of his father. They had been a very strong influence in Flint's decisions and choices. Had he been brainwashed? But the thought of the grave, his grandmother's grief and the terrible treatment of his ancestors was something that had to be paid for, avenged.

Most of the students returned to their morning's work. Flint was left on his own to wait for his instructions about using the special containment laboratory.

He thought back to his trips to London. Three visits and there were three very different impressions. With Bibi he has seen wealth, power and imperial splendour. The second visit left him with the impression of society in disarray, depressing and, at times, threatening. The last visit had shown another facet of the city. There was new construction work and the bustle of the street market. He had an impression of optimism. He thought about the older woman who had prepared such tasty food.

As his mind drifted he suddenly realized that that was the same area where he intended to put the bacteria. Did the grandmother live in that area? Would she use the water there? The pretty girl who served the food to him, was she her granddaughter? Did she live there and use the water there? The answer to all these questions had to be yes. Could he warn them? How could he warn them? How could he get them out in time?

Flint felt horribly trapped. There was nothing he could say or do without arousing suspicion but they should not be the victims. They had done nothing. They could have no connection to the events for which he wished to wreak revenge.

He decided he would go to their market stall next time he went to that area of London. He would talk to them, find out if they were at the market regularly, and perhaps find out if they lived there.

"You OK?"

Flint jumped. He had been unaware of the presence of one of the other students who shared the office with him.

"It's just you've been sitting there staring at the wall, twiddling that pencil between your fingers for ages."

"Yeh, yeh. I was just deep in thought," Flint managed with something approaching a smile.

"You haven't forgotten about the lecture on the use of biotechnology in clearing land contamination, have you?" she continued.

Flint had forgotten. His mind had been completely consumed with other thoughts.

He went to the lecture but it was a subject that did not interest him. It was merely something to occupy his time until the tutor was available. Then, he could have his introduction to the special laboratory.

Fortunately, immediately after the lecture, the tutor came to find Flint. She was very apologetic about the delay but explained that it was due to an urgent meeting with Professor Able.

The introduction to the laboratory was straightforward. Flint knew the theory and it was just a matter of putting it into practice. He was allocated his own enclosed laboratory bench and his own spaces in a special fridge and freezer. He was told about the use of a face shield and protective clothing. The tutor was very thorough in her instructions and told Flint if he had any doubts or worries to get back to her.

Flint thanked her and assured her that he would follow all the precautions.

During the afternoon Flint moved culture tubes containing small plants and various bottles of the reagent on to his new laboratory bench. To the observer it would look as if he was working on plant culture, probably on genetic engineering of crops. He also moved some racks of tubes into the refrigerator and freezer spaces which had been allocated to him. He spent some time getting everything organized to his satisfaction. He had always been a very thorough laboratory worker and in this environment used all his best practice.

Later in the day, when most of the people had finished their work and were leaving the laboratory, Flint sat back and surveyed his work. He was satisfied. No one had noticed him take two small plastic vials out of the freezer and add a small amount of culture medium to each so the little pieces of dirty paper were submerged. He had put these in a rack at the back of his bench. There they would be safe and hidden from view by larger items on the bench.

Flint now had to wait, but waiting would not be easy. Had the bacteria survived?

He thought back to the day when he had prepared the pond sludge paste and bacteria. He had had no chance to check that the technology that he had devised to transport the bacteria would work. Everything had been done in such a rush. Certainly nothing had been suspected as he came through the airport. That aspect had worked. However he did not know if he had prepared the sludge adequately. Would he discover that a whole lot of pond bacteria and algae would grow, and would overgrow any cholera bacteria? What about the time spent getting to Sillfield? Had the bacteria survived those days at the warm temperatures? Would they have been affected by altitude, the low pressure, in the aircraft?

Everything had been done at the last minute after the community elders had been persuaded to back his idea about coming to Sillfield. It all felt like a long time ago and a long way away. Now Flint could only think of so many things that could have gone wrong.

Chapter 42

Life was changing for Louise. She was moving from research student to inventor and business woman. She was at the stage where her invention needed to be made into a usable device. This would be the prototype which was to be built at the Sillfield workshop. Dan had agreed that there would be funding for this step. He had made the arrangements for them to talk to the appropriate person in the workshop. There would have to be a lot of design work to produce a device which could be used at the outlet from the reservoir. There would have to be discussions about the volume and flow rate of water to be handled. The device would have to be built to the water company's specifications. The research idea needed to be transformed into something usable. Louise felt very excited about this step.

Dan organized a meeting between himself, Louise and Jo at the workshop. Louise realized that she did not know where, on campus, the workshop was. She had never been there, let alone seen the inside. When they got there she was surprised by the size of the place. Somehow she had imagined a shed behind one of the university departments but, instead, they were confronted by a large industrial building. The sign outside the building said CONSTRUCTION CENTRE, UNIVERSITY OF SILLFIELD. The 'workshop' was merely a nickname.

They went inside to a small entrance hall. One of the doors in the hall was labelled J. S. SANDS. Dan was about to knock when the door was opened.

"Ah, you must be Dan Norton and Louise Browning. I'm Jo Sands. Please coming in," said a small woman with a mass of blonde curls.

After the introductory handshakes they went straight into business. Dan had already sent some specifications to Jo but now she wanted to know more. They considered the shape and size of the structure, and how it would be moved and fitted into the building at the end of the reservoir. Dan had some pictures of the reservoir outlet and Louise looked at the images of a beautiful lake in a remote area of Wales. Then she caught her breath. So that was where her idea would be put to the test. Theory and reality would suddenly be coming head-to-head there.

Jo started to sketch out some ideas on a sheet of paper. Louise and Dan moved round to stand behind her to get a better impression of her design. Louise admired Jo's skill in using a few pen strokes to convey the idea. Dan had stepped back from the table slightly to get a better view of the drawing and he started to discuss the materials which would be used in the construction. Louise noticed how his eyes roamed over Jo's body. He was not just admiring her design. He was admiring her. He moved behind Jo to get a different view of the drawing and Louise saw how he leant forward so his body brushed against Jo. Jo moved slightly to avoid his touch and continued to discuss timescales for the work. Then she turned and smiled at Dan.

"It certainly is a beautiful area. I go climbing near there. It's one of my husband's favourite climbs."

Louise and Dan instinctively looked at Jo's left hand.

"I don't wear a wedding ring. It could get caught in the tools we use during construction. Engineering workshops are dangerous, you could lose a finger or worse," Jo answered their unspoken questions.

The conversation returned to manufacture and installation, however, Louise noticed that Dan did not touch Jo again.

By the end of the meeting a timetable for the work had been drawn up and Dan and Louise arranged future meeting dates with Jo so they would be able to monitor the progress.

As Louise and Dan walked back across the campus they felt confident that there would be no major problems with making the prototype. Dan said he would visit the reservoir and make sure everything there was ready for the installation.

"Your pictures of the reservoir were lovely. I'd never been to that area; looks spectacular," commented Louise.

"Yes, and Jo was right, there are some rock faces in the locality. Very popular with people who like high risk activities where you can break your neck," laughed Dan, "they also do hang gliding in the area. Looks like flying with no control to me."

Louise thought about the conversation at the Construction Centre. It was as if her idea, her invention had been handed over to someone else. She was listening to what was going to happen. She would have little control. Until now all the ideas, all the developments had been hers with some suggestions from Charlie and help from Dan. Her emotions were confused and mixed. Was she happy, sad, relieved or some strange mixture of these feelings?

While they walked back across the campus to the School of Biotechnology Louise became aware of the first signs of spring. Crocus and snowdrops were in flower between the trees and, in a sheltered spot, daffodils were beginning to come through the ground. She mentioned this to Dan and by the time they got back to the School they were in deep discussion about the beauty of the countryside in the coming months.

Later, Louise thought that this was the first time she and Dan had discussed a topic which was not related to her work. It had been a pleasant conversation. Also his pictures of the reservoir reminded her of the time when she and Jake had admired the images of the American Rockies. That was a long time ago and so much had changed.

Chapter 43

Nothing had grown. The culture medium in the little vial was clear. When he examined it under the microscope there was nothing there, no cholera bacteria, not even some contamination from the pond sludge. How could this be? Flint sat staring at the vials. What had he done wrong? Had he added the wrong culture medium? Had he been unlucky in his choice of vial, the wrong slip of paper? Could the other pieces of paper in the other vials contain what he was looking for or had nothing survived the journey to Sillfield? Had he done something wrong in the preparation of the samples on the paper before he left home? Could it be that he had not collected the right test tubes from his old university? The two test tubes he had collected from that laboratory, what if they had not contained anything?

Flint knew he could not go back and repeat most of these steps. All he could do was check that he was using the correct culture medium and try to find the bacteria using more slips of paper. So there was nothing to do but to wait for a few days. He sat staring at the laboratory bench with a feeling of despair. He had been so stupid to think that everything would work easily. His frustration was so intense he forgot everything else. Then he realised how fast he was breathing and how rapid his heart was beating. He must retain his composure. He must not do anything which would attract attention or cause someone to ask questions. That evening, when everyone else had left the laboratory, he would take two more vials out of the freezer and set up the culture again.

The other jobs he needed to do were to get Louise's extremophiles and their special culture medium. He would wait until she was not around and there was no one working in the laboratory where she had her bench. That should not be difficult as she seemed to be spending most of her time at her desk. Yesterday she had been out of the building for a long time and he had seen her walking across the campus with Dan Norton. They had been in an animated conversation, laughing and smiling together. They had stopped and looked at some small white flowers growing close to a tree.

Louise had changed from the quiet swot to somebody much more extrovert and sociable. It was as if two people were wrapped in one body. Then Flint thought he should perhaps point the finger at himself. Here, in England, he was careful, very reserved. At home he had been considered clever but he had been gregarious at school and university. The change in his apparent personality had only taken place after he left school and he had concentrated on performing this mission.

Flint worked busily into the late afternoon and early evening. He was concentrating on his plant genetic engineering project. The facade had to be maintained; plus he wanted to do well on this course as success at Sillfield would be important for the future.

From time to time he had a need to go to other areas of the building. Louise was always there either at her desk or moving things around at her laboratory bench. There was no chance for Flint to touch her stuff.

Flint took two small vials out of the freezer and carefully added culture medium until the slips of paper were submerged. The vials were put out of sight at the back of his bench. He was very glad he had managed to obtain the place in the special containment laboratory as these steps would have been extremely dangerous in a normal situation. He could have been infected with the cholera and this would have spread to others working with him.

When Flint had finished setting up this culture he wandered out of the laboratory. Louise was still in the building. He would not be able to do anything that evening. Altogether it had not been a good day.

That evening Flint was making a coffee for himself when Bibi came into the kitchen.

"You alright?" she asked, "Don't look very happy."

"Just my project's a bit slow," Flint replied aware that he must avoid the subject of his disappointment with what had happened, "maybe I'm doing the wrong stuff. Perhaps I should make a change."

As usual Bibi's calm voice edged the conversation into what would really interest Flint and challenge his intellect. The discussion kept coming back to the suggestion of work on biochips.

The rest of the evening was spent talking about where Bibi and her fiancé were going in Australia. She suggested Flint should contact them and see if there were any projects being undertaken that might interest him. If so he could apply.

Bibi always made quiet logic thought Flint. She gets me to consider things from a different point of view and think about my life from another perspective.

As he lay in bed that night he wondered about his future. In the past his ambition had been to fulfil the wishes of the elders in his community. Perhaps he had been groomed for this single end. Maybe he had never had the chance, or was it the courage, to form his own ideas and ambitions.

In any case, what was he going to do after he had spread the cholera in London or, at least, tried to do so? Where was he going? He certainly could not continue his career in England. Although most of the people he had met had been pleasant he would never be able to feel comfortable. Then there was the climate. He could never spend the rest of his life anywhere so cold and dark.

At Sillfield he had developed the image of a scientist interested in crop genetic manipulation. However that was a facade, just a cover story, to get him into Sillfield. It had worked very well but it was not his real interest. His real ambition would surely lie somewhere else. The intellectual challenge posed by the development of biochips excited him.

To be able to work on such an intriguing problem, surrounded by other people working on challenging ideas, would be something he would like. To be able to do this in a place where there was sunshine. All that would fill his own personal ambition. Tomorrow he would find out more. He would see if there were positions in the Australian organisation for which he could apply.

Yes, tomorrow would be exciting as he tried to build his dream, his own personal dream.

Chapter 44

The next morning was an abrupt return to reality as Flint remembered that he had an assignment which was due to be handed in by that afternoon. There was no time for laboratory work, little chance to monitor Louise's movements and no opportunity to find out about the biochip work going on in Australia. Flint felt it would be a day when he would achieve nothing, a least nothing that he wished to achieve. Perhaps tomorrow would be a more productive day.

As he got out of bed the first thing he noticed was the light. Even before he opened his curtains it was bright. When he looked out the sight was wonderful, a cloudless blue sky, a brilliant sun shining throughout the leafless trees showing the skeletal form of their branches. The ground was covered in a pristine coat of white snow. Everything was perfect and untouched. The beauty of this morning could make up for a lot of dark grey days.

When he went outside it was cold, very cold, but the sunshine compensated for this. Everyone seemed to be in a happier mood. There were shouts and laughter as a group of students became involved in a snow fight. Someone got rolled in the snow. Flint stood for a moment staring at all the activity. One of the girls laughed and suggested Flint could make a snowman or snow angel. He said he knew what a snowman was but what was a snow angel? She lay down in the snow and moved her arms up and down to produce the pattern of angel wings. Everyone was laughing.

By the time Flint got into the School of Biotechnology he was cold and wet, but he had to admit he had enjoyed the childish stupidity which the snow had brought on. However, this was only a preamble to a day of hard work on the assignment which was due in that afternoon. Tonight maybe he could go online to see what information there was about working in Australia. At least he might achieve something which would be of use to him.

When he handed in his assignment late in the afternoon the lecturer's comment was something about leaving things to the last minute to midnight, but Flint did not care. He had met the deadline, just.

As he prepared to return to hall he walked past the School's main notice board. There was a new poster about a lecture by a visiting professor. The title was 'The use of biomolecules in advanced electronics'. That sounded very interesting. Flint would make sure he did not miss that.

Trudging back to hall in the dark, through melting snow, was not fun and the evening was frustrating as he tried to find out about the work in Australia. It became apparent that the institution where Bibi was going was a private organization and details of their work were not published in the scientific literature.

The next morning the snow had gone and with it the bright sunlight. Flint was determined that there would be no distractions today. He would get on with what needed to be done. He would check for growth in the little plastic vials and he would monitor Louise's movements. He would not get diverted by thoughts of working in Australia. He would wait for the lecture on biomolecules in electronics and then he would look for opportunities in that field. The other thing he decided was that he must visit London again and check the progress of the work laying the water mains. Perhaps he could visit the market and get a taste of home. That would be pleasant.

First it was the little plastic vials. He rotated a vial in his fingers to swirl the liquid contents. Yes, the culture medium looked slightly cloudy. He checked the second vial and it looked the same. Something was growing, but what?

Flint carefully transferred a drop of the cultural onto a slide and examined it under the microscope. He could see tiny bent tubular-shaped bacteria which were moving about in the droplet of water. This was exactly what he had been waiting for. Now he had some material to work on. He started to formulate plans. He would check more of the vials he had brought from home in the hope he could increase the size of the culture. Then he would have enough material to work on, to genetically modify with the genes which Louise had found in her extremophiles. Flint's work on genetically engineered plants had gone well and he was seeing the modified plant cells growing in their culture. He felt confident about the technology. What he could do for plant cells he could do for bacteria.

He would grow a new strain of cholera bacteria which would not be killed by the chemicals normally used to keep drinking water safe. His final step would be to introduce these genetically modified disease causing bacteria into the water supply in London. That would be job done and he could be on a plane home before the disease would develop.

Then, if the outbreak was as virulent as the one seen at home, the victims would be dead within hours. The speed of the disease caused by this strain of cholera would mean that the local healthcare services would not have the time, or capacity, to respond adequately.

The only major hurdle to be overcome now was getting access to Louise's material.

Chapter 45

"You've been very quiet this morning, Flint. Surely you must have some views about the public's perceptions and worries when it comes to genetic engineering. After all you are working in the area of the genetic modification of plants," said the tutor at the end of the seminar.

"I found it very interesting listening to the rest of the group. It was such a good lively discussion," replied Flint.

"Yes, it was good to hear a whole range of views, for and against. I suspect that some of the group were playing devil's advocates," smiled the tutor.

Flint was only too aware of the power of this science for good and evil. Part of his laboratory work was designed to produce plants which would withstand pest infestations. This could increase crop yields in countries where the destruction of the harvest frequently leads to food shortages and famine. Then there was his other work which would deliberately lead to death.

As Flint walked out of the seminar room he contemplated this conflict. How would, how could, he resolve the fact that he was working on these contradictory outcomes? Then his thoughts were suddenly jolted into the present as he found Louise and a group of her friends in the corridor. They were in a discussion about going out that evening to celebrate a birthday. As Flint paused to look at a notice board he heard them deciding they would finish work in good time that afternoon. Their laboratory and office should be empty by four o'clock. An opportunity had just been delivered to Flint.

Through the afternoon Flint kept looking out of the window. He waited until Louise and her friends had walked away from the building then he went into the laboratory where Louise worked. Her bench was clear. All the signs of the extremophiles cultures had gone. Yes, she had finished the laboratory studies and her work on the technology to be used by the water companies, her patented invention, but she would not have disposed of everything, he thought. Samples of the extremophiles and their special culture medium must be stored in the refrigerator or freezer. First he looked in the refrigerator. Everything was very well organized. It was clear where everyone working in the laboratory stored their material. But there was no shelf, nothing marked with Louise's name. The same applied to the freezer. Flint felt his mouth go dry. He had to control his breathing and heart rate as he walked casually along the corridor. Where was her material? It had to be somewhere, he thought. At that point he realised he was walking past the room where glassware and chemicals were stored. He remembered there were large refrigerators and freezers at the back of the room. That was where things were put for long term storage. Flint pulled open the heavy freezer door.

There, encrusted in ice, were racks of test tubes bearing Louise's name. The tubes were labelled with the scientific name of the extremophiles. Flint carefully removed three test tubes at random from the racks. He took them back to his laboratory and stood them in a beaker of warm water. Then he returned to the storeroom and opened the refrigerator door. There were several large bottles labelled with Louise's name and listing the contents as the culture medium for the extremophiles. Flint stood for a moment considering the bottles. He would not be able to carry one of them back to his laboratory bench without the worry of someone seeing what he was doing and querying his actions.

He went back to his own laboratory bench and collected a flask and a pipette. Then he returned to the storeroom where he carefully transferred some of the extremophile culture medium from one of the large bottles into his flask. Flint carried this essential ingredient back to his laboratory bench.

By now the contents of the test tubes had begun to thaw. He decanted the liquids and ice from each tube into a fresh tube and put these at the back of his bench close to the cholera cultures. Then he pipetted some of the extremophile culture medium into Louise's tubes and returned these to their positions in the rack in the freezer. In a few hours the contents would be frozen and the tubes would be encrusted with ice. They would be indistinguishable from the rest of Louise's carefully preserved samples.

Flint went back to his laboratory bench where he made sure his precious possessions were labelled with his name and coded so he knew the contents. He felt tired but happy as he mentally ticked off his achievements. He had live cholera and extremophile bacteria. He had culture media in which each would grow. As part of his course at Sillfield he had learnt the techniques used in transferring the genetic material, DNA, from one cell to another. Louise had told him enough about the genetic structure of the extremophiles in the seminar she gave to the School so he knew which piece of DNA needed to be introduced into the cholera bacteria. In addition he had identified the site in London where he would place the deadly bacteria.

He had all the pieces of the jigsaw. Now it would be mainly a matter of time while he waited for things to grow.

He would be able to check that his cholera bacteria could withstand the chemicals used by the water industry. That would be a simple procedure in the laboratory. There was no laboratory test to show if his bacteria caused the lethal disease. That would only be demonstrated when he had contaminated the water and it had been consumed by members of the public.

Chapter 46

The next visit to London confirmed that the work on laying the new water pipes was still ongoing.

As Flint paused to look down into the latest trench a voice behind him said, "They're running late with this lot. At this rate they won't get water into those new places before people start living there."

Flint turned to his elderly companion, "I'm sure they will get everything connected in time."

"Well, we got our new pipes two months after we were supposed to," complained the old man, "and then the water was dirty and we were told to boil it for the first couple of days. We are supposed to have decent stuff the whole time."

Flint did not comment but thought about the state of the water which would be delivered in a few months' time.

He made his way back to the market to find the stall which served the wonderful food with the aromas that were a reminder of home. The same old woman and young girl were preparing and serving everything. As he approached the stall he wondered how he could warn them and protect them. Perhaps he could find out where they lived and see if they were in the area of maximum danger. He decided he would start a conversation with the girl. However, a group of young people who were obviously friends of the young girl arrived at the stall at the same time. They started to laugh and joke with the girl. Clearly they were going to hang around for some time. Flint would not have a chance to find out what he wanted to know.

He ordered his food then strolled through the market in the direction of the station. The taste of the pineapple and spices drove his mind to think about home. It would be nice to see his mother again and it would be very good to see his sister with her new baby. The latest news his mother had sent included the fact that one of the community elders had died and another was seriously ill. Flint pondered the fact that the old men who had encouraged and supported him on his mission were dying; the group was getting smaller. Then the thought struck him that soon there might not be anyone who thirsted for revenge. To most of his generation the events that had happened were a long way in the past. Things had moved on, times had changed.

Flint walked on glancing at the range of stalls. Some sold new clothes and others second hand clothes, books and ornaments. One had a lovely range of cakes and breads, but Flint noticed that the busiest stall was the one selling fruit and vegetables. This one was loaded with a wide range of produce and the stall holder had a van parked in the side street behind his stall. The van still contained crates of stocks which were being used to replenish the stall. Flint paused and watched all the activity. As he stood there the stallholder pushed past him with a crate.

"Out of the way, boy. Can't you see you're in the fucking road!"

Flint tried to apologise but as he stepped back the stallholder continued to swear at him. Some of the customers took the stallholder's side. They all seemed to blame Flint for some sort of obstruction to trade.

Flint walked away briskly. It was clear he was not welcome there.

On the train back to Sillfield he thought about what had happened. He had done nothing but these people seemed to object to his presence, to his existence. He began to sympathise with the feelings of the elders. Perhaps nothing had changed. Nothing had moved on. He still had his mission and he would carry it out to the best of his ability.

When he got back to hall Flint looked at the timetable for the coming week. There was an assignment to be handed in but that was nearly complete. There were a couple of lectures and seminars but the highlight of the week would be the lecture by the visiting professor. Flint decided to do some research and find out more about this speaker. He discovered that he was from Canada and he had an impressive number of publications on the use of biomolecules in computer memories. The more he read the more he became fascinated by the subject. He would try and talk to this visitor. He would endeavour to find out what opportunities there were to work with him. Could he go to Canada instead of Australia?

Of course there was still the laboratory work but most of that was a matter of waiting for things to grow. He would have some time to devote to looking at his future.

CHAPTER 47

It is strange how habits do not die even when they are no longer necessities. Flint continued to monitor Louise's movements and activities. He was very quick to see her one morning, on the front steps of the School with Professor Able. A few minutes later they were joined by Charlie. Not the usual Charlie in old jeans and a tee shirt, this was the well dressed Charlie with grey trousers and shirt. As they waited, a car drove up and parked in front of the building. A very smart woman got out and Flint recognized her as the woman who had attended Louise's seminar and had joined the discussion with Professor Able that afternoon. The other passenger in the car started to unload camera equipment. Then Flint noticed that Dan Norton had joined the group.

Some photographs were taken on the steps of the School and then they all walked across the campus out of Flint's sight.

Flint was fortunate that the window by his desk overlooked the front door of the School. He decided that he would dedicate the rest of the morning to finishing the outstanding assignment. His decision was rewarded when he saw Professor Able and Charlie leading the rest of the party back to the School. This time they had been joined by a small woman with a mass of blonde curls. Flint wondered who she was as Louise and Dan were in deep conversation with her. Then a van, bearing the logo of the water company that Dan worked for, followed the group. It stopped in front of the School and the woman with the blonde curls and Dan appeared to give the driver instructions.

Flint watched in fascination and with a degree of envy. Flint made the assumption that the van contained the device based on Louise's patent. This seemed to be such a highlight for her studies. The outcome of her work was being acknowledged. He wished he was working on a project which could lead to public acclaim instead of secrecy.

When the van had gone, Professor Able and Charlie came back into the School. The woman with the blonde curls walked back across the campus and, after a few minutes, the smartly dressed woman and photographer got into their car and left. Louise and Dan stood talking for a while and then walked away together.

That evening Flint could not stop thinking about the events he had observed and the conclusions he had drawn. Louise was realizing her ambitions. What about his ambitions? He certainly had a mission but was it his ambition or was it just something that had been instilled in him by the community elders at home. Had it ever been his desire or had he been brainwashed since childhood? What would he like to achieve? Where did his own ambitions lie?

The discussions he had had with Bibi has excited his imagination. The ideas about using biological molecules in computers were compelling. To achieve something in that field of research could be a substantial contribution to science and technology. Tomorrow was the day of the lecture by the Canadian professor. Would this open the door to an ambition which was really his, his own, not just something instilled in him by a group of old men?

The lecture more than stood up to Flint's expectations. The work underway and the vision of the future excited Flint's imagination in a way no other research had inspired him. During the discussion which followed the lecture Flint asked some of the most probing questions, even more so than those asked by the students doing Ph.D.s in the area.

Flint was determined not to let this chance pass. He followed the lecturer out of the lecture hall and asked if he could talk to him some more. Professor Pierre Tremblay liked the eager student and a meeting was arranged for the next day. Flint spent the evening deciding what he wanted to ask the professor. He organized his thoughts into an orderly agenda.

The meeting went on much longer than Pierre Tremblay had expected. Flint had asked so many questions and he had steered the discussion through a comprehensive analysis of the research and development which was going on in Professor Tremblay's university department. Then matters turned to whether it might be possible for Flint to become involved in this work. By this time they were on first name terms and Pierre had already decided he could find funding for such a bright enthusiastic student.

"When do you finish here and when do you expect to head home?" asked Pierre, "I guess you would like to visit our labs and see at first hand what's going on."

This was exactly the invitation Flint had hoped for and very quickly they arranged dates.

Before they finished their discussions Flint said he would like to ask one more question, "Is it very dark in the winter where you are? I mean do you have less daylight hours than they do here in England in December?"

Pierre put his head back and laughed, "Have you seen our latitude? We are much further south than here. We have great winters, lots of sun, lots of snow. It's as cold as hell but you can get out and enjoy winter. I love to ski!"

Chapter 48

There were no words to adequately express Flint's excitement at the idea of research in Canada. That evening he went to Bibi's room and knocked on the door.

"I've got wonderful news, great offer," exclaimed Flint as he stepped into the room without an invitation, "I'm going to Canada. Professor Pierre Tremblay, amazing research, I'm visiting the labs on my way home after leaving here." Flint paused as he caught sight of Bibi's computer screen. She was on a video link with her fiancé. "Oh, I'm sorry I'm interrupting," he trailed off.

"Don't worry. Just let me finish this call then we can have a drink together and you can tell me about this Canada idea."

Later that evening Flint sat with Bibi telling her about this life changing offer he had had and now his ambition was to contribute to this area of science and technology. Bibi recalled earlier conversations they had had and said she felt that this sounded perfect for him, rather than plant genetic engineering.

By the next morning Flint had come to the realisation that he had to plan his timetable for the next two months, not just the week ahead.

He knew which day he would leave England to fly to Canada. It was imperative that he got his modified bacteria into the water mains on the preceding day. He had been told that all his laboratory work had to finish two weeks before he finished his course at Sillfield so his laboratory bench could be cleared and cleaned for the next set of students who would be studying at the School. It was not just the bench that had to be cleared but all his samples which had been stored in refrigerators and freezers had to be removed.

That left six weeks for Flint to complete his preparations. He was confident that he could achieve this but he would have to stick to a strict timetable. There was also the work connected to his course. He could not afford to let that get behind. He needed the qualification that would be awarded at the end. This qualification would be important as he built his future career.

He decided he would do one more visit to London. He knew that the date on which he had to put the cholera bacteria into the mains water was set regardless of the progress the water company had made laying the pipes. There was so much that was out of his control but he would need a plan of action for that day.

Another problem was that in six weeks' time he would have to remove his deadly bacterial culture from the School and store it somewhere for two weeks before it was used. How was that to be done? There were so many decisions to be made.

The laboratory work went well. He had sufficient material to do the genetic transfer of the extremophile DNA into the cholera bacteria. The genetically modified cholera grew well. Now was the time to visit London and see how the work was going there. He would identify the exact site where he could get to the new water mains.

How could he have been so stupid? He was a scientist who had done some clever genetic engineering. He was about to become involved in some of the world's leading technology, but he had made a crazy error in his planning. Flint despaired of himself. How did he think he was going to get the cholera into the water supply? The water in the pipes was under pressure. Even if he managed to find an access point to the mains he would have to find the stop tap before he could open the system. Otherwise he would get a fountain of water up to forty metres high. If he could find the stop tap and cut off the water supply it would be registered immediately and the reason for the interruption investigated. His actions would be detected and his mission would fail. He might be caught.

It was no use just looking down the trench in the road at the newly laid pipes. His bacteria would only be effective if they were introduced into the water which was going to houses and apartments. All this work, all this planning to fail at the final step due to naive thinking.

Flint turned and walked back towards the underground station. He did not go to his favourite food stall. In fact, he did not go past any of the stalls. He walked along a back street that ran parallel to the market. He needed time to think or was it to develop a new purpose.

The more he thought about it the easier the whole thing appeared. After he had cleared his laboratory bench and refrigerator he was no longer faced with storing a large amount of liquid. Now it would be a small volume. He needed to find a cool secure secret storage space. It could not be in the hall. That was too dangerous. Then it occurred to him. Although the weather was warming up the countryside was only just waking up. The soil was still cool, wet and soft under the hedgerows bordering the fields.

Flint found clearing his materials in the laboratory a straightforward task. He had rehearsed in his mind what he needed to do. He made sure that all the sample tubes, small vials and surfaces which could be contaminated with the cholera bacteria were sterilized and either washed thoroughly or put in with the rest of the material in the laboratory's hazardous biological waste. He was making doubly certain nothing was left that could cause a problem in the future for the laboratory or for himself.

The mood among the students could almost be described as festive. It was the end of term, of the academic year and they were about to go home and start new jobs.

"You going home?" asked one of the students.

Before Flint could reply others were joining in the conversation.

"I've got a wonderful job in genetic engineering of rice to develop a strain which will grow at high altitude in places like the Himalayas. Their present crops are infected with insect pests. Great research opportunity and I will get the chance to go to Nepal!"

"I won't be going to anywhere so exciting but I've got a job with a pharmaceutical company developing new vaccines using the latest technology. The money's good so I will be able to live like a real person not just squeezing by as a student."

"I am going to do some work which is essential for the environment. May not sound as exciting but it is necessary that we clean up the oceans and get rid of oil contamination and plastic. Biology will be able to partially deal with the situation but will need a helping hand. The department I am going to is looking at what organisms, already in nature, are attacking these problems. We will be trying to promote their activity."

Flint took a pause in the discussion, "I'm going to Professor Tremblay's department in Canada to see the work they are doing there before I head home."

"Tremblay? Was he the guy and who gave a lecture on using biology in computers, biochips?"

"Yes, I found it very interesting."

"But do you think it will ever work?"

"Look at the stuff they're doing here. Nearly got it to work."

"Maybe," said a doubting Thomas.

As most of the students left the building to enjoy the pleasant summer weather Flint went back to the laboratory and puts some tubes, which had been thoroughly wrapped in plastic, in his pocket. He walked out of the School of Biotechnology and out of the University grounds into a small lane. He ambled slowly and to the passing motorist he was just a younger man enjoying the countryside. He paused by a tree in the hedgerow and looked down into the muddy ditch. He crouched down and pushed a small plastic wrapped package into the soft mud, making sure it was out of sight. He took a branch that was lying nearby and pushed it into the hedge so it pointed at where the package was buried.

That evening Flint started to pack ready to leave the room he had occupied for nearly nine months. He looked at the clothes he had been wearing to deal with the English winter and smiled. In Canada he would need even warmer clothing. The Canadian winter would be interesting, very interesting. Then he saw it. The orange jacket with the logo of the water company was still in the cupboard. How was he going to dispose of that? He could not leave it behind. Someone would find it and questions would be asked. He had to get rid of it so there would be no link back to him.

Chapter 49

Bibi had suggested that they had a meal together on her last evening in hall. She promised to cook the food that would remind Flint of home. Needless to say the meal was delicious but Flint noticed how bare Bibi's room looked. The clutter of student life had been packed away.

"Are you flying home tomorrow?" Flint asked.

"No, I'm staying with friends who live close to Heathrow tomorrow night. Then it's a long journey as the flight has a stop in Saint Lucia," explained Bibi. "At least it is quicker than some of the options which go via Holland!"

"And then when you get home?" quizzed Flint.

"It will be hectic. We are getting married ten days after I get back," Bibi smiled. "My family has made all the arrangements but there will be a lot of last minute things to do."

Flint nodded as he thought back to his sister's wedding a year ago.

"It may seem strange for a couple who are both travelling abroad and who are involved in high tech but we are having a wedding which will involve some traditions from home. The bride and groom's families have separate rites to ensure the prosperity of the marriage. There is a dye which is blessed then smeared on our bodies to give restorative and cleansing powers. Of course I do not believe in this power literally but I think the symbolism is important." As usual Bibi dug deeply and thoughtfully into the underlying significance of symbols and actions.

After the meal Bibi and Flint sat in Bibi's room discussing their time at Sillfield. The door was open and other occupants of the hall stop by to join in the conversation as they walked past.

"Thank you for all your help," said one of the students and Flint recognized him as the man who had berated Bibi in the communal kitchen a few months ago. Now this attacker had become one of Bibi's friends as she had supported him through difficult times.

Gradually the room filled with fellow students who all wanted to offer their thanks to Bibi and to wish her good luck in the future. Flint admired the way in which everyone felt so relaxed in Bibi's presence. By the end of the evening there were nine people packed into the small room, two perched on the window sill, two on the desk, two on the bed and one leaning on the doorpost. Bibi and Flint occupied the only two chairs.

Flint would have liked the evening to last forever but eventually he had to return to his own room and think about the water company jacket and all his other plans. In addition he must get a good night's sleep. He would need to be wide awake tomorrow.

However Flint did not go to sleep immediately. Instead he lay in bed thinking about the evening in Bibi's room. It was the first time he had talked to the students who had been his neighbours for the last nine months. He had isolated himself for the whole time but now he realized that he had missed out on the company of an interesting group of people. That small pale woman who had occupied the room opposite his was a chemical engineer who was engaged in research into carbon dioxide capture. During their brief conversation last night she revealed that she worked for a company which polluted the atmosphere and she had suddenly realized that something had to happen to reduce their contribution to global warming. She had spent the last year working with a group at Sillfield to solve this problem. Now she was looking forward to implementing these ideas at work. She was adamant that industry had to solve the problem they were causing.

Flint regretted that he had not spoken to her earlier so he could have shared her energy and drive. He thought of the time he had spent exploring Tep's ideas about getting a boat and setting up a tour guide business. If Flint had been completely making his own decisions, if there had been no pressure from the elders and his family history, he might have joined Tep in such an exciting business venture.

The discussion during the evening had extended to what people would be doing during the summer. Two were going diving and planning to film the creatures they found. Flint had a chance to describe some of the wildlife in the coral reef at home. Why hadn't he videoed any of that? He could have shown them the wonders of the sea around his island. Flint felt this was another opportunity lost. He had been forced to concentrate on his mission to the exclusion of so much else. After he left England he would make up for this and grab all the openings that life offered. He would have freedom to explore.

Another fifty six hours and he would be on the plane and his new life would begin.

The next morning he did his packing and stripped his meagre possessions from the room. He had done little to decorate this student space. He had done nothing to make it his own. It had been stark when he arrived and had remained unadorned but he realised he would miss the view from the window and the ability to watch the change in the countryside as the seasons changed. The bare skeletons of the trees and the morning when everything had turned white would remain in his mind. The dark of the winter months had been an interesting experience but he did not wish to live permanently at this latitude. But, on the other hand, the wonderful light evenings when there was hardly any night was something he was enjoying.

He folded the water company jacket and placed it at the bottom of his backpack. It was to be covered with his overnight stuff. He could not make any definite plans for its disposal but hoped a suitable opportunity would arise in London.

The last item to be packed would be a plastic wrapped package containing test tubes.

The evening was the perfect time to go out for one last walk in the countryside. Flint decided not to go directly to the hiding place. He would make an excursion via a path across a field and then return by the lane.

Flint breathed in deeply as he walked along the path across the field. It smelled pleasant. Was it the smell of the grass? He picked up a few blades and rubbed them between his fingers. Yes, the smell was pleasant. His eyes searched the sky for birds. Of course there was nothing like the huge ocean skimming birds he was used to but there were some smaller grey birds. Their wings had white stripes and were tipped with dark grey feathers.

As he approached the hedge he heard the high pitched calls. He saw a small brown bird on a branch. Its head and wings were dark brown and it seemed to be shouting out to proclaim its presence or was it to proclaim its territory? Flint smiled.

He passed through a small gate back onto the lane and headed towards where he had hidden the precious parcel. He admired the trees which formed part of the hedge along the field. There was one huge tree which was just behind the hedge. Flint stopped to admire its gnarled trunk and the spread of its branches. This must be an oak he decided and he stood in the lane wondering how old this giant was. Then suddenly he became aware of it. It was coming straight at him with wheels as tall as himself. Flint leapt to one side onto the verge and partly fell into the ditch as the huge yellow tractor went by. As he pulled himself back onto the lane he became aware that he was bleeding from a scratch on one arm. He looked back at the hedge and saw a long thin stem covered in prickles. He must have fallen against that! If he was going to retrieve the plastic package he needed to concentrate on his surroundings and take care.

Eventually he saw it, the marker branch. He dug into the mud and found what he was looking for. He wiped it clean on the grass and put it in his pocket.

Back at hall he slid the package into a side pocket of his backpack.

It was still another thirty five hours to his new life thought Flint. He felt a fresh burst of confidence. Everything would fit into his plan.

Chapter 50

It was all arranged weeks in advance: the day when Louise's system would be switched on at the reservoir.

Dan Norton could not have been more helpful. He had chosen the site. It was a small man-made lake high in the mountains in a remote area of Wales. He had always considered it the perfect location for a reservoir. The rainfall was consistently high due to its geography. The prevailing winds from the west produced an unremitting stream of air which had picked up moisture from the expanses of the Atlantic Ocean. Then, as the air was pushed up over the mountains, the water vapour turned to droplets, to clouds, which grew until they fell to earth as a constant supply of pure water tumbling from the heavens.

The sides of the mountains were polished slate which offered little opportunity for plant growth and even less scope for animals. There was nothing contaminating the run-off. A lane ran along part of the mountainside but it only led to a few isolated farms and cottages. It was barely more than a track and used by very little traffic. No litter-dropping tourists ventured this far. Dan had once joked that the greatest source of contamination was feathers from the red kites which circled the mountain peaks.

The reservoir supplied part of Birmingham. The water flowed from the purity of the mountain environment to the polluted city. Such a source of pure water did not really need any treatment to protect its consumers. However, Dan was aware that all the regulatory precautions must be observed. On the other hand, if these were relaxed for a few days, nothing disastrous was likely to happen.

He had arranged for all the preparatory work to be done in advance. All Louise would have to do was check the installation and make all the final adjustments to the settings. Then, of course, there would be days, and perhaps weeks, of work making sure everything was functioning correctly.

Dan had made bookings for Louise and himself to stay at the hotel closest to the reservoir for the first few days.

"It's quite comfortable, decent food. I've used it quite a few times," he assured her. "You'll be close so you can get on with the work."

They set off early in the morning and Dan drove the water company van straight to the reservoir to give them maximum time to get everything set up and running.

As Louise got out of the van she drew in a breath of fresh air. How wonderful to be in such spectacular countryside on such a superb morning. The sky was blue with just a few white clouds to accentuate the colour, and the air was clear. Louise could see every detail of the mountain across the water. There were the polished sheets of slate. The still water surface acted as a mirror to reflect the peaks giving a perfect repeat of the image.

Louise would have liked more time to enjoy the scenery and, perhaps, to walk along the edge of the lake. However, this was a day for work not relaxed enjoyment. The only concession she allowed herself was a short walk to the edge of the lake. She could see the pebbles through the transparent water. She dipped her hand into the reservoir and felt how cold it was. The temperature of this mountain lake never rose sufficiently to encourage the development of life. The water waited there cold and pure, ready to supply the needs of a city.

The rest of the day was fully occupied with activity. Louise had to adjust all the equipment, check and re-check all the settings. Dan acted as her assistant. He seemed happy for the reversal of roles. Louise gave the instructions and took the responsibility while Dan took the more subordinate position.

Louise was too busy to contemplate this shift in authority until they took a short break to eat some sandwiches and to have a drink. As she sat on the stone wall beside the water pumping station she smiled. Yes, this was the situation she wanted. She was in charge of the project, growing the business. Her shoulders went back, her head a little higher. Of course the financial rewards would come later, she would enjoy those but, perhaps, the greatest reward was the freedom to make her own decisions. These were responsibilities she felt confident she could handle.

"Better get back to work."

"You're a hard task-master," laughed Dan.

"It's getting hot and humid," Louise pushed her hair away from her face and adjusted the clip which held it in a short ponytail.

"Forecast mentioned thunder later."

"Shouldn't affect our work."

The afternoon's work went well. Louise's system was switched on without a hitch and everything was running smoothly. All the months of preparation had been worthwhile.

By late afternoon they were monitoring the readings every half hour. Between readings Louise went outside the pumping station for a short rest. She was feeling very hot and her T-shirt clung to her in the humidity. She could see a dark cloud between two of the mountain peaks.

"Looks as if the forecast was right."

"How many more readings do you plan to take?"

"A couple, so we should be finished, for the day, in an hour's time."

"Do you want me to put these things in the van while you do those?"

"Yes, then we can go through everything and enter the data into my laptop when we get back to the hotel."

Louise heard the first roll of thunder as she took the last reading of the day. Dan, who seemed very ready to get to the hotel, did the last round of adjustments and checks at the reservoir outlet. He and Louise were in the van, heading for the hotel, before they saw the first flash of lighting and large raindrops hit the windscreen.

Chapter 51

Mrs. Bethan Hughes had always had her septic tank pumped out once a year. Her friends and neighbours said it was not necessary, especially now that she lived alone in the little cottage which had once accommodated her late husband and the four growing sons. The sons had long ago departed to areas with mains sewers and mains water supply.

"Well water not good enough for you," Mrs. Hughes had said when her sons commented on the pump in her kitchen.

The procedure was the same each year. Emrys Pritchard, the farmer who lived in the valley on the other side of the reservoir, would bring his old tractor pulling the tanker up the steep narrow lane beside the reservoir. He would pump out several domestic and farm septic tanks and slurry pits before returning home, past the reservoir, to his own farm.

It was a beautiful morning when he set out for the day's work. The sky was a pale blue with just a few narrow white clouds streaming like pennants from the peaks of the mountains. He could not hear the cacophony of bird song above the noise of the tractor engine but he did see a red kite circling high above the still waters of the reservoir.

The temperature rose as the day wore on and the blue of the sky became richer.

"Lovely day," he commented to the cottage owner who was the last of the morning's clients.

"Yes, but the forecast is for storms, thunder."

"Summer – two good days and a storm - they say. More like one hot morning and a storm here."

"Yes."

"Still I expect I will be home before the storm hits."

By the time Emrys had reached his last client of the day, Mrs. Bethan Hughes, the heat and humidity had risen considerably. Emrys was beginning to feel he was too old to be working in these sultry conditions.

"Clouds gathering," Mrs. Hughes commented when he arrived.

Emrys turned to see what appeared to be huge black balloons appearing between the peaks of the mountains. With luck he would have finished the day's pumping and would be well on his way home, beyond the reservoir, before things deteriorated.

"Thank you very much. See you next year," were the last words of Mrs. Hughes to Emrys as she paid him for his work. There were already some rolls of thunder and a few large drops of rain gave the old tractor and tanker a polka-dot appearance.

Emrys wiped his brow, perhaps the rain would cool the atmosphere and make the journey home more comfortable but, on the other hand, the cabin on the old tractor was rusting and hardly waterproof.

Emrys carefully negotiated the track between the cottage and the lane and, just as he raised his hand in a farewell wave to Mrs. Hughes, the first flash of lightening danced round the circle of mountain peaks. The rain started in earnest, not isolated drops but sheets of water. By the time Emrys had gone a mile the little mountain streams had turned into torrents. By the next mile the whole mountain side had turned into a waterfall and the lane was the pathway for a gushing current of water.

Emrys was glad he was in his tractor and not having to struggle through the water in his car. The only other vehicle he saw was a Land Rover which pulled into a gateway to allow him to pass.

Over the low stone wall, which marked the edge of the lane, Emrys looked down to the reservoir. What a change from the silky blue water he had passed in the morning. It was now a black surface flicked with small white crests as the increasing wind picked up waves of ever swelling size.

The windscreen wipers on the front of the tractor were proving ineffectual in this downpour and, even if they had worked efficiently, the surface of the road was invisible. The numerous pot-holes and the crumbling edge of the road surface were hidden from view under water.

No one saw the tractor, its driver and the tanker laden with the contents of the day's clearance from septic tanks and slurry pits, slide over the edge, ricochet off the rocks and break up as it entered the waters of the lake. Everything was submerged beneath the surface of the turbulent reservoir, a few yards away from where the water was taken off to start its journey to the taps of Birmingham.

Chapter 52

They agreed they would have an early dinner then spend some time going through the day's work.

As soon as Louise got to her hotel room she decided her priority was a shower. She put her laptop on the small bedside table and threw the notes and charts from the day's readings on the bed.

It was only as she allowed the shower water to run over her head and shoulders that she realised how tired she was. They had started off early that morning, perhaps she had not slept well the previous night with the contemplation of the significance of the work to be done. Then she had worked hard, concentrated intensely throughout the day.

As she sat in front of the mirror drying her hair she looked at the reflection of the bed. It looked inviting. A pizza and an early night would suit her, but no, she was a business woman growing her own company. She needed stamina; she could not give in to the feelings of fatigue.

Louise put on a short grey skirt and crisp white blouse. Her hair was sleek and shiny, and a little make-up was applied. She was ready, she hoped, for dinner followed by a couple of hours work.

When she reached the bar Dan was already there, waiting for her.

"Got you a glass of white wine. Hope that's OK."

"Yes, thanks, fine." Louise usually drank white wine but, perhaps, if she had been asked before the drink was ordered, she would have chosen something longer. The heat and work had left her thirsty. She took a long sip.

"I've brought that article I mentioned to you. It's full of statistics about the increase in water consumption."

Louise looked at the document and took another long drink of wine.

"It also shows how water use has grown in the developed, industrialized world. Other countries are even worse than the UK."

Louise was close to the bottom of her first glass of wine.

"I thought the facts and figures would be useful data to use in your business plan to show to the venture capitalists."

Louise looked at the graphs and charts showing the consistent rise in the demand for water. She hardly noticed that a waiter had brought a second glass of wine. "Yes, yes, this is just the kind of information I need. Lots of hard figures to give to those fellows."

Louise was beginning to feel very relaxed but she did think it was time they studied the menu. Even after ordering it would probably be some time before the food was ready in this small hotel.

"Terrible weather," Louise commented to the waiter as he brought her third glass of wine.

"Yes, we get a lot of rain here but this storm is the worst we have had for some time."

Louise was on her fourth glass of wine by the time they started the meal. The food was good with lots of fresh local produce. Trout from a nearby lake, lamb from the surrounding mountains, goat's cheese produced by a farm in the valley. Louise and Dan ate very well.

"Coffee? Do you want coffee here or should we go up to your room and get on with the work to be done? We could have coffee or something there."

"Yes, that's fine," Louise was easily persuaded by this time. She did not notice Dan pick up the bottle of wine as they left the table. It was only when they reached her room that she noticed him emptying the bottle into two glasses. He gave her the glass with the larger share.

"I think I've had enough to drink," but Louise took the glass. She sat on the bed and opened up the laptop.

Dan stood beside her studying the notes from the day's work. "These are the ones to be entered."

Louise looked at the papers. She was having trouble concentrating.

"Look that's where we switched over." Dan leant forward and pointed to a mark on the chart. As he handed the paper to Louise his arms wrapped around her shoulders. The kiss was warm and Louise's response was more primitive instinct than judged decision. She returned the caresses of this experienced lover.

Was it the ultimate act of a day's cooperative work or was it alcohol-induced lack of judgment? Louise did not know, but she did know that the man, whose physical advances she had held off for years, was in her bed following an act of strenuous love making.

Through the night Louise was awoken several times by the apparently insatiable demands of this Casanova. She was amazed at his stamina but found herself responding and enjoying the attentions of this able lover. She had denied herself this physical pleasure since Jake had left her feeling so wretched. All her energies and attention had been directed to academic and business success. Now she was well on her way to attaining these: her Ph.D. was almost complete and she was confident about the quality of her research. She had finished the business course at Sillfield with flying colours and now it looked as if her own business was well under way. Why should she not enjoy the pleasures of life? A good meal, pleasant wine, then a night with a competent lover, she could and would allow herself these indulgences.

Chapter 53

London was a familiar place for Flint now. The moving staircase which took him to the bowels of the earth, the rush of wind as a train entered the station, the crowd of people pushing to get onto a train were just usual parts of travelling on the underground. There was no confusion when he reached the station that was his destination. Flint knew exactly where he needed to go. He knew the layout of the streets and could see the lines of fresh tarmac where the new water pipes had been laid. Ahead he could see the new tall apartment building.

There were fewer stalls in the market than Flint had seen on previous visits but the fruit and vegetable stall was in the same place and still attracting a lot of customers.

This time there was no aroma of his favourite food from home. The old woman and young girl were not there. Flint felt a sense of relief.

He walked towards the end of the road and his way took him past a pub. When he approached he could hear loud voices through the lounge bar's open door. Just as he was level with the door a woman staggered out in front of him.

"Wanna bit of fun?" she slurred as she lunged towards Flint.

Flint froze in horror at the sight of this ugly woman confronting him.

"You wanna fuck?" she started again as two men ran out of the pub.

"Ah Maisie stop it! Don't bother the young gentleman," said one of the men as he grabbed the woman but it was too late. She lurched forward and vomited.

Flint recoiled at the smell and he looked down to see if his trousers had been fouled by her disgorge but it was just his shoes, his trainers, which had been splashed.

"Sorry, sir, sorry," said one of the men as they pulled woman away. "You OK? Oh your shoes. I'll get something to wipe them. Sorry, sir."

In a moment someone had come out of the pub with some paper towels so Flint could wipe his trainers.

He watched Maisie being led away and he was left with the impression that this was just the latest time that she had propositioned a young man while she was in a drunken stupor. He wondered if it was sad or disgusting, or was it a combination of these. One thing, in retrospect, surprised him, he had been called a gentleman and addressed as 'sir'. The event seemed to have raised his social status. What a contrast to the attitude of the vegetable stallholder he had encountered on his last visit!

Flint crossed the road and as he walked on he tried to focus his mind on the job which had to be done, disposal of the water company jacket. He turned down the street which would bring him to the site where the water company workers had parked their vehicles on his previous visits. They were parked there as usual. He went on slowly trying to give the impression that the new building was the focus of his attention. However, he did notice that the back doors of the two vans were open and the small group of men wearing the water company jackets were walking away from the vehicles towards a trench further up the road.

Flint turned down a side street and stopped, apparently to give his shoes another wipe, but at the same time he reached into his backpack and pulled the orange jacket to the top. Then he doubled back and came out opposite the vans. There was nobody close to them so Flint crossed the road to pass between the open doors. As he passed the back door of one of the vehicles he slipped the jacket out of his backpack and placed it in the van, then he walked on down the street away from the apartment building. His heart was racing and his breathing fast. He realized he had to control these signs of stress and he must appear calm.

He walked slowly along a street parallel to the market and then turned into a narrow side street which would bring him to the fruit and vegetable stall. As usual the stallholder had parked his van in this street and left it open so extra crates of supplies would be easily available. As Flint passed the reserve fruit he looked at their busy stall ahead of him. The stallholder and his customers were being distracted by a young woman and her new baby.

Flint slid a small plastic package out of his backpack and, as the group of people in front of him admired the new arrival and congratulated the mother, he empted a tube of liquid containing genetically modified bacteria over the produce. Then he went round to the other side of the van and reached in through the open window. He poured the contents of the test tube containing the culture of the original cholera bacteria over the steering wheel, dashboard and the inside of the door.

Flint turned away and ambled back down the side street dropping the test tubes and the plastic wrapping down into a drain as he went. Then slowing his breathing and calming his heart rate he meandered back to the underground station and got onto a train to Oxford Street station.

When he emerged above the ground he noticed a change in the weather. The blue sky and warm sunshine had been replaced by a thin layer of cloud and he thought he detected an increase in humidity. As he wandered through the streets of Soho he noticed a drop in light level as a thick layer of dark cloud developed. Then he felt the first drops of rain and he decided it was time to go to the airport hotel where he was going to spend the night.

He had completed his mission to the best of his ability and in fifteen hours he would be on the flight to Canada.

CHAPTER 54

By the time Flint got to his hotel the rain was torrential and as he entered the hotel lobby there was a flash of lightening followed by an immediate crack of thunder.

The lobby was full of people but there was only one topic of conversation, the impact of the storm.

"My flight to Brussels has been cancelled!" said a smartly dressed young woman

"Well I was supposed to be going to Delhi tonight," joined in an older man.

A very distressed woman was starting to cry "I've got to get to Sydney by the weekend for my daughter's wedding and no one can tell me when I can get a flight."

"My elderly mother is on a flight that has been diverted. No one seems to know where they are or what is happening," said someone else.

Flint checked on his phone for an update on his flight. There was no new information. He tried to make his way across the lobby but was in blocked by a large red-faced man who was proclaiming to no one in particular and everyone in general, "Bloody airlines! All the modern computer technology, all the detailed weather forecasting but they cannot see the storm coming and reschedule their flights in advance! Damn incompetence!"

Although no one interrupted the monologue several people nodded their heads in agreement.

When Flint managed to reach his room he did think about what the man had been saying. Perhaps he had a point. This storm must have been predicted but it seemed a lot of people had been left in the lurch, and what about tomorrow? There was still no change of schedule on the airline website.

Flint lay in bed listening to the rain pounding on the window and to the loud rumbles of thunder. The illumination from the lightning found a way round the edges of the blackout curtains into the room. Flint tried to tell himself there would be no disruption to his plans for tomorrow especially after he had accomplished everything he wanted to do today.

His sleep was fitful and included a nightmare involving an ugly old drunken woman pouring some liquid out of a test tube over him while a large red-faced man stood by and directed operations. Eventually he fell into a deep sleep until woken by his alarm. It was quiet outside except for the distant roar of aircraft engines. He pulled the curtains back far enough to reveal sunshine and a clear blue sky.

Everything was on schedule.

During the flight Flint sat between two Canadians, an older man and a younger woman. When Flint told them he was hoping to become a student in Canada they were very interested. The younger woman was particularly keen to tell Flint about life in Canada. She described the opportunities to go canoeing in remote areas where you can see bear, deer, moose and other wild animals. For Flint it was so pleasant to sit back, relax and enjoy the conversation. He had nothing to hide. When he arrived at the airport in Canada he would have no worries. He was just a student who had been invited to a university to discuss research opportunities. He had the letter from Professor Tremblay.

At immigration Flint was stopped and taken to one side by an officer. His passport was examined and a second officer was called over. Flint started his routine of controlling his heart rate and breathing. He hoped his facial expression showed concern but not too much worry. The two officers consulted a computer screen then they nodded in unison.

"Yes, that's fine. We don't see many people from your islands. Enjoy your visit to Canada," said one.

Flint walked out of the airport terminal and took a deep breath. So this was Canada, but if he was honest it smelled just like any other airport, jet engine fumes.

He had been given detailed information about the buses which would take him to the university residence where he was to stay. Everything was easy to follow and Flint soon found himself in an anonymous student room. He had planned to explore the university campus that evening but jet lag and the stress of the last few days suddenly caught up with him and all he wanted to do was sleep.

The next morning he made his way across the campus. It was a perfect day, blue sky, warm sunshine, and he was in plenty of time, his body was still on UK time. He had woken up early. He strolled at a leisurely pace and paused to look at the trees on the campus. There was one with a silvery white bark which looked beautiful in the sunlight. Then there was another with large green leaves that spread out like hands. Flint recognised the tree from the Canadian flag and realized it was a maple. He thought back to his undergraduate days when they had studied the biochemical changes that took place in leaves as they changed from green to yellow to red. He thought it would be very interesting to observe these changes in reality.

Then as he paused he saw it. A small grey animal with a long fluffy tail ran down the maple tree. When it got to the ground it squatted on its haunches so Flint could see its white belly and short front legs. He wondered what it was. He had heard about skunks which inhabited Canada and he knew they were to be avoided at all costs because of their disgusting smell but he did not think this was a skunk because it did not have white stripes on its back and also he did not think skunks climbed trees. Perhaps it was a raccoon. He knew that raccoons could climb and could use their fore paws like hands. However he thought the pictures he had seen of raccoons showed a banded tail. As he walked along Flint realized he knew all the species of fish which inhabited the coral reef at home but he would have a lot to learn about the animals in Canada.

As soon as he reached Professor Tremblay's department he was met by one of the research students who showed him around the department and into a room scattered with a collection of sofas and comfortable chairs.

"I tell you mycelial communication is via electrochemical stimuli not by the slow chemical diffusion," came the voice of someone slumped on the sofa.

"It may be but I still don't think the fungal mycelium can be considered a brain. Toadstools don't have brains!" someone argued from a chair across the room.

"But they seem to be able to sense sources of food and grow toward it. There is some form of communication and response," came a third voice.

Flint and his guide paused to listen to their discussion. Flint was fascinated. Although his undergraduate course had touched on the subject of mushrooms and fungi he had never previously considered them a subject of interest.

As they left the room Flint caught part of another conversation. "Extremophiles might be a source of suitable enzymes. They can survive heating, drying. Their enzymes do not appear to be denaturised. We could try them."

Flint thought back to Louise and the work she had done on extremophile, the work which he had used. He wondered how things were going for her. He knew that the day after he had left Sillfield she was due to try out her patented technology at a reservoir in the mountains. She should be seeing the first results by now.

Pierre Tremblay's research group was a revelation to him. Flint was used to university researchers working in near isolation as each individual works on their own project but here there was total co-operation with several people working on different aspects of the same problem and sharing their results and suggestions.

After the first day in this atmosphere Flint lay in bed thinking back to the days when he had considered plankton and the amount of information packed into each cell. Now there was another biological mystery, fungi. Communication over long distances by organisms considered primitive and largely ignored by science.

Chapter 55

"It's a squirrel," one of the students said when Flint ask about the little grey animal. "They're all over the place and will come into houses if they think they can find food."

"They're not as bad as coons. A coon got into our summer cottage and trashed the place," joined in another student.

Flint wondered what a coon was then suddenly realized it was raccoon behaviour which was being discussed.

A desk was allocated to Flint but he did not get any dedicated laboratory space. Instead he was encouraged to see what other people were doing. He could go into most of the laboratories except the clean room. The air pressure in this special laboratory was kept slightly higher than that outside to prevent any contamination entering the room. The people working in there were completely covered in white overalls and face masks. Special training was required before anyone was allowed inside in this environment.

"That's where biology and computer hardware actually meet each other," joked his guide.

Flint considered the difference between this clean room and the special contamination laboratory that he had worked in at Sillfield. One was designed to stop things getting in while the other was preventing things, bacteria, getting out.

Flint found the atmosphere in which people collaborated, where there was a lack of competition, fascinating. He was sure it helped to speed up the research and improve their flow of ideas. However the thing that impressed him above all else was the freedom of thought which was encouraged. Were fungi like brains? What a preposterous idea that was but they did have long thin mycelia, root-like structures, which transmit information over long distances. Were they a biological network for information?

He had been fascinated by a discussion about chlorophyll in plants. The way it absorbed energy from sunlight and then the energy was transferred to other plant pigments. Could this transfer of energy be mimicked in computer systems?

It seemed to Flint that no idea was dismissed as crazy until it had been thoroughly discussed and tried out in the laboratory. He found his mind was completely absorbed by all the novel concepts. He had no time to think about other things. There was no chance to go out and explore the Canadian countryside. That would have to wait for another day.

On the last afternoon of his visit Pierre Tremblay came to find him. "Well, what do you think? Does our work interest you?"

"Yes, yes, it is great and I like how everyone collaborates."

"So, do you think you could contribute?"

"Yes, I think so. I hope so."

That was the total extent of the interview.

Professor Tremblay said he had funding to support Flint. The only question left was when he could start. Flint said he was on his way to visit his family but after that he was free.

On the flight home Flint could not believe everything had been arranged so quickly. He almost believed he had dreamt about the visit to the laboratories in Canada and the offer of a position. It all felt too good to be true. Then, suddenly, he returned to the present. The plane would be landing soon and he knew he would be met by two of the elders. What would he, what could he tell them? He had not managed to get the cholera into the water supply. He had not even looked at the news to see if there was any report of an outbreak of cholera in London. Flint began to feel rather sick. He would have to put on a brave face and admit where his plans had gone wrong.

As expected the elders were waiting for him. They greeted him with great smiles and warm handshakes. When they got to the car they poured congratulations on Flint for the success of his mission. He admitted had not seen the news yet.

Flint was taken to the cottage where the elders held their meetings. They were all there and were very excited. Flint was shown the news reports. Yes, there were reports of a serious outbreak of illness and there had been deaths already. However, this was happening in Birmingham and it appeared it was dysentery not cholera that was causing the problem. Flint was puzzled. He sat for a few moments trying to understand what had happened. The elders were oblivious to any anomalies. They saw the disease and deaths. That was all they wanted. They did not question Flint about how it had been done or why it was in Birmingham and not London.

Flint felt tired, exhausted, but he felt a sense of relief, as he gazed at the black feathered cockerel strutting past the open door of the cottage. Now all he wanted was to see his mother, his family.

It was good to be home and to feel the warmth and love of his mother and sister. Then there was the contented sleeping baby and that smell of his mother's cooking. What could be better? Of course they wanted to know about England. He tried to describe how cold and damp the winter was. He attempted to explain what London was like with its underground trains and huge buildings, but they had seen pictures of these things and he could not convey the actual feeling of being there. They did not ask much about Canada and the research he would be doing but he had the impression it was so far away from their lives that they had little understanding and probably no real interest. His mother and sister were content to live in this place with the community which shared the same ancestors who had always lived on these islands.

There was one bit of news they did tell him. There had been an accident with one of the boats that took the cruise ship visitors to swim close to a coral reef.

"Someone got hurt," said his mother.

"No, they died," corrected his sister.

"Whose boat was it?" asked Flint.

Neither of them knew. Flint hoped Tep was not involved but at that moment he felt too tired to try to find out the details. He would check tomorrow.

After the best night's sleep Flint had had in months he decided to catch up with all the news. First he tried to find out exactly what had happened in England. Quickly he found the news about Birmingham. As he went to the latest update he saw the names. Dan Norton and Louise Browning had been arrested and were helping police with their enquiries concerning criminal negligence at a reservoir in Wales.

Louise, criminal negligence, no that was not possible. She was such a thorough, conscientious scientist. Flint could hardly believe the report.

Chapter 56

The cause of the outbreak of dysentery in Birmingham was traced to a reservoir in Wales.

At the same time it was reported that an elderly farmer had gone missing in the area of the reservoir. It appeared that Mr. Pritchard had spent the day pumping out the contents of septic tanks and slurry pits for the community which lived beyond the reservoir. After a search a body was found in the cab of a tractor at the bottom of the reservoir. A tanker of the sort used by Emrys Pritchard was found nearby.

An examination of the reservoir showed that the device based upon Louise Browning's patent had been installed at the outflow. However, it appeared that on the night of the storm the water did not pass through this device. The controls had been left in a position which allowed the flow from the reservoir to go directly into the water supply serving Birmingham.

Dr. Dan Norton, the research director of the water company, who was onsite that day, was held responsible for this failure. Louise Browning, as a student working under the instruction of Dr. Norton, was not to blame.

Louise was stunned. She was told she was free to get on with her life but she did not know what the rest of her life would be. She needed to rethink her life. She decided to go home for are few days.

Life at home was exactly as it had always been. Her bedroom was unchanged. The meals her mother cooked were familiar as was the conversation. Louise was told of who had died, who had got married, who had had a baby. There was a bit of scandal about a woman who had left her husband for another man. To Louise it all seemed very narrow. Her mother and her friends were only interested in the events that happened within a five mile radius of their front doors.

Louise felt very out of place in this environment and she was certain there was no future life for her in this introvert community. She had to get out of the house for a time and decided to see how Max was doing.

Louise was still in contact with Emma and was aware that Max was in a very happy stable relationship with a man, Phil, who was about four years older than them but had attended the same school. Louise remembered him performing in school concerts, a talented musician whom played a range of instruments, violin, piano and guitar.

To her surprise Max was sitting outside in the sun when Louise reached the farm. Gone were the torn jeans and T shirt. He was wearing green trousers and a matching shirt. His hair, usually an untidy mess, was held back in a neat pony tail.

As soon as he saw Louise Max got up and walked up to her with his arms open. Nothing was said but Louise collapsed in tears in his embrace. Nothing was said as Louise continued to sob. Then Max led her back to the bench where he had been sitting.

They sat in silence until Louise lifted her head, "Oh Max this is the first time I have cried since it happened," she said.

Max waited patiently and quietly while Louise gathered her thoughts.

"It's been awful, terrible. Things were going so well and then this. The police, the arrest, I can't take it in, a nightmare," she said between sobs, "What am I to do now? All gone, people dying."

Max said nothing while Louise sobbed, then, "From what I have heard your work was going well, good sound science.

Then there was a combination of the worst events which were not your fault – the storm, the tractor crash and the controls left in the wrong position by Dan. You could not have foreseen those happenings."

"No, but"

"You'll need time."

"But."

"We can talk about everything over the next few days but in the meanwhile let me show that you something."

Max lead the way into the office then paused. The door into the back room was open and Louise could hear voices. It sounded like a man and two children. Then there were the sounds of a violin being played followed by some rather scratchy attempts at copying the music. Louise peeped into the room and could see Phil sitting opposite two young children, Emma's children. The children each had a little violin. They were watching Phil intently as he gave them a music lesson.

"Phil is thoroughly enjoying teaching the youngsters and they are doing very well, picking it up quickly," said Max as he and Louise walked back outside. "The children are coming on wonderfully in all respects. Next month they are off to Colorado to stay with Jake and Al. It is a business trip for Emma but it's been expanded into a family holiday. By the way Jake and Al are expecting twins."

"Jake, twins!" said in Louise in surprise. "I've never thought of Jake as a father, and" she laughed, "two already and soon there will be four."

The laugh was not lost on Max.

"How long are you planning to be home for? It would be nice if you could come over and see Emma."

Louise was easily persuaded to go to the farm every day for the next week. She sat outside talking to Max in the warm evening sun and, gently, slowly, Max persuaded her that the fault had not been hers. She could not have expected the torrential rain which led to the accident in which an elderly farmer's tractor and tanker went into the reservoir. It was disastrous misfortune that the toxic pollution went into the area where the supply was taken off by the water company. Her technology had not failed. The water did not go through her system. She had not been responsible for leaving the controls in the wrong setting. Dan had been responsible for that.

During their conversations Louise marvelled at the change in Max. When they were at school he had been angry and impatient with the world but now he was so kind and understanding. Was this change due to the Phil's influence or was it an indication that business success was allowing Max to relax? Louise had no doubt that Max was still as ambitious as ever but recently he was realising his goals.

Sometimes the children would be playing outside while Emma finished work in the office. Louise looked at the seven year old boy. Was this clean, neatly dressed, healthy child the same one that she remembered as the toddler wandering around half naked in that filthy smelly room while pouring the dregs from beer cans over his head for amusement? It seemed that some miraculous transformation had happened.

One evening the two children came over to talk to Louise.

"We're going to Colorado in America," explained the boy, "Colorado has very high mountains and we are going there to see the wild animals. Mum says there are bears and moose and deer and coyotes."

"And sheep with big horns," added his little sister waving her hands around at the side of her head in explanation.

The children's excitement was infectious.

"And there are mountain lions so you will have to be very careful," teased Max.

"We will be very careful. Don't worry," assured Emma who had joined the group, "Come on children it's time to get home."

"Bright kids," commented Max after they had left, "Should go far with Emma behind them."

Over the next few days Max gradually turned the conversation to Louise's future, "How much more work is needed to complete your thesis? Is it nearly ready for presentation?"

"Well, it just needs a thorough checking," confirmed Louise.

"Then it will be the viva, I suppose."

"Yes, I dread that. Three years work being picked over by the examiners."

Louise and Max sat back quietly for a few minutes until Max said, "Remember Ann at school?"

"Yes, wanted to do medicine."

"Wanted to work with children in Africa."

"Yes, but her plans to do medicine did not come off and she went to work with a charity on a remote island somewhere. I remember Jake told me she had died."

"There was a problem with the water supplied there, contaminated and no purification."

Louise realised she had made the decision to return to Sillfield, to carry on, to get her Ph.D.

Chapter 57

Dr Roger Charles sat leaning forward, elbows on his desk and hands clasped in front of him. In all his years of academic life he had never encountered a situation like this he thought. Generally he liked working with his research students. He would see the results of his guidance as the majority of them completed their Ph.D. theses. They became scientists and would go on to have successful careers. Of course, most students had problems along the way. There were frustrations during periods when there did not appear to be any positive research results but Charlie felt he had convinced them that negative findings could be important in getting a complete understanding of the truth. Sometimes students needed to step back from their laboratory work for a day or two to get the wider picture of their studies.

There had been a few occasions on which students thought they could complete their thesis and write some scientific papers on the basis of a few favourable experimental results. He had to convince them that they needed more confirmation of their findings, good solid repeatable results.

Charlie thought back to his days as a research student. He had been one of this group that, on the back of a few weeks work, felt he should get a Nobel Prize. Then he had gone through the process of learning how much evidence needed to be accumulated to prove a theory. He had to learn to be a thorough scientist. In the end he came through this process with well defined ambitions. He was not interested in power and money. He did want to become an internationally recognized scientist whose work was valued and respected.

From time to time he had found himself involved in some of the personal problems, usually money problems, of his students. Three years of low income could be oppressive when your school and university friends had well paid jobs. Often friends could afford to get married and buy a house.

In spite of all these challenges Charlie enjoyed his work with clever, ambitious, young people. However, today he would have to face one of the most difficult days of his career. Dan Norton who had helped fund the research of many of Charlie's students had been sacked from the water company, was in police custody over the deaths in Birmingham and now there were rumours, on the academic grapevine, that he was being investigated in connection with improper sexual behaviour.

Charlie felt a deep underlying regret that some of his students, including Louise, could have been exposed to such a creature.

Louise was expected to come back to the School after all the terrible business in Wales and the disaster in Birmingham. The police had decided that Louise was a not to blame. She had done nothing criminal but what about Louise's own thoughts? What did her conscience say? What could be said to raise her self esteem?

Charlie sat at his desk trying to compose suitable things to say and suggestions to make. Nothing came to mind. He did not know how to approach this problem. He would just have to walk along to the laboratory and see if Louise had arrived.

He stood up, took a deep breath, attempted to pull his shoulders back and walked out of the office. As he approached the laboratory he could hear the sound of voices. He slowed down to make sure he could see what was going on before walking in.

There was Louise surrounded by her white coated colleagues. Charlie paused to examine the notice board opposite the door to the laboratory. Everyone was assuring Louise that the blame was not hers. Her own research and developments for water purification were of the highest standard. She should be able to hold her head high and continue her career. Yes, she might want to change direction but she was a good scientist.

Charlie continued his walk along the corridor. The student group was saying all the things that he wanted to say to Louise but they were saying it better than he could ever have done.

Louise successfully completed her Ph.D. but after graduation she decided not to pursue a career in business and research. Instead she joined a charity working to provide access to clean water across Africa.

Chapter 58

Flint felt he must see if anything had happened in London. There were no major headline reports. Perhaps everything was overshadowed by events in Birmingham. Eventually he did find something. It was a report of the sudden death of a well known market trader. The article was about how much he would be missed. Nothing was said about the cause of his death and there was nothing to suggest there were other deaths or even an outbreak of illness in that area on London.

Next he started to look at the reports of the accident involving a cruise ship passenger. It appeared an older man had claimed he was a strong swimmer but he had been swept against the coral reef by the waves. He had been cut, started to bleed badly and the situation was made worse as the old man was on medication which had the effect of stopping his blood clotting. The bleeding was so bad that he had died before reaching hospital in spite of the best efforts of the crew and some of the other passengers. Flint was relieved Tep's boat was not involved but it appeared that the excursions to swim by the coral reefs had all been suspended. Flint realised Tep's business would be involved.

Flint wandered down to the beach. He walked to the water's edge and let the warm ocean wash over his feet. He looked out to sea and watched a pair of booby birds skimming over the waves. It occurred to him that he had not seen the sea while he was in England. England had not felt like an island.

He sat down on the trunk of a fallen tree. He had time to think. Poor Louise, for all her success in research and development her ambition was now shattered. Her future must be very uncertain.

Then there was Tep, had his business gone?

He thought about the old men in his community. They believed that their joint ambition had been fulfilled. They thought they had had their revenge. They could all die happy.

His thoughts went to his mother and sister? Didn't they have any ambitions, or perhaps their ambitions were to keep things as they had always been. They wanted to be the stuff of which stable communities and families were built. They were succeeding in that ambition wonderfully.

Next his mind drifted to Bibi. She was the kindest, gentlest person Flint had ever met. She was probably the most academically brilliant student he had come across. He felt certain that all the doors were open for her. Perhaps the only ambition she had left to fulfil was to marry the man she loved and that wedding was happening tomorrow.

Finally what about Flint? Had he found his own ambition? Not something suggested by others, by background, but something which had grown within himself. He thought back to the ideas he had had when he first started university. About all the information which must be packed in every tiny living cell to instruct it to do everything that is necessary for life. Then it had the mechanism to implement these instructions. It would be wonderful to replicate this ability. Perhaps now he would be on the pathway to find out more. Even if a fungus, a mushroom, was not really like a brain its biology might be able to teach us something. Was this area of research his ambition? His answer was yes. His future would be dictated by his own personal ambition. The job in Canada offered the opportunity. The research to develop a new generation of computers was fascinating.

Canada gave him an academic challenge as well as a chance to satisfy his interest in biology. He settled in quickly and easily. He enjoyed the social life at the university and, during the summer, he used every opportunity that was offered to go to the lakes to canoe and camp. He wanted to see the wildlife of Canada. His first sighting of a moose standing at the edge of a lake left a lasting impression. The only disappointment was the winter. It was not dark like England, in fact the reflection of the sunlight off the snow made it very bright; however, it was the cold. He wanted to ski but the experience of breathing intensely cold air seemed to freeze the inside of his nose. He could not stand it; he could not ski!

Professor Pierre Tremblay was delighted with the contribution made by Flint. His work was inventive and thorough. He fitted into the daily life of the research team quickly and easily. There was only one thing that was puzzling. Why had Flint gone to England, to Sillfield, to study? The work he had undertaken there did not seem to fit in with Flint's strengths and interests. Had he been influenced, persuaded by someone else to go there? Flint was not willing to talk about that part of his life. Perhaps, for Flint, it was better lost and forgotten as he followed his chosen line of research.

Val Owen

Val Owen was born in England in 1942. She studied at Liverpool University and was awarded a Ph.D in plant biochemistry in the late 1960s. She subsequently moved to Canada and worked in the medical laboratory sector.

Returning to the UK in 1980 she did research into biosensors before getting involved in technology transfer, getting research ideas out into commercial products.

Since retirement she has lived on the north coast of Anglesey where she is an active member of the Copper Writers group.

Printed and bound by CPI Group (UK) Ltd, Croydon, CR0 4YY
25/07/2025
01924273-0001